LIMITLESS DESIRE

THE DESIRE SERIES BOOK 10

BARBARA DONLON BRADLEY

ONE

The command center bustled with activity. Heather wasn't paying attention. She found her mind wandering back to their crazy trip through time. It had been a few months ago, but there were times when an odd memory from one of the alternate timelines reminded her that she and Storm belonged together. With the exception of one timeline, she didn't have to worry about what Reasta would do throughout the changes. Ever since Reasta came to their planet, she had made life on Vespia difficult.

Most of Vespia was now in the caverns beneath the surface. The moment they escaped from Reasta's ship with the elders and a few of the ancients, the woman changed her tactics and put the planet on lockdown. No one was allowed to move without her permission, so they slowly started bringing everyone underground, leaving just enough to make the towns look populated while they waited for the crops that were planted above ground to be harvested. Heather wasn't about to let Reasta have the chance to steal those crops.

Heather hated that. The thought of anyone getting hurt because of Reasta's desire to capture her bothered her. She looked over at the android she found several months ago.

Mac had told her there were seven computers she needed to find to beat Reasta. Since she learned that, she focused on trying to find them. Unfortunately, nothing was that easy. She had been told she would find them as she needed them so trying to force the issue wouldn't allow her to find them faster. So far, she had found Cim and Mac. Finding the other five was paramount but not having them wasn't going to stop her from blocking Reasta every chance she got. Clashes between Vespians and Reasta's security kept happening as their people fought against the stifling laws. Heather wanted that to end.

She had found an out-of-the-way corner in front of a computer and sat, staring at the maps of the underground complex. Her desire to find the other computers was a palpable thing, and she worked on it every spare moment she had. Not finding what she was looking for she went looking for Mac, who was working on an assignment Heather had given her.

"You wish to speak to me?"

"Yes." Heather loved the way the android anticipated her needs. "I wanted to ask you about the other computers. Do you know what each of them are?"

"I know what they are capable of."

"Could the ancient ship be one of the systems I need to find?"

"My system says all the computers are on Vespia," Mac's feminine voice responded. "If one has been moved, I am not aware of it."

Heather nodded. Not what she wanted to hear, but Mac had told her several times she didn't know where the other computers were, so the computer's answer didn't surprise her. Walking back to her quiet corner, she continued to study the maps she had pulled up earlier. She still had another half hour on her shift and wanted to take advantage.

"My heart, you have been studying those maps for hours. Why don't you take a break?" Storm came up behind her and placed his hands on her shoulders.

"I know." She sighed as she sat back. "This is driving me crazy. There is a lot that hasn't been explored down here, and I think that is where I need to go to find them."

"Didn't Mac say you will find them as you need them?"

"She said they would make themselves known to me, but we don't have time to wait for that."

"So now you want to push. Do you think that will work better?"

"No." She tilted her head back so she could look up at him. "But I feel I need to do something."

"I know something we can do that will make you forget everything but us." He smiled down at her.

She laughed as she turned in her chair. "But we're still on duty."

"Then I guess I need to just heat you up a little." He gave her one of his bone-melting smiles. "That way you won't forget my promise."

She stood as she smiled back. "The last time you tried that we got in trouble."

"Ah, but we did have fun before that happened." He stepped close enough she could feel his breath against the skin above the collar of her uniform.

"You are incorrigible."

"And that is why I'm your heart."

"Do you two ever give it a break?" asked a familiar voice.

"No." Heather and Storm turned to face the man who spoke.

"Kuarto, you know you're happy we feel the way we do for each other." Heather leaned against Storm.

"He sure has a funny way of showing it," commented Storm.

"I'm here because the two of you are needed in the main hall. The elders are going to make their first appearance since coming back, and Heather, as part of that council, you need to be there."

"Which is why I came to get you." Storm wrapped his arms around her. "But seeing you so focused without us being intimate distracted me."

A light blush filled her cheeks. "Let's go."

They changed into their proper clothing and met Anseri in the main hall of their underground complex. It was good to have her and the rest of the council back.

"Good." She greeted them with a hug. Whispering in Heather's ear she asked, "Are you ready for this?"

What did she mean by that? "Yes, Anseri."

She cupped her cheek. "You're going to do fine."

That comment made her nervous, but before she could ask what she meant it was time for them to take their places. Heather went to where the rest of the council stood but found only three chairs. Odd. She ended up standing with Storm and Fridon off to their left.

Anseri stood, grabbing everyone's attention.

"My children, I am happy to say we are safe and home where we belong. We thank everyone involved in our rescue." She looked out over the sea of faces. "You have been trying hard to take back our planet without declaring war. We want to fix that. We are declaring war on Reasta. We will take our planet back."

A shout filled the hall.

"That being said, the elder council is stepping down."

Murmurs filled the hall. Heather grabbed Storm's hand. She wasn't sure what was coming next but was pretty sure she wasn't going to like it.

"It is temporary, my children. We are a peaceful council, working for the betterment of Vespia. We have no business dealing with war. As we have done in the past, we will appoint a war council. One from the elder council and one from security, but this time we will add one more. Our choice from Security is Fridon. He has done so well when he was head of security and far exceeded what was asked of him. Our second is my son, Storm, the future leader of this planet and current head of security. The third is Heather, a member of the council and mate to the future leader of our planet. Heather's background in Earth's security gives her exactly what we need on this war council."

Heather locked her feelings inside as Storm took one hand and Fridon took the other. They moved together toward the chairs. Heather wanted to fight when they turned, and she found she was in the center chair. How did this happen? She had no right to be the leader of this.

"I leave you in good hands," said Anseri. She turned toward them and bowed. Then the sea of people did the same thing.

With Storm's subtle signals, they all stood and bowed back before they walked behind the stage that Anseri had set up in the large cave.

The heat of her mate's hand on the small of her back let her know he was close. She wanted to scream. No one asked her opinion on this. They decided to broadside her instead. "Why was I in the center?"

"Mother's choice."

"Uh huh, normally the center chair is the leader," she spoke softly so no one would hear, but she knew her mate's sensitive hearing would pick it up. "Anseri always sits in the middle."

"We are all equal, my heart, but because you are on the council it was decided to put you in the center so the people will know the council has you to speak for them."

"I could have sat anywhere, and they would have thought that."

Storm wrapped an arm around her waist. "How about I show you where we will be working?"

He wasn't going to explain why she was in the center. At least not right now so she nodded. "It might not look like much right now, but more will be added as we build our staff."

"Staff?" She looked at him.

"Each of us will have nine staff members that we choose." The doors in front of them opened, and they entered. "They will be our elite teams."

"And the criteria?" The large room he escorted her to had nothing in it but a table and three chairs.

"Anyone who has been in Vespian security."

"Oh, then my first choice is easy." She smiled as she sat. "I want Latimer."

"No." Storm frowned at her when he heard her choice. "Choose another."

"Did you want Latimer?" she asked Storm. When he shook his head, she turned to Fridon and asked him the same question.

"He is an interesting choice, but I had someone else in mind."

She turned back to look at Storm, waiting for an answer.

"He's not a good choice." He crossed his arms over his chest.

Heather recognized his intimidation tactic, but it wasn't

going to work on her. They had worked with the man since Reasta had arrived. He and their daughter were the ones to fix the timeline Susan Harris kept trying to change so she could end up with Storm. Storm had grudgingly admitted that Skye was very good at his job, but Skye still rubbed Storm the wrong way at times. She also knew that Storm still didn't like the fact that she had put a fake memory of her and Skye as lovers in his clone when she was a prisoner on Reasta's ship. Heather didn't care. Skye had skills she admired, and she knew she could trust him. "He is for me."

Storm stood and slammed his hands on the table. "You are my mate!"

"Yes, I am." Heather placed her hands on the table and stood as well. "Is this going to cause a problem in our relationship if I choose Skye?"

Fridon stood as if this was his cue to leave. "Excuse me for a moment."

Heather knew he was leaving before they started to argue. At least he was used to them.

"You know how I feel about him," Storm groused.

"I do. And you're telling me that feeling hasn't changed even after working with him and seeing how good he is at his job?" Storm didn't answer her. If he thought the silent treatment was going to make her back down, he was wrong. There was only one way to handle this.

"I see." Heather wiped her hands on her council robes before she turned toward the door.

"Where are you going?" Storm moved so he blocked the door on her.

"I need to speak to your mother." She looked right at him, daring him to stop her.

"Why?" He frowned at her.

"I am your mate. I can't maintain my station as your

mate and fulfill the role the Elders expect me to fill." Before she could move, she found herself pinned to the wall.

"My mother just told everyone that you were the elder's choice to be on this council and now you're going to tell her she made a mistake?" There was a hint of a growl in his voice.

"What am I supposed to do?" She paused, trying to pick the right words. "Shame my mate or stand up for what I think is right."

He let her go and sighed. "As my mate, you do what is expected of you and you do it well. You have to do the same thing when you represent the elders."

She could ask if he was going to allow her to do the job the elders wanted her to do, but knew she needed to get to the heart of the matter. "Why are you against Skye as my second?"

He looked at her. They had never kept anything from each other. With all the obstacles that wanted them apart, they didn't want to add to the problem by keeping secrets. "He bothers me."

"How?" She pushed.

"He stares at you a lot."

"Storm." She pressed her hand against his heart. "That's because he's afraid I'll turn into some sort of crazy mind monster."

"I know, and that bothers me." He wrapped his arms around her and held her close. "You have the kindest heart and would never do what he keeps expecting."

"But you have been with me since this power of mine started to develop. You've seen what I've gone through because of it. He hasn't."

"He shared some of that process when you were captured by Reasta. He knows what you go through."

"I frighten him and sometimes myself."

Storm pressed his lips against hers. Gentle, sweet, and making Heather sigh. The moment she opened her mouth he took advantage and deepened the kiss. Their tongues twined together, dancing the way they always did.

Heather found her back against the wall as Storm's lips moved to her mark. "Storm, we're not in our rooms."

He lifted his head and looked at her. "I know, my heart. Too bad you can't use your mind to lock those doors."

"That would be Skye's area of expertise."

"What do you mean by that?"

"His gift. I have a feeling it's with computers." She saw Storm's confused look. "You know how I can touch minds? He is starting to do that with computers."

"So soon he won't be able to think of you as a threat if he has the same problem." He brushed his fingers along her jaw. She watched a shadow cross his eyes.

"What?"

"You know you could have anyone you want?"

"I only want you." She knew he meant any sex partner she wanted as she looked up into his eyes. Her words started her favorite glow in his eyes.

"My heart." His warm lips pressed against her mark. The soft pressure felt wonderful. When he pulled the delicate skin into his mouth she sucked in her breath.

The doors opened, and Anseri stepped in. By the way she looked around, Fridon must have warned her they had been arguing. She smiled when she saw them in an embrace. "Good, you're not busy. I have something for Heather."

Heather touched his face then stepped away from Storm.

Storm's father came in carrying a box. He set it on the table then stepped back.

Anseri pointed to the box. "For you, Heather."

She stepped up to the table and opened the box. Inside she found a uniform much like the one Storm wore, but in the dove grey color of the dresses she wore when she was with the council.

"I thought wearing your council robes would be a bit cumbersome for you when you were working and this would be more comfortable yet still remind the people you represent the council when they saw you."

"Thank you, Anseri." The material was soft to the touch.

"Try it on, my child."

Heather peeled off her council robes and pulled the new uniform on, but not before she saw the spark of arousal turn into a low flame in her mate's eyes. Seeing her body, even as quick as it was always aroused him.

She swung her arms over her head then did a squat. Her new outfit was quite comfortable. She looked at Storm. She would like to see how easy it was to work out in. Without having to say a word or send a thought Storm held his hand up above his head. Heather smiled. A quick warm-up loosened her up enough to jump and side-kick his hand.

"You like it?"

"Very much." Heather smoothed the material. When she first started working with the council, she wasn't sure what color to wear. Anseri always wore white, and the rest of the council wore block colors of white, gray, and tan. Then one day she just decided to wear a solid color. The light gray dress was one she got a lot of compliments on and became the one she wore a lot. She still mixed it with the block colors like the rest of the council wore but had been going to the solid gray more and more. "Is gray my color?"

"It does look good on you." Anseri looked at her son

before looking back at Heather. "Have you chosen your second?"

"That was what we were discussing when you walked in."

"And your mate wasn't happy?"

"No Mother, I wasn't. I also realize that I shouldn't treat the representative of the council as my mate when we're here."

"I'm glad to hear that you realize your heart is here for a reason. I know your desire to protect her is strong, but she is a strong woman. That's why we appointed her."

"And she will do the council proud."

"I know." She smiled at her son. "She will do you proud, too."

He slipped his arm around her. "She does that every day."

"Then I shall leave you to your work." She touched them on the cheek before she headed out the door.

Storm turned Heather in his arms. "I want to see where the seals are on this uniform."

She laughed. "You created these suits."

"Not this one." He brushed his hands along her shoulders. "This was created by my mother, and she always had different ideas than I did."

The doors opened and Fridon stepped in. Heather looked at his face and wanted to laugh. He didn't know if he should stay or not and wasn't sure if he should ask.

Storm grinned as he released his mate. "We can pick this back up later."

They sat at the table. Storm looked at Fridon. "Ready to pick your second?"

"I have an idea, but I'd like to see who you two pick first."

The intercom interrupted. "Heather, we have an incoming communiqué from Admiral Barrister."

She looked at Storm. Why was he contacting them now? "Put him on."

"Commander Drexel, on behalf of the UCE we received your missive and are here to help you with your war. We can't offer much, but I have a ship filled with security officers who volunteered to help."

"But we didn't ask for help." What did Earth want now? She had kept her communications to a minimum but had broken their silence months ago. She didn't want to get Earth involved in this war.

"Our government believes in helping our allies."

Now that sounded like a memorized speech. She knew if she questioned him, it could cause trouble. "Thank you, Admiral. I will speak to the council on your behalf."

Once she closed the commlink, she looked at the computer. Bear was sending her data on the people he brought with him. Heather looked through the different files as she thought. Vespians didn't allow off-worlders on the planet, and Bear knew that. Why was he here?

The council had stepped down, but as leader of the war council, she couldn't make this decision on her own. She pressed a button and waited for Anseri to answer. "You are needed in the war room, Anseri."

"Of course."

Heather then pressed the button on her new uniform. "Kuarto, you are needed in the war room."

"On my way."

"You want your brother here?"

"We need to talk about this and will need his medical input." She looked at her mate. "We've never allowed non-Vespians on our planet before, but we could use the numbers. I want as much input as we can get before we decide to let them join us or send them away."

It took Anseri and Kuarto a few minutes to arrive. They stood when Storm's mother entered the room.

"You wished to speak to me?"

Kuarto came in behind her. He waited until Anseri sat before he took a chair as well.

"We have been contacted by Earth. They have sent a ship filled with soldiers to help us with our war."

"They're already here?"

Heather nodded. "We have never allowed a non-Vespian on the planet."

"That's not quite true. We have allowed Bert to live here," said Kuarto.

"True, but he is ancient. They have been on the planet before, and he doesn't interact with the population. Just with us." She focused on Anseri. "I want to make the right decision. I understand why you don't want strangers here. Besides the pheromones unmated Vespians emit that affect all other races, everyone here is honest. I don't want that to be changed by a bunch of humans, but we could use their help. It would allow us to fill out enough elite teams to do what we want and get the last of our crops so we can get all of our people underground."

"We have found that the shots or inserts other planets have used to counteract our pheromones doesn't last more than a few hours," commented Anseri.

"True. Bear sent me data on some new drugs they have been trying to extend the time out. Kuarto, that's why I wanted you here." She handed him a pad with the data.

"I figured as much. I have toyed with the idea of coming up with something permanent, but it is rare that we are around off-worlders that much. A couple of hours at a function here and there." He looked through the data.

"Do we want to have something to dampen the pheromones or stop the reaction?"

"There are a lot more of us, and if we dampen the pheromones we could interrupt people finding their right mate."

"I can do this. It will take me a couple of hours unless I run into trouble."

"Let me know when you're ready."

He stood and left the room.

"I will leave you to make the right choice." Anseri stood and headed out as well.

Heather looked at Fridon and Storm. "Now we need to decide whether or not to let them on Vespia. I know your instinct is to tell them to go home but spending time in Earth's security I have seen the positive aspect of using others to help in your quest."

"You think they will be more of a benefit than harm?" asked Storm.

"I want to know what you two think. But understand if one of you comes up with a negative reason the other two are to come up with a positive one and vice versa. If there are more negative than positive, we'll send them back to Earth." Heather leaned forward. "I'm going to start with the big one the reaction to our pheromones, but we're coming up with something to fix that so neither one of you can use that again."

"Alright. Reasta continues to clone her people, increasing her ranks. Adding the humans will allow us to build ours as well," said Fridon.

"But our battle plans call for small teams, not a large contingency like Earth security is used to," countered Storm.

"Earth has used both strategies to their best ability," Heather reminded them. "If you tell them what you want, they will follow. They are soldiers and as soldiers, they are more than willing to learn if it is something that will make them better."

"Our leaders don't expect our people to follow blindly. We want their input."

"Storm, humans want their soldiers to think on their feet. They are given orders designed to keep them safe but sometimes changes have to be made. They would be our guests, and this is our war, not theirs. They have been trained to follow orders. If you ask for input, they will respond." Heather smiled. "And I think we can use that to our advantage."

"How so?"

"We know Reasta has been trying to get a mole in our ranks, but our people are too loyal to give her what she wants. What if we give her one?"

"Use one of the humans?"

"Why not? They have a history of being traitors. She has to know that there is a ship out there waiting for our approval. What she won't know is that we'll be in control of that mole, so she'll only get the information we want her to have. It might allow us to find out how she's able to continue to clone. We've had to have put a dent in her supplies, yet she continues to make those stupid clones. If we can stop that we can level the playing field."

"You think Earth's security will go along with this idea?"

"All we have to do is ask."

They continued to go through the pros and cons until they decided to let the humans in.

Bear loved the idea of the mole and gave her a list of people who would be good candidates to use. Now, she needed to be sure they had safe passage. Reasta had to know they were out there, and she couldn't capture them before they had a chance to set everything up. They were getting ready to launch a ship to escort them in, but she wanted to be sure they weren't intercepted.

"Bert? There is a ship coming from Earth. You should be picking them up on your screen. Can you make sure they land safely?" She smiled when he promised to help. "Thank you," Heather stood. "They should be landing in fifteen minutes."

Storm and Fridon rose and followed her out of the room. She sure hoped this worked. It would give them a leg up in their battle against Reasta.

"Why do you think he's here?" asked Fridon.

"My guess is Earth wants to make sure their supply of our grain continues."

Fridon nodded. "Are humans that shallow?"

"I know that's how it looks but they need the grain, and they fear we could cut them off once we win our war if they don't offer help but someone else does. They want to prove they are willing to get in the trenches with us and aren't using us for the grain."

The admiral disembarked from his ship and stopped in front of Heather. After he stepped off the ship, soldiers who had joined him on the mission came down the gang-plank and started to get in line. He noticed her uniform and raised a brow. "Commander Drexel."

She saluted him. "Admiral Barrington."

"On behalf of the UCE we offer our help to retake your planet."

"Thank you, Admiral." Heather smiled. "We need to secure your ship, sir."

"Of course."

Heather nodded to the security team who started moving into the ship.

"Nice cave."

"Most of Vespia has moved underground for protection." Heather noticed there were still people streaming out of Bear's ship.

"And the ships that greeted us about three hours ago?"

"We're at war, sir, they are there to warn those that don't know and protect those that want to help."

"Is that why Latimer came aboard our ship and added something to our sensor array?"

"Yes, sir." The people were lining up in rows of fifteen then standing at attention.

"Well, there are three more ships waiting for permission to approach."

"Three more? Are they near our borders?"

"No. They're waiting on Earth. Once you give permission, they'll take flight."

"We don't really need the ships, Admiral."

"When I told the members of Earth security that I needed volunteers to come here and fight I had over two thousand volunteers. I thinned the number down, but there is still six hundred more that I felt were worthy. UCE was proud to let us use these ships. They're our new troop movers. They hold more soldiers than any of our other ships. They hold two hundred in total. Do you have room for three troop movers?"

"Three more? I need to speak to the rest of the council to see where we could fit them." She gestured for Storm and Fridon to move off with her. Heather spoke softly so Bear couldn't hear them. "Do you think we need that many extra people here?"

"It would allow us to build more elite squads," said Fridon. "But you must make the decision."

"We need to speak to Kuarto."

They nodded.

She pressed the com in her collar. "Kuarto, they have six hundred more people who volunteered."

"That many? Good Lord." He was quiet for a moment. "I can replicate enough to cover everyone if you want that many people joining our ranks."

"Thanks." She looked at Storm and Fridon. "Thoughts?"

"Our squads are the best Vespia has to offer." Storm looked over his shoulder. "If he took that many of those who volunteered then they can't be the best Earth has to offer. Not all of them will qualify. What are we supposed to do with the ones that don't?"

"I'm sure this is the best of the best and we wouldn't put anyone in a squad who didn't qualify." Heather thought for a moment. Bear wouldn't have brought people he thought would be a detriment. Storm might not understand, but she had worked with these people, and she knew they would do what was needed. She smiled. It was time to show her mate just what type of training Earth's security had been through. "I know just what to do. Is the room available?"

"For two hours."

"Perfect." She turned to her commander. "Admiral, we're honored to have your team here. I know how hard Earth's security has trained, but the Vespians have only seen them during exhibitions. I would like to put our people through some of the toughest tests the Vespians have to create their elite squads. Show them what we're capable of."

"Of course. I chose only the best of the people who

wanted to come. I'm sure they would like to show what they can do."

"Wonderful." She smiled. "Once this council has seen the quality of these men and women you can send for the rest."

"But there is something we need to address before you start," said Bear. "Some of these officers are higher rank than you."

"And they understand that no matter my rank I am the liaison, and I know what the Vespians want, sir. It won't be a problem."

"True." He shifted his stance to attention and the rest of Earth security did the same thing. Heather followed suit. "But I have the authority to do a field promotion. Commander Heather Drexel you are raised to the rank of captain."

"Sir." She saluted and he returned it.

Bear then stepped forward and shook her hand. "I've been wanting to do that for a while."

"Thank you, sir."

———

Heather led the people from Earth to their creation room. She had used it to prepare for the rescue of the elders. Now she would use it to show how good Earth's security was. They stood at ease in rows of twenty.

"Each Vespian who wants to be part of an elite team must score in the eighty and above percentile in order to be considered. You must score the same. In this room, I have altered the gravity and air to Earth's. There should be no excuse."

She loaded their first challenge into the system, scaling a rock wall. "This might look simple, but you will climb it in the dark and the hand and foot holds will shift and disappear as you scale it."

"Row one, step up to the wall." Heather waited until each person was ready to climb. "Computer, turn the lights on when the last person hits the top. Lights out." She paused for a moment. "Go."

There were a few curse words and a grunt or two, but everyone made it to the top. The lights came on and the next group prepared to climb. Once they were plunged into darkness Heather's mind brushed against her mates. *Are you watching them?*

Of course, my heart. They need to be safe.

Has any of them given you cause to fear for their life?

No. They have been as agile as any Vespian but wanting to know if I was spying on them wasn't the reason you touched my thoughts. I can sense that. What did you want, my heart?

I want to do hand-to-hand and need our troops to spar these people.

Want to show me they can fight the way a Vespian can?

Our groups work with each other all the time and know each other's moves. I thought a fresh challenge would make all of them work a little harder for it. Can you also contact Sam, Skye, and anyone else you feel will be a good judge?

Judge?

We will be responsible for keeping tallies of the score. The one who scores five points first will end the fight.

I will make sure it gets done.

My heart.

The lights came on as the last person climbed to the top. The next group lined up and they went through it as well. Once the last group finished Heather checked the scores. "Your next challenge is hand-to-hand. We have brought in the best Vespia has to offer. They know our ways. I taught them. The first one to five points wins."

The main doors to the lab opened and soldiers poured in. They wore their Vespian uniforms. Helmets on. Heather knew Storm told them to wear them for effect. Sam, Skye, and a few choice others came in to help judge. She paired everyone up and broke them into groups quickly.

The judges gathered around her.

"They are very good at hand-to-hand. Our goal is to see how they handle working with our soldiers. The scoring isn't as important as the way they learn from each other. Once the matches are done, they're going to do the two challenges again but in Vespian air and gravity. The top ten percent will be added to elite teams right away." She gave her mate a bright smile. "I would like to give them a demonstration first."

He smiled back. "I can arrange that."

"I already know who I want to do the demo."

"You and Skye?"

"In the beginning. Skye will show them how we want the match to go. Then I want you to spar me." She saw his smile become predatory.

"And I get to show them what we don't want to see?"

"Yes."

He laughed. "I shall enjoy this."

"You always do."

They headed back to the soldiers waiting for them.

"Next is hand-to-hand. This is what I want to see." She signaled for Skye to step up and they started to spar. Slow easy hits that became more complicated. They picked up the speed they struck to a point where some couldn't keep up with the strikes, but they could see Heather or Skye's reaction. Once she thought they had seen enough they stopped and shook hands.

"Now this is what I don't want to see." She didn't have to signal her mate. He had already wrapped his arms around her. His hold was possessive. She smiled. Her mate was marking his territory. These soldiers knew who he was but had no idea what it would be like to fight a Vespian. The only thing they had ever seen was news feeds. "No holding. No restricting hands."

She slipped out of his hold and turned to face him. Storm charged her and pinned her to the ground. "No charging, tripping, or pinning. You're here to fight."

He gave her his bone-melting smile, and she knew he wouldn't let her up until he got a kiss from her. Her human counterparts had no idea what their real relationship was like, but now they would. She would never deny him anything.

His head dipped toward hers. Need unfurled as his lips touched hers. Her government might frown upon her behavior while in uniform, but she wasn't on Earth or in their military now. His lips brushed softly against hers. She opened her mouth, and his tongue swooped in, searching for its mate. They danced together, heightening their desire for each other. When Storm broke the kiss, his eyes were glowing, and she was having problems stringing thoughts together.

He touched her jaw with gentle fingers before climbing off her and offering her his hand.

She took his help and gained her feet. Wiping her hands on her outfit she gathered her thoughts. "No shots to the groin." She turned to Storm, grinned, then kicked him. "The suits Vespians wear protect their bodies so they don't feel a thing, but the payback is hell."

"It sure is." Storm wrapped his arms around her and lifted her off the ground.

"I have taught Vespian security Earth techniques." She slid out of his arms only to find herself in another hold.

"You can't think that you'll do something they've never seen."

Storm let go and allowed her to touch the floor. She broke the soldiers into groups of five and paired them with a Vespian and a judge. "Once you're finished have a seat against the wall."

Watching her group, she listened to the different calls being made so she could keep track of when a judge was free.

Her group finished and she joined Skye and Fridon. Their groups had finished just before hers. "So anyone stand out?"

"Yes," said Skye.

Heather handed him her pad. He marked the ones he recommended. Fridon took it next and marked the ones he recommended as well. She watched the rest as they sparred, marking the ones she saw something in. Once they were all done, she asked the rest of the judges to mark the ones they felt would excel.

Then she put them through it again, this time with Vespian air and gravity. Once they finished both tests Heather gathered the judges to her. They gave their input on the contestants and helped Heather decide on about twenty-five who were ready to be placed.

"Each test will advance a certain amount of you. We have our first group picked, but before I assign anyone to a Vespian team you need to understand the Vespian way. I know you've seen the newsfeeds that make it sound like Vespia has orgies in the streets.

"There is no truth in those newsfeeds, but their viewpoint of sex is different than the way Earth views it." She looked at her mate. "These people have accepted me as their own. My mate helped me acclimate to their way of life. I'm going to try to do it for you in the few minutes we have. So listen closely.

"Vespian's don't understand why we keep our sex such a secret. They view it as a beautiful way to express their feelings for each other, even if it is just for a moment. That is why they don't hide it. They also don't understand the concept of rape. Why would you force someone when so many give so freely? Remember that. If I hear that any of you tried to strong-arm a Vespian into having sex with you I will personally kick you off the planet." She paused for a moment. "Understand, the way they see sex allows them to express those feelings wherever they feel comfortable. In their society, it can be anywhere. A discreet corner, a garden. It is not to be gawked at." She saw heads nod in understanding. Good, they understood. "Now the following people are to step forward. We have a new assignment for you."

TWO

Heather spoke to Bear while Storm picked another test for the human soldiers.

"As much as I'd like to let you bring more people here, I don't think it is wise." Heather looked at him. "Reasta allowed your ship in because we had a little help, but she'll stop another one and then press those soldiers into her military."

"I can't leave those people on Earth. Too much media has gone into them leaving. It also allowed Earth to bring in more into the academy. More people are being fed and housed."

"This is about the grain, isn't it? We had to stop the shipments when she started to fight us openly and things are starting to go backwards at home. Earth wants their grain."

"You know how bad it was when we signed that treaty, and the grain helped. We were able to feed the needy, which gave them hope. It allowed a good number of them to be healthy enough to find jobs. A lot of the people wanting to help are personally touched by the grain. They either were ones who were finally healthy enough to join security or had family members who were improved by it."

Heather was touched by his story. "Then let me see if we can use a few ships of our own to bring them here. It would be safer, but I'll need a little time to see what I can do."

Bear didn't want to give in. She could see it on his face. But he nodded his assent. Heather smiled. "I'll go talk to who I need to, and I'll find you once I have an answer."

She headed out of the room and stepped into the first room she found vacant. Pressing her collar, she contacted their friend. "Bert?"

"Yes, Heather."

"First I want to thank you for helping that earth ship arrive safely."

"Of course, my friend."

"Bear has told us there are more troops who want to join us, but I fear they will be stopped if another Earth ship tries to approach the planet again."

"Reasta has increased her patrols of Vespia's space border since their arrival," said Bert. "I've been tracking everything she has been doing."

"How ready is our new ship?"

"Ah," Bert paused for a moment. "Our beautiful new flagship will be completed in three days. You wish to take it to bring your human friends here?"

"It would be a great way to test it."

"Send me the information from your admiral, and I'll get a crew together."

"Umm, I'd like Skye to captain the ship. I think his presence will make it easier for the humans to understand the use of our ship."

"I think he will be very happy with your choice. He's been wanting to take it out for a run for a few weeks."

"I'll get the info from Bear and send it to you as soon as I get it." Heather closed the link. She looked around at the room she was in and frowned. It didn't look familiar. Where was she? This wasn't one of the rooms they had built. This one was naturally built. "Okay, how did no one find this place?"

"Because only you could be the one to find me." A young Vespian male stood in front of her.

"Me?" Fear filled her as she went into a combative stance. Was he one of Reasta's soldiers here to try to kidnap her?

He tilted his head at her. "I frighten you? Why?"

Heather didn't drop her guard. "Who are you?"

"I am Arc. Artillary Remote Computer."

"What?" She relaxed her stance. "You're one of the seven computers I have to find?"

"Yes." He paused for a moment. "You have now found the third one."

"And your area of expertise is weapons?"

"Correct."

Heather smiled at him. Wait till Storm found out.

———

She got the data she needed from Bear and gave it to Bert. Heading back to the room where they were testing Earth's security, Heather brought Arc with her. They stepped into the bustling area, and she headed straight for her mate.

"We have another group to release to our elite squads," said Storm when he spotted her. He handed his pad to her. Noticing the Vespian male behind her he arched a brow at her.

"Good." All she could do was smile. "Where is Fridon? I wish to speak to him as well."

"Behind you," he said.

She turned to face him. Stepping away from the soldiers' training, Heather waited for Storm and Fridon to join her. "I found another one."

"Ancient computer?" asked Fridon. He turned to look at Arc who had followed Heather as well.

"Yes." Heather gestured for Arc to join them. "Arc this is Storm and Fridon. They have clearance."

"You give it this freely?"

"I trust them with my life. You have access to the files now. They will prove why I give them clearance." She noticed Skye was finished with his group. "Latimer."

"Yes?"

"You've been reassigned."

He fought a frown as he approached her. Before he could speak, Heather handed him a pad from inside her uniform. "This is your new assignment."

Skye looked at the screen then at her with a big smile. "Yes, ma'am."

"Dismissed." That was the first time he called her ma'am, but they were surrounded by their peers, and she did just get promoted. She looked at the pad Storm had handed to her.

"What else do you have hidden in that uniform?"

She felt the warmth of his breath against her neck. Heather looked back at her mate. "Only your favorite playground."

"Which I can't wait to see."

"And I can't wait to show you." She rested her head on his shoulder.

"We could sneak away," he said softly as he wrapped his arms around her.

Heather laughed. "You do have a one-track mind." She turned in his arms. "Who will decide who will make the elite squads while we're occupied?"

"We have Fridon."

"Who won't make that decision without us."

He frowned at her. She had kept her voice soft so no one would overhear them. Storm spoke softly as well. "You have mentioned the one thing that will keep us here, but you know you will pay for it later."

"I sure hope so."

It was his turn to laugh. "You like my punishments far too much."

"You do too."

"I know." He captured her lips with his for a quick kiss. "We will finish this later."

She smiled and brushed her fingers along his jaw.

Fridon cleared his throat. "Everyone is done."

"Right." Heather looked at the pad. "Send the ones I checked through. We'll keep testing the rest of them."

———

Their shift was finally over, and Heather and Storm walked down the hall toward their room with Arc following behind them. Heather turned to Arc and released him until she needed him again.

"And where am I to go?" he asked.

"You can go back to the room I found you in for now if you'd like. Unless you wish to have a room to wait in until you're needed."

"No."

"Then we will see you later, Arc," said Storm as they stopped in front of the door to their room.

Heather walked through their private door and let out a sigh.

"You alright, my heart?"

"Yes." She turned to smile at him. "I'm just glad that is done."

"We will have to do this again when Skye comes back with the rest of the troops."

"I know, but we've now perfected the tests." They now had a permanent room that was large enough for them to have a sitting area as well as a sleeping area. Heather sat on the small couch they had in their room and stretched her legs out in front of her.

"What are you doing?"

"Resting my feet?" She knew that he wanted to pick up where they left off earlier, but she loved to push him when it came to their intimacy. He loved it, too. Most of the time, it allowed him to be the dominant one.

She reached down to release the seal on her boot when she found her hand encased in Storm's larger one.

"Now what are you doing?"

"Removing my boots?"

"No, you are trying to annoy your mate. This is a new uniform that I didn't design. I need to study it. Find the closures, see where they lead." He knelt by her feet and pulled one then the other boot off. He softly caressed the arch of her foot then slid his fingers up under her pant leg to find the seam.

Each soft brush against her skin made her very aware of his touch. Storm eased the seam apart on the outside of her left leg. Warmth filled her. He slowly worked his way up her leg until he hit her hip then worked on her right leg.

Each touch melted her a little more, and she knew he did it on purpose. It didn't take long before she was naked. "And what about you?"

He stood and broke the seals on his uniform, so it fell to the floor then he scooped her up in his arms. "Mac, we wish to use the shower."

Heather waited for Mac to remind them they didn't need to shower together if their goal was to save water. She guessed Mac finally understood that they wanted to be intimate in the shower. The space appeared without a word.

Storm carried her into the alcove and allowed her to set her feet on the ground. He announced the strength of the spray and the temperature before turning his attention back to her. "Now. I believe I promised to punish you."

"You did," she smiled at him. A little thrill filled her when he smiled back.

He backed her up against the wall then lifted her so they could look each other in the eye. "You are so beautiful when you're excited."

"My heart." She touched his jaw. "You are the one who made me this way."

"What I did was create a monster who craves my touch."

"You say it like it's a bad thing."

"Oh, it's not. It makes me very happy. You are no longer that shy woman I was intimate with when I first met you. You know what you want and aren't afraid to let me know." He lowered his mouth to her mark. "But I also know how to make you silent."

A sigh escaped her when she felt the heat of his mouth against her delicate skin. He did. All he had to do was bring her to the edge of an orgasm. That took her breath away. The thought of feeling one again notched her desire up a degree. "And you're very good at it."

Steam swirled around them as Storm worked on arousing her more. His hands roamed to his favorite places, a brush here, a touch there. Each one had her wanting more. "My heart."

"Sorry, my heart, this is where the punishment happens. I have my desires too, and I want a scream. The best way for me to get what I want is to deny you what you want until I have pushed you to the limit." He inhaled next to her throat. "You are close, but not quite there yet."

"I feel like I'm there." She tried to move, but he still had her pinned to the wall.

"My nose doesn't lie. I know the scent you give off when you are where I want you to be, and that scent isn't present yet." He pressed his lips to her mark again. "But I know I'll smell it soon. Very soon."

His hands skimmed her skin, caressing all the sensitive spots he could get to.

"Storm." She wanted to take it. Allowing him to have his way was always a win-win situation for the both of them, but she couldn't take much more.

"I see I'm going to have to take measures to keep you still. Mac, can you give my mate a shelf to stand on?"

Heather felt the wall slide out under her feet, giving her something to put her weight on. It also allowed him to ease his weight off her when she would no longer slide down the wall to the floor because he wasn't holding her in place. He lifted one arm, drawing soft circles against her skin, and pressed it against the wall. Once he had her where he wanted her, he took one finger and pressed it into the wall triggering a reaction that allowed him to draw part of the rock wall out and around her wrist. He did it to her other wrist and ankles as well.

"I love the little things we've learned about this cave system." He used his foot to push the small shelf they no longer needed in. His hands spanned her waist then lifted her up the wall until her breasts were even with his mouth. The restraints he created out of the wall slid up with her.

"That's because you can manipulate me any way you want now without having to release me."

"How about that." He ran his fingers over her abdomen, down over her hip and into her folds. His mouth latched onto one of her breasts. Heather felt the heat of his mouth and the magic of his fingers deep inside her, making her want more.

His tongue swirled against the tip before he pressed a kiss in the valley between her breasts then he focused on the other one. It had Heather squirming. His fingers slipped into her folds again to caress her as he focused his attention on her breasts.

"Now, now, we can't have any of that. You could hurt yourself." He braced one arm against her torso, so she had to keep still.

"My heart."

"Not yet. I know what you can take, and I know how to push you to where I might get those elusive screams."

She wanted to plead but knew he would ignore her. His desire to bring her to new heights each time kept her quiet. Deep down inside she wanted it as much as he did. The magic he worked on her body was something she always wanted.

Soft caresses against her core had her sucking in her breath. The arm bracing her against the wall relaxed and started to wander her body, touching all the spots that ignited her need. She felt the cooler air on the breast Storm was honoring and knew he was working his way down her body. He placed a kiss against her right ribcage then her belly button.

He slid her up the wall a little more before she felt the heat of his mouth on her core. First, he lathed her then suckled her, switching between the two and pushing her toward her orgasm. Each time she got close he would switch, frustrating her for a moment before ratcheting her desire for release a little higher.

"Storm." She wanted to be released and riding him. Her body craved to feel him deep inside her.

He knew what she wanted through their connection, but he wasn't willing to give in yet.

Heather pulled against the restraints, wanting freedom, needing to take control. She craved relief from the exquisite torture he was putting her through. A moan escaped her when she felt two of his fingers slide deep inside her again. They stroked against the sensitive spot he always went after. It had her shaking as her orgasm raced toward her.

Storm pulled her down toward him and drove into her just as she climaxed. She would have moaned if she could have uttered any sound. He held her there as he set a nice strong pace for them.

"Mac, release her."

Heather was able to move her legs and arms again. Her legs went around his hips so she could meet him thrust for thrust. Her arms wrapped around his neck. She felt the heat of his lips on her throat, drawing another moan from her. She wasn't sure she could take much more. Her release was so close, but it evaded her.

Storm changed their pace, moving faster, but driving just as deep. Her breath hitched. She felt it build inside. Slowly filling her with warmth. Her release bubbled up and filled her senses, flinging her out to the stars. She felt boneless, floating along with her climax. It was glorious.

She sighed as she became aware of her surroundings again.

"My heart." Storm brushed his knuckles along her jaw.

"Sorry, there was no scream."

"You really have to stop doing that. It is something I strive for, but it doesn't mean it has to happen every time. As long as you have that out-of-body experience every time, I know I have done my job."

"But you work so hard to get it. I hope it happens as much as you do."

"Yet I'm never disappointed when it doesn't happen. I look at it as an added bonus."

She sighed again. "You make my body sing for you."

"And it is beautiful music."

"It is."

———

Heather walked the hallways that led to their war room. Arc was right behind her. She had found him outside their room when she stepped out this morning and wondered if he had stayed there all night. Storm had gone to see his mother before he would join her and Fridon.

Several children ran past her, and she smiled as she stepped aside. How she missed her children. Terrik and Zuni were isolated from the rest of the children here and she wanted to change that. She entered the war room to find Storm already there.

She greeted her mate with a hug.

"Now is that any way to greet your mate?"

"And how would you like me to do it this time?"

He grinned. "Since we know Fridon will be walking in those doors any moment I will settle for a kiss."

She smiled as she leaned into him. He wrapped his arms around her and pulled her against his body as he lowered his mouth toward hers. Their tongues danced together as they focused on each other. It took Fridon clearing his throat to get them to separate.

"Morning Fridon," said Heather as she took her seat.

"Morning, Heather, Storm." He sat in his chair. "We have the stats from the testing ready to view. We must also finish picking our staff."

"I have decided who I want as my second," said Storm. "I think Bear would be a good fit."

"I do too," said Heather. Now she had to say this right. "He must have been thrilled when you asked him."

"He was."

"And who is your choice, Fridon?"

"I wish to choose Sam."

Storm nodded then looked at his mate.

"You know who I want." Heather looked at her mate, expecting him to argue with her once again.

"I know, and you know how I feel about it." He returned her gaze.

"I do." He didn't say no this time, which she took as a good sign.

"So have you thought about who your tech will be?" asked Fridon.

"I would like Loli," said Heather.

Storm nodded. She knew it didn't surprise him. "She's not held a leadership role before."

"But she is one of the best techs I know, and I have faith she can excel at this." Heather leaned back. "And I assume we all want Kuarto for medical."

The men nodded.

"With Micali as his assistant?"

More nods.

They finished picking their staff and Storm stood. "Time to announce our decision to the council."

"I wish to speak of one other matter first." Heather was the only one who remained seated.

"Is it about our choices?" growled Storm.

"No. I was walking the halls earlier and saw some children run by."

Fridon headed toward the door. Heather knew he didn't want to hear them shouting at each other again.

"This is the safest place for them." Storm sat back down. "You want to bring the twins here?"

"I'm just wondering what type of message we're sending, telling all of Vespia this place is safe for your children, but not ours."

"My heart, they don't know the children exist. You blocked that from everyone's mind to keep them safe."

"I know, my heart, but our children are isolated. They have no one to play with. Bert and Dian are giving them an excellent education, but what about their social skills?"

"And what about Bert and Dian?" asked Storm. "They have become quite attached to our children. I think they would be very sad if we took them away."

"Who says we have to take them away? I've been doing some research and have found a cave big enough to house his ship."

"His ship?" He looked confused. "You want to bring the whole compound down?"

"Why not?" She propped her elbows on the table. "Reasta can't detect it, and it is big enough to hold everyone here if she were to attack the compound again. We'd also have instant access to them."

"And how do you plan on explaining their presence?"

"The same way we're explaining Earth security." She smiled. "They came to us, wanting to help."

"To do what?"

"Teach our children?"

"And how will we explain the sudden presence of our children?" He seemed to be agreeing to her plan.

"I've thought about that and believe I can use the same technique on the parents that I used on Sam when we were trying to figure out what Reasta was up to. When they are outside of Bert's ship they won't remember the twins, when they are inside, they will remember that we wanted them near us, and with the addition of our new guests, we felt comfortable enough to bring them here. I think they would be safer here, and I'm not just talking about our children."

"And where do you want him to land that massive ship of his?"

Heather grinned.

———

Heather took her seat on the dais before Storm and Fridon took theirs. For someone who wanted to blend into the background, she sure happened to be at the center a lot.

"We have deliberated and chosen the rest of our council to face our enemy." She looked at the sea of faces in front of her. "Fridon's choice for his second is Sam."

Her daughter stepped forward, bowed then stepped behind Fridon's chair.

"Our future leader chose Admiral Barrister."

She could hear the whispered surprise of Vespians and humans alike as Bear did the same thing Sam did.

"My choice is Skye Latimer, who is on assignment right now." Heather then named the rest of their staff who stood when their names were called, bowed then joined the other members of each of the staff. Now she needed to address the additions to their ranks. "We have been fortunate.

Several of our allies have requested to help us in our fight against Reasta."

She saw several people nod.

"Earth has pledged over a thousand of their best fighters to join us. Some will be integrated into our elite squads. The rest will be assigned security duties that will take advantage of their skill set.

"We have been approached by another ally who wishes to help us. They are scientists so security isn't something they would be able to join, but they have offered to teach our children while they help us with scientific research. That will allow those caring for our children more freedom to help with this war."

More nodded. She hoped they were some of the people caring for the children. No one seemed upset with the plan which helped calm her. Hopefully, there would be no questions about the ancients when they arrived. Bert was preparing his ship to be converted to fit in the underground cavern she and Storm had offered him. "The rest of the Earth soldiers will be arriving later in the week. Our other guests will be here in a few hours. Welcome them as you have welcomed me."

Arc followed Heather everywhere and it was driving her crazy. "Arc, you don't have to be with me all the time."

"And where am I to go?"

He had asked that before. "When Mac isn't needed, she steps into the wall and rests."

"I do not have that option."

"Why not?" Heather knew she couldn't have him standing outside their room every night. It would attract too much attention.

"It was not built into me."

"But if Mac was first, why wouldn't you have the same abilities with a few upgrades?"

"Mac was the first one you found. It doesn't mean she was the first one of us created. Each computer has different abilities due to their programming."

"Well, we need to figure out what to do with you when you're not needed. Standing outside my door at night will make people talk."

"And that is a problem for you."

"Our people need to feel safe. Having a guard outside our room will make them wonder if we're in danger." Heather looked at him as they headed to security command. "You won't go back to the room I found you in. I can't get you to fade into the wall. There has to be some-thing you can do to not look so conspicuous."

"Why do you wish to hide me?"

"How am I to explain an advanced android when we don't have that kind of technology yet? You are ancient in design, and they are smart enough to figure that out. It could start rumors I don't want circulating."

"I'm not sure I understand."

"The ancients haven't existed for years. The knowledge of your existence would raise their curiosity. They will want to know what you or Mac could tell them about the ancients, what their lives were like when the murals and writings were done. I know they would mean well, but it would interfere with your purpose."

"And why do you think this will happen."

"The same thing happened to me when I first came here. Everyone wanted to know about the little human. It happened again when Storm and I started working with everyone here in the underground caves. The moment I became readily available I became the center of attention."

"Yet you are bringing the ancients here to mingle with the Vespians." The android looked at her. "You are subjecting them to the same thing you are complaining about now."

"Not completely. Bert and his friends will probably stay on their ship so the people they will deal with will be limited. We need access to Bert's technology without risking leaving the planet anymore. It will also give our people a place to go if Reasta figures out how to attack this compound. His ship will protect everyone here." She stopped just outside the opening to their command. "It also will give our friends the chance to be with our children. Something I know they would enjoy immensely."

"But you could be jeopardizing everyone."

"I have thought it through, and I believe it is the best move. Besides, if Bert thought this was a bad idea he would have said no and wouldn't be moving the ship." There were times when she got annoyed with these computers. She knew they were only being curious, but sometimes they persisted when she wished they wouldn't. She started moving again, heading into the command center.

The guard on duty came toward her. "Your guests have everything ready. They are going to land in our second landing cave then transfer their equipment to the caves you have set aside for them."

Heather nodded as she stepped to the main screen with all the data. They sure did work fast. Bert was waiting for permission to land. She signaled all clear and notified the staff in the second cave of their arrival. Storm had made sure the only people there were ones who knew about the ancients, which really was him, Fridon and Sam. It would be difficult for the three of them to do the job that normally took ten, but she was confident they could do it. She would do what she could for them from the command center.

Bert landed the ship and with the help of the rest of the ancients unassembled the sections and placed them in the cave she gave them. She was amazed at how fast they did it. It wasn't long before Bert and Storm came into the command center.

"Thank you for your hospitality, Heather."

She knew he said that because of the people around them. "I hope you found the area we gave you suitable. When you're ready we'll introduce you to the children here."

He nodded. "My people are quite excited about it."

"Good. I'll assemble the children with their parents."

———

Heather brought the Vespian children and their parents to Bert and his friends. She explained to their people that their new guests were educators, which wasn't too far from one of the many things they enjoyed doing. Once Heather finished explaining Bert and his friends, she offered to show the parents the area that had been set up for the children.

Heather led the parents and their children into the compound where Storm stood with the twins. The moment everyone was inside, the doors were sealed. The parents looked around and noticed the twins. Now she would know if they would only remember the twins in this area.

Murmurs were heard as they realized the royal children were there with their children. Heather told everyone that their twins had been away getting special training, but when their friends wanted to come and teach the Vespian children they decided to bring the twins home so they would be taught with the rest of the children.

Storm had talked to the twins earlier and explained they needed to let their mom be the leader she was expected to be. They stood beside him with big smiles on their faces.

His mate introduced Bert to everyone, and he introduced the rest of his friends. Bert approached the twins first.

"These two are yours, Heather?"

"Yes." She smiled at their children. "Terrik and Zunni."

Bert crouched down in front of them. "Nice to meet you."

The children looked up at Storm before they answered in unison. "Nice to meet you, too."

Heather introduced Bert to the other parents and children. Zunni pulled on her father's hand.

"Can I walk with Mommy?"

"Have you asked her?"

"Yes, but she told me to get your permission first."

"Go." He kissed the top of her head before she scampered to her mother. Her small hand slipped into her mother's, and she walked proudly at Heather's side.

His mate finished with the introductions and Bert offered to show them some of the subjects they planned on teaching. Storm took his son's hand, and they walked behind everyone.

———

Heather walked beside her mate. Everyone had dropped off the children with Bert and was heading back to the command center. She leaned into him.

"Is this the way it's going to be?" she asked softly. "Me telling everyone what to do?"

"I would think you would revel in the power."

She just looked at him. "I'd rather just be a soldier."

"You are a leader, my heart. You proved that by having Zunni at your side. It relaxed the rest of the parents to trust Bert and leave their children with him."

"That was your daughter's idea. She could tell they were nervous and wanted to help calm them." Heather put her arm around his waist. "She's showing signs of being a great leader at a very young age."

"She is a lot like her mother," said Storm as he slipped his arm around her shoulders.

Heather looked up at him, giving him the perfect opportunity to capture her lips with his for a quick kiss. He wanted to deepen it; she could tell by his thoughts. "Your mind is betraying you, my heart."

"No, it's not." He brushed his knuckles along her jaw. "It's telling you the truth. I want more than a caste kiss. I want to feel your heat accept me in. Listen as your breath catches." He pulled her against his side. "Watch as your release washes over you."

She wished they were alone too. When he talked to her this way his need was high and always spiked hers.

"But we have work to do." He stopped walking and held her close. "All I can do is stoke your need so high that when we are alone you'll explode in my arms."

The parents following them moved around them, leaving them alone and blocking them from view.

"You normally can't wait when you want me."

"My heart, I want you all the time." He captured her lips for another quick kiss. "But we have learned how good it can be when we have to wait."

"Then the rest of the day is going to be long and torturous."

"And this evening will be glorious."

THREE

Heather watched the training of her human counterparts. Several of the people who would be able to be their mole had made it into some of their elite teams. Each time a team went out they were always a target for Reasta's soldiers, so this could work. She just wished she felt better about it. The idea was great when she first came up with it, but seeing how hard Bear's people were working to prove themselves made her second guess the idea.

Is this what it meant to be a leader?

"Heather?"

She turned to find Mac standing a few feet away. "Yes. Mac?"

"May we speak?"

"Of course." She stepped away from watching the training and walked with Mac.

"I sense Cim."

"Can he sense you or Arc?"

"No. We are shielded from that system until you have us all together."

Heather nodded. That was good to know. It had worried her, and she had made a few adjustments to Cim so he shouldn't be able to sense them anyway. "He is here, but he won't come into contact with you. He has been assigned to stay with Bert and help with the children. He may not leave that area without talking to me."

Mac nodded. "You must be sure it doesn't happen. He cannot know about any of us until you find the last computer."

"Will you explain why? I would think he being aware of you would be a good thing. He has been very helpful in the past."

"I only know what has been programmed in me."

Heather nodded. "Am I to keep all the computers separate until I have found number seven?"

"That is up to you."

Wonderful. No right answer to this. Then, for now, she'd keep them apart. Arc was always nearby, but he hadn't approached her, and Mac wouldn't do anything without her permission.

Arc was different from Mac. She was easy to talk to, like Cim, but Arc was the exact opposite. If he had emotions, she'd swear he was mad at her.

"There is more. We have found another cavern."

"Show me."

Mac handed over the pad with the data for Heather to look at.

"We've been there before. How did we miss it?" Heather studied the data. "Who else knows about this?"

"I alerted you the moment it showed up in my system. It hasn't been detected by the Vespian/ancient system yet."

"Good. Keep it that way." She handed the pad back. "It needs to be checked out before I allow anyone else in there."

"Of course."

My heart? Heather connected her mind with Storm's.

Yes?

Mac has found another cave. According to her data, there are weapons in it.

When do you want to investigate?

This evening, after our meeting with the teams.

———

Heather donned her old Vespian uniform for their excursion to the new cave. Storm teased her about it. She could have worn her gray uniform. Their helmets and gloves would have fit it as well. She didn't wear it because everyone knew about her new uniform. It stood out a little too much for her. If they wanted to do this discreetly no one should know who was in their uniforms once they sealed them.

They headed to the air bikes they had requested. The bikes came in handy in the caverns when they needed to travel. They were quicker than some of the larger transports they used and easy to maneuver.

Heather powered up her bike. She loved riding them. The freedom she felt on them was something she couldn't explain.

"You take point, my heart."

Heather grinned as she snapped her helmet on, then attached her gloves. She took off with Storm right behind her. They zipped through the main cavern, keeping their bikes above the people working below. She maneuvered down several corridors until they hit a less-traveled area.

"After our kiss earlier, I thought about just taking one bike, but not being able to touch you through your sealed uniform and being that close would just frustrate me more."

She laughed. "You are insatiable."

"You say it like it is a bad thing."

They landed their bikes at the edge of the explored areas. From this point on they would walk. Once they could map out the area, it would be added to the database and a flight pattern would be created for it.

They kept their uniforms sealed as they worked their way through the cavern, allowing them to see in the darkness. It wasn't as large as they thought it would be.

"This is odd. What Mac downloaded doesn't seem to match." Heather scanned the area a second time. "You think something is shielding this area? Her data did show weapons."

"Possibly. The weapons she said were here are not visible." Storm ran scans as well. "We know they are here so we'll have to keep this place off-limits until we can locate them."

Heather nodded.

"How was this area kept from us?"

"I'm thinking it's linked to Arc. He has told me he is the weapons computer." Heather looked at the scans she did. "I had hoped this cave would be big enough to house all the humans together."

"You want to isolate them?"

"No, but I do know that most will gravitate to each other anyway, and this would let them have their own place. Some will want to live with our people, but I don't want to force them into anything that would make them uncomfortable."

"Those on an elite team should stay with their team." Storm looked at her.

"Yet, you and I only do that when we're on assignment."

"Our roles are different than other elite team members."

"And adding humans to the teams changes everything too. Humans are used to having their own space. Unless they are on a mission, they don't stay with their teams all the time."

"They are on a mission," he reminded her. "To help us defeat Reasta."

He was right.

"You think I'm coddling them when I'm just trying to give them the same amenities our people have. We need more living space with the people from Earth joining us, and you know it."

"Soft heart." He pressed his hand against her heart.

"Your heart." She did the same to him.

He wrapped his arms around her. "One of the things I love about you."

Heather smiled. It sounded strange to hear Storm use the human word love, but ever since he had time-traveled to Earth at the turn of the twenty-first century and had spent time there he had started using it. It was rare and it touched her heart when he did.

Storm released her. His gloved hand caressed her shield with gentle fingers. "Ready?"

She nodded then placed the small reader they used to measure the caves on the ground in the center of the room. Beams shot out of it, marking and measuring every inch of the cave. Data streamed into her helmet.

"It's still not showing the size that Mac estimated. We're going to have to go and do it by hand."

"Where do you want to start?"

She looked at her screen. "That far wall is where the readings are off."

He took her hand and ushered her to the wall in question. "It seems to match the readings we just took."

"And that doesn't make sense." Heather stepped up to the wall.

"Let's set up the lights in here so we don't have to wear our helmets all the time." Storm went back to the bikes and removed the equipment they brought. It didn't take them long to light up the cavern. Once they were done, they pulled their helmets and gloves off.

Heather knew he wanted access to her body, and with the helmets and gloves on he didn't have that. She stepped back up to the wall and studied it.

"And it has aroused your curiosity, hasn't it?" His voice, close to her ear, sent frissons of heat through her.

She looked up into his glowing eyes. "And you are just aroused." They hadn't had any time to themselves since they dropped the children off with Bert. With no one around Storm could take advantage of the situation.

He just smiled at her. Storm pulled her against him as he captured her mouth with his. He caressed her lips with his tongue. When she opened her mouth, his tongue swooped in to deepen the kiss. His swirled and danced with hers. She felt his hands working on the seals for her uniform, easing it open so he could move the collar that blocked her mark.

He broke the kiss then worked his way across her left cheek, down her throat to her mark. One hand slipped inside her uniform, gently caressing her breast. She felt it to her toes. Just as she was willing to do whatever he wanted he shifted his hold and pulled her close, but he wasn't pushing for their intimacy. "Storm?"

"Why don't I get everything set up for our stay while

you explore a little more? I'll come get you when I'm ready."

They had planned on staying there for the night so she could explore all evening. She knew he was ready now yet was willing to let her try to figure out why the readings weren't matching. "I can wait."

"So can I." He brushed his knuckles along her jawline. "I want your full attention and know you would be distracted by not knowing why the readings are different."

"I'll be as quick as I can." She pressed her lips against his then dashed off.

"Tease."

She looked back at him with a smile, before she turned her attention to one of the corners that had the strange readings. Heather found an opening that led to another room. This was what Mac saw but their scans couldn't detect.

"Storm, you need to come in here." The walls held weapons she had never seen before. Pulling one off the wall she examined it to see what it was supposed to do. It seemed pretty straightforward. She shifted one bar and armed it. Pressed a few buttons to figure out the strength of the blast and how fine the beam could be. She looked up to find Storm at the opening banging on it. What the hell was going on?

———

As she approached it her skin started to crawl. The closer she got the worse it got. Heather didn't want to get too close and wondered how Storm could handle the creepy-crawly way it made her skin feel. She signaled to him, asking him if he tried to connect with her mind, and received a nod as an answer. Okay, so the barrier affected their mental connection.

"Arc, I know this is your doing. Show yourself."

No answer.

"Fine. I'll blow everything in here up." She grabbed a small cylinder, activated it, and set it back on the shelf she found it on.

"Why are you trying to kill yourself?" Arc hadn't appeared, but she knew she got his attention when she heard his voice.

"I've been told I can't die. I might end up with some major damage, but I know I'll heal." She crossed her arms over her chest, totally ignoring the activated ordinance. "Now show yourself."

Arc stepped out of the wall opposite her.

"Why are you testing me?" Heather picked up the bomb and deactivated it but kept it in her hands. So, he could hide himself when he wanted. Why did he tell her he didn't have that function? Computers can't lie.

"Why would you think that?"

"You have been questioning what I do at every turn. I'm not sure what you expect from me, but you're not happy with what you have seen so far."

"You are supposed to be a great warrior, yet you let your mate control you."

"You expect me to walk around like I'm going to war all the time?" Heather shook her head. "You have access to my files, why do you think I can't be the warrior you expect?"

"I do not have access to any files. Cim did because of what he was created for. Mac only has what you have given her and until we connect, I can't access that data."

"You have been following me around for the last few days watching as we work with the humans who have joined our ranks. What have you learned about me in the process?"

"You are too friendly with your soldiers. You laugh with them at a time when they should see you as their leader."

"Arc, I might have a different way of doing things, but they all lead to one place. Defeating Reasta. That is my goal, and we will achieve my goal."

"But are you the leader I've been told you can be?"

"We've come back to you not being able to see my files." She pinched her nose. "Now that you're activated why can't I just give you permission to access my files? Is it just in case one computer fell into enemy hands?"

"Because there is no specific order for you to find us. If we were set up so we could access each other's data without a physical interface, then you could have the data from all the computers through one if you knew how to get at that data. Although that could be beneficial, you need the computers as well to achieve what you want, and our creators didn't want to tempt you."

Whoever created them knew her well. With Reasta fighting for control of the planet she would take any shortcut she could to get rid of the woman.

"If I allow you to gain this knowledge from Cim or Mac wouldn't we still have the same problem? Reasta could still steal you away, and you would have this knowledge."

"The reasoning behind it was if she found us before you did, she wouldn't be able to activate any of us. If we had been connected and she got us before you did, then she would have the firepower designed for you."

"For me? These systems were created for me?" She had suspected this since Mac told her about the seven computers, but this was the first time one of the computers confirmed it for her.

"You knew this."

"I knew I needed to find all of you to activate the whole system so we could defeat Reasta and suspected that their creations were to help me, but this is the first time one of you has actually stated that you were made for me in particular."

"We are ancient in design as you are. A Vespian might have been able to find us, but they wouldn't have been able to activate us. You know that because of Cim. You were the only one to find him and the only one who he would respond to."

What he said was true. The Vespians had been searching for the underground complex for years before she showed up and found it rather quickly. "So now that I've found you it's safe to let you interact?"

"With all but Cim. Reasta is aware of our main computer and until you have all of us connected that is still a danger."

"Even though Cim is underground with us? There is no way Reasta can get to him?"

"What if he has a program that sends her information?"

"Then she'd know about the ancients and would have already captured them." Heather wondered if she should allow them to meet. She needed to speak to Storm. He was her sounding board. When she looked over to where her mate stood, still pounding on the invisible wall, and mouthing something that couldn't be good. She knew she needed to let him in soon or his anger would be hard to control. "You see that man out there? Tell me who he is."

"Storm, your mate."

"And?"

"I'm not sure I understand the question."

"Storm is the future leader of this planet and head of Vespian security."

"And?"

"You said it yourself. He's my mate. As his mate, I'm supposed to defer to him in front of his people. Leader of the council doesn't change that. I'm not going to go against that protocol because I'm considered the leader. Had you thought about that?"

"No."

"That's it? No?" Heather shook her head. It wouldn't do for her to get angry when Storm was mad enough for the two of them. She pointed to her mate. "You see Storm?"

"Yes."

"You need to let him in. He's very angry right now and just might tear you limb from limb. Drop that damn barrier before he fights his way in."

"You need to figure out how to remove it."

"I just might beat him to it." Not what she wanted to hear. Her first thought was to blast it but was pretty sure it wouldn't work.

"Beat him to what?"

"Tearing you limb from limb." She went to the barrier and signaled Storm, letting him know about this new wrinkle. He didn't look happy but nodded.

Heather looked at the weapons around her. What would remove the barrier? She could grab one of the big blasters and try to zap her way through it. She turned to Arc. He expected something. Turning back to the weapons, she tried to figure it out. He expected her to be some sort of super warrior. Common sense would figure this out.

If whatever created the barrier was in the room, it should be close to the wall. No matter how advanced the technology it would still be at its strongest if the source was close and that barrier was thick. It also made her skin crawl but didn't seem to affect Storm so it must be close to the door and on this side of it.

Heather moved to the wall next to the opening. "You know the moment I let Storm in he's going to want to take you apart."

"Why would he do that?"

"Because you threatened me? I am his mate, and the leader of the council. He is supposed to keep me safe."

"I would never harm you."

"Yeah, yeah, I'm the future. I've heard it before." She looked over her shoulder at him. "That isn't going to stop my mate from showing his displeasure at you separating us."

"I don't understand."

"And that's the problem. You are looking at this the wrong way, but you don't know what we have been through. Storm has always been there for me when I needed him. He's my advisor, my protector. I trust him with my life. I also trust his judgment."

"I must be satisfied that you are the woman you are supposed to be."

"Fine." This conversation had happened too many times. Heather turned back to the wall. "According to Bert and all the other ancients I'm coming along nicely."

"You have an odd tone in your voice."

"Do I?" She picked up a small orb to study it. "Perhaps it's because I feel like a specimen under a microscope and not a person. You expect me to run around like She-ra or something."

"What is a She-ra?"

Heather didn't know how to explain the fictional character. She had seen old videos of the animated series when she went back in time and to Earth to find Storm. "Never mind."

There was nothing out of the ordinary about the orb. It didn't glow, hum, or feel warm, yet she knew she had the right one. She pressed three keys.

Storm charged into the room and advanced on her, wrapping her in his embrace the moment he was close enough. "Are you all right?"

"Yes." She smiled up at him. His hands caressed her as if he was checking to see if she was real or a figment of his imagination. "Better now that you are here."

"Is that what blocked the opening?" He kept one arm around her as he reached for the small orb she still held in her hands.

"Yeah. Most of the items seem to be grouped together by what they do." She slid her fingers over the smooth surface.

"And how do you know that?"

"I don't know." She shrugged, not looking up. "I just do."

"Which one will blow a hole through his CPU?"

Heather laughed. "I can show you one that can do some damage, but nothing that would destroy him. You remember what Mac told us?"

"Unfortunately." He glared at Arc for a moment before turning his attention to his mate. "But he needs to be taught a lesson for isolating you that way. You head the war council and are the eyes and ears for the elders. You cannot be out of communication for any reason."

"Perhaps I should distract you?" Her words had the right effect because his touch had become more intimate as he held her.

He dipped his head to her mark. "Maybe I should be the one distracting you."

"You are very good at doing that." She pressed her hand against his heart.

"But you want to deal with this walking computer first."

"He does need to be dealt with." She pressed her hand against his heart. "Once I'm done with him, I can take care of you."

"And I can take care of you." He slid his fingers along her jaw.

Heather knew the glow in his eyes meant their intimacy would be wild in the beginning. It was so bright she was amazed she was still dressed and on her feet. But she had to deal with Arc first. She turned to face the android. "You were built for me, correct?"

"Yes."

"Then that means you are supposed to obey my commands." Her mate slipped his arms around her waist and pulled her back against his chest. His hands worked at the seals of her uniform.

"You haven't issued commands."

That explained a few things. With Mac, she didn't have to act like a superior officer. All she had to do was suggest what she wanted, and Mac did it. So did Cim. "You're right. I had assumed you would pick up on the nuances of my voice and know when I was giving you a command without sounding like it, but I now know that was wrong. You want it in black and white. Here it is. You are to go back to the room where I found you now and stay there until oh six- hundred tomorrow morning then you are to come to the war room. I want you to stay in the background. Be inconspicuous. No one is to know you're there. If you draw attention to yourself or disobey any order I give you, I will allow my mate to mangle this form of yours and I will deny you the ability to create a new one so you will not be able to interact with the rest of Vespian society. You won't be able to learn the way you're supposed to."

"Am I to take this as a threat?"

"I am stating a fact. You don't understand the basic nuances in voice inflection and polite conversation." Storm's hands had opened enough of her suit to slide inside, inching their way to her core. Keeping her focus on Arc became more difficult as he caressed her. "Each time I wanted you to stop following me was a directive. I was just too subtle for you. Mac and Cim understood the underlying command. You don't have that program, so I want to be sure you understand when I give you an order. I will not tolerate you disobeying or ignoring me anymore. Is that understood?"

Arc bowed and faded into the wall.

Heather knew she now needed to give her mate her undivided attention but didn't want to move as he continued to stroke her. Need took over as she got closer to her release.

"Storm."

He turned her in his arms, and she expected to feel the wall of the cave against her back. Instead, she found herself swept up in Storm's arms.

"I know you enjoy it when I lose control, but I need to prove to myself that I can maintain." He nuzzled her throat as he carried her to their temporary bed. "I promise we will still have our wild moments, but not right now."

He allowed her to stand on her own and she laughed when her uniform fell to the floor.

Storm peeled his uniform off, wrapped his arms around her, and set her on the bed. He pressed her back as he joined her.

"You amaze me at times."

"Only at times?" He brushed a few stray hairs from her face. "I must be slipping."

"You? Never. I just can't figure out how you can get me out of my clothes so easily. You were carrying me."

"I have my ways, my heart." He pulled her into a sitting position so he could release her hair from the braid she always wore now. His fingers slipped through her soft tresses as he loosened it so her white-blonde hair hung loosely around her face. "You have such beautiful hair, especially when it is loose like this."

"You like the way it fans out around my head when we're intimate." She reached back and touched his face.

"I won't deny that." He lifted a section and brushed it against his face. "And it feels like silk against my skin when you're above me."

Heather loved the feel of his fingers combing through her hair. She leaned her head back against his shoulder and looked up at him. His tenderness when he was ready to explode made her feel loved. Storm's mouth claimed hers as his hands touched every sensitive spot he could reach.

Storm broke the kiss and touched her face. "I'm sorry, my heart, but I can't wait."

Heather turned in his arms and wrapped her legs around his hips, letting him know she was more than ready for him. He helped her center herself, and she slid down his erection. A smile spread across his lips as he leaned her back once again.

Storm set a strong pace that had her shaking. Each thrust filled her with need. She hiked her legs higher, wanting more, which Storm gave her. They raced together toward their release. It got closer and closer but still was just out of reach. Storm hit one of her more sensitive spots drawing a moan from her.

"So close."

Heat pooled in her belly before it flowed out through her body, flinging her into the stars. Her heart beat hard in her chest as her body became boneless. A satisfied smile spread across her face. Only Storm could bring her to these heights.

His fingers brushed against her face. "My heart."

She wanted to speak but it was beyond her at the moment. Her mate smiled at her. He knew.

"The way I take your breath away each time fills me with joy." He pressed his lips to her mark.

She sighed. He held her close, his hands wandering where they wanted to, igniting her for a second round. He always wanted to make it up to her when their intimacy was a bit wild. Now they would take their time with each other, filling the other with need and then joy as they reached their climax once again.

———

Heather looked at all the ordinances they had moved from the cave. Her plan was to turn that cave over to Earth's security, but not until they had removed every weapon.

They had put everything into the war room so they could be studied by her council. She found them intriguing. They were a combination of Vespian, Earth, and Ancient technology, and exactly what they needed right now.

Arc had followed her commands and now stood toward the back of the room, watching.

The shield that trapped her was the one they were reverse-engineering first. Fridon was very close. If they could utilize the technology the way they wanted to, they could cut off Reasta's grain supply. The lack of grain would mean she wouldn't be able to control her troops as easily as she could at the moment since she synthesized the grain for a mind-control drug.

"Heather?"

She turned toward Fridon, who was the one doing most of the work on the shield. He must have asked her a question, and she wasn't paying attention. "Sorry. I was thinking how helpful that shield will be if we can enlarge it enough to protect our crops."

"It's the thickness that will be tricky. I can make it large enough but making sure our suns' light can penetrate without a person going through is going to take some work."

"The light from our suns travels at the same speed all the time, can you set it for speed?"

"I can, but I worry that our enemies will figure that out."

"True." Heather picked up one of the weapons. There was something about it that she liked but didn't know why. "Earth has been doing cross wavelengths for years. I'll get the data for you to make this easier."

Fridon nodded. "I'll also pull from our border technology."

Storm came into the room. "Our ship is landing with the rest of your human security."

"Then we should go meet them." Heather waited until Fridon stood before heading out the door. She signaled Arc to follow.

"She still doesn't like being in control, does she?" Fridon asked Storm as he fell into step behind her.

"Oh, she does at times, just not now."

"I can hear you," she said.

"You were supposed to, my heart." Storm wrapped an arm around her waist. "I like it when you take control."

Heather could feel the heat of a blush fill her cheeks.

They entered the large underground hanger and waited for the ship to be cleared and powered down.

"You know I like that color that fills your cheek."

"I know." She rested her hands on the blush that wouldn't go away.

The gangplank lowered while Heather tried to control her emotions. Bear joined them and one look from him had her going into soldier mode.

———

Storm watched his mate as she locked her emotions deep inside. He didn't like the fact that she had to do it because of the humans. She should be able to be herself.

Skye stepped off the ramp and joined Heather. Storm and Fridon stood behind her, showing their silent support. In groups of four, the people from Earth stepped off the ship. Turning their heads toward Heather and Bear, they saluted as they passed them. Storm noticed several of the soldiers took note of the two of them standing behind his mate.

They lined up outside the ship in rows of ten and waited.

His mate knew her job well because she stepped away from them and moved until she stood in front of the new arrivals. "All of Vespia thanks you for volunteering to help us defeat our enemy. I know many of you have families relying on the grain from Vespia to live. We have a cave set aside for you. The next few days you will be tested. Show the Vespians what it means to be in Earth security."

A large group of Vespians lined up behind her. "These soldiers will escort you to your new living quarters. Get settled and I'll be by to explain the Vespian way of life and what is expected of you. You are dismissed."

The troops filed out.

Heather walked up to her mate and placed her hand on his heart. She placed her other hand on Fridon's shoulder. "My sentinels."

"They needed to know that Vespia supports you." Storm placed his hand on top of hers.

"And I think they got the message."

Loud voices came from inside the ship. Heather turned toward it. "I thought everyone was off the ship."

"Latimer just went back in," said Bear.

"Is he arguing with someone?"

The sound got louder, making Storm wonder the same thing.

"Look, Mr. Latimer, I don't care if you are the king of Siam. I brought some very delicate items that I refuse to leave on this ship."

"Henry?" asked Heather as she looked at Bear. She knew that voice anywhere.

"He wouldn't let me leave him behind," said Bear. "Even enlisted so we couldn't turn him down. It took everything I had for him to wait until I got approval to join you."

Heather turned toward Storm and gave him the smile that always took his breath away. She ran to the gangplank. Henry, the man he had met on Earth when Heather was pregnant, came into view, wearing an UCE uniform.

"There's my girl." He came down to embrace her in a fierce hug. "Now, I don't want to be naming names, but that Latimer won't let me bring my gear down."

"What did you bring that has him stopping you?" Heather knew Skye was just following protocol. Nothing was allowed on the planet without being approved. Skye must have scanned his items and knew there was something he would need to clear before it could leave the ship.

"You knew everything needed to be listed and checked before you came."

"You too? I added them to my cargo list." Henry shook his head. "I brought some seeds I'll need to grow food for these people. You know they're not used to Vespian food and no one in their right mind would eat CG food when they can have the real thing."

CG? Heather heard in her mind.

She knew Storm had no idea what that stood for. She looked at her mate, then Fridon and saw the same confused look. She laughed mentally.

You and Fridon asked me the same question at the same time through our mental connections. It means computer generated.

Storm smiled. "That is one thing that humans and Vespians agree on. Your seed needs to be checked out first, Henry. We have kept diseases from my people by following this protocol."

"And if your scans harm my seeds?"

"I promise it is a very delicate procedure, and you will be made aware of any problems the moment it is found."

———

The cave Earth's security was given was huge. It could hold a lot more than the group now residing in it. Mark Russell wanted to know why they were being so giving when Vespians were known for their secrecy. Did Captain Drexel have something to do with it?

He set his gear on one of the bunks. She was just as pretty as he remembered, and he could tell she was fit but still just as thin. There was something different about her though. Heather was more sure of herself. Maybe it was because of those two Vespians standing behind her. They were massive. Tall, well-muscled. He bet there wasn't an ounce of fat on their body. Did Heather look the same? He sure would like to find out.

He wondered if she would remember him. He had been half in love with her before Susan started spouting her vile lies and he had fallen for it when they were in school. The pain in Heather's eyes when he acted like all the others cut him to the core. It was one of the reasons he volunteered to come here. To ease his conscience. He also wanted to see if they could start anew. Was she lovers with both men? Would they allow her to take on a third?

Only time would tell.

FOUR

Heather stood in front of their guests. Now she had to explain about the way Vespians viewed sex and put to rest those fake stories of orgies in the street. She used the same speech she gave the first group. Then she went into what they should expect in the next twenty-four hours. "Tonight, we will have a gathering that will allow you to meet your Vespian counterparts. I expect everyone to be on their best behavior. Training will start at oh five hundred Earth time. Any questions?"

"Dress code?"

"We will issue modified Vespian uniforms for you to wear. In here I will allow you to wear rank, but not on missions. Our enemy doesn't need to know that you're not Vespian. There is an on-duty and off-duty uniform. No civilian clothing unless specified. All your data is loaded into the fabric of the uniforms issued to you so there is no borrowing. You are responsible for the proper care of your uniforms."

"Are your monkey suits any more comfortable than these damn things?" asked Henry.

Heather laughed. "I find them quite comfortable, Henry, but I've been wearing uniforms for years. You'll get used to it."

"I hope not."

Several people laughed at his comment.

Heather turned to the Vespians holding the new uniforms. "Once you change drop your old uniforms into the recycle bins. I want no evidence that you're human. From this point on everyone is a Vespian."

"Yes, ma'am." They responded in unison.

Heather turned on her heel and exited the cave. Storm and Fridon followed her out.

"Where do you plan on having this gathering?"

She flashed him her best smile. "That's my next challenge."

———

Somehow, she pulled it off. Finding a room large enough to house several thousand people was part of the problem, but she was able to use the mess hall as well as several surrounding halls. Being in charge had its perks. No one balked when she made her requests, they just hurried to get it done. Too bad Arc didn't seem to be learning from this. He was there, following her command of being inconspicuous but other than that he seemed oblivious.

Everyone had changed into their off-duty uniforms, including her. The dove grey version of the Vespian outfits made her stand out a little more than she wanted, but she was doing this for the people. She was the council right now and had a suspicion it would be like this for the rest of her life.

Storm stood beside her. "Human alcohol? Are you sure that is wise?"

"This will show us who can keep themselves in check. Anyone who gets out of hand shouldn't be on any elite teams. The smart ones will stay away from it completely." She smiled at different people as they milled about. "They will figure out they're being tested."

Bear came and joined them. "It feels strange to be wearing someone else's uniform."

"It looks good on you, sir."

"You aren't going to be able to call me sir anymore since Storm has chosen me as his second."

"I don't know if I can call you by your real name, sir. Been trained too well."

Bear laughed. "Well, you're going to have to figure something out because I will correct you every time. No matter when you say it."

Heather knew he was right, but she couldn't call him by his first name. Could she call him by his rank? "Well, I know what I want to call you."

"Oh, please, I've worked hard to get rid of that name."

"Yet the moment any child calls you that, you melt and don't care. Most of security calls you it behind your back anyway." She was talking about the twins, but no one outside of Bert's complex knew they existed.

"I know." He frowned. "Fine."

"It's part of your last name, sir. There is no disrespect by it."

He nodded but didn't look pleased.

Mac stood close by, waiting to speak to her. Heather excused herself. "What did you find out, Mac?"

"The Earth seeds will grow in Vespian soil, but they won't be as healthy as on Earth. I can make the changes needed, but our suns will be too powerful."

"Then we need to find a cave that can be converted into

a grow space." Heather wasn't happy with the setback. How were they going to do this?

"You do have the cave the humans are in."

"I know, but I had hoped we could plant immediately."

"You do plan on moving a lot of the humans into elite squads, and command positions. They will be moving out quickly."

"True, but with all the new people. We might need that area for housing anyway."

"I will continue to see what can be done."

Heather nodded then headed back to her mate.

"You do not look happy." Storm wrapped his arms around her. "Shall I make you smile, my heart?"

"All you have to do is be near me and I smile." Heather placed her hand against his heart. "I'm trying to find a place to give to Henry so he can plant his seeds. It's becoming a little harder than I thought it would be."

"There are plenty of caves to still explore. I can assign a small contingent to look for something he could use."

"I thought the same thing, but you know I have to clear each one before it can be used. I might as well be the one to explore them."

"And you don't have the time because of the war council."

"You see my problem." She looked around at the people around them. "We seem to have drawn some attention."

"Those staring are the humans."

"They're not used to seeing their commanding officers acting like we are." She smiled up at him. She had gotten used to his attention at any time and wasn't about to change that. This was something her human counterparts were going to have to get used to.

"It is something they will have to understand too

because I will never stop touching you when I want or kissing you when I want."

"Or being intimate with me when you want?"

"If I could do that, I'd keep us locked in our room forever." He pulled her closer. "But I have wonderful fantasies of what I would do with you if I could lock our door for a few days."

"Why are you fantasizing, my heart?" She wrapped her arms around his neck. "Have I been remiss in making sure we have enough time alone?"

"I'm humbled you have been able to give us as much time as you have, knowing all we have to accomplish." He bent his head and captured her lips for a quick kiss. "I'm not talking about the quantity of our time. That I have no complaint about. I just remember before all this started, I could sweep you away from time to time and keep you all to myself."

"We still had jobs to do. We didn't really have that much time to ourselves."

"I know, but that is part of the fantasy." He smiled down at her. "We have all the time we want so I can bring out a few of those screams I love so much."

"Do those fantasies involve restraints?"

"And oil." He dipped his head to hers, capturing her lips with his. He slipped one hand inside the waistband of her pants to cup her buttocks while the other slid up under her blouse to the nap of her neck.

"Please tell me I don't have to hose you two off."

A growl escaped Storm as he released his mate. Heather just grinned at her brother. "Good to see you, Kuarto."

He kissed her cheek.

"Are you ready for tomorrow?"

"Yes." He stood beside his sister after she disengaged

from Storm. "Once the orientation is done, we'll insert the Vespian com device, tracking devices, translator as well as the new inhibitor."

"Good."

"Why haven't you told our guests about tomorrow?"

"They are soldiers, Kuarto."

"You are testing them."

She gave him a bright smile. "I have worked with some of these soldiers. The smart ones already know what to expect and know they are being tested."

"And the rest will figure it out in the morning?"

"Exactly."

———

Heather was beautiful. Mark had wondered if her body was as honed as these Vespians. Seeing her in her off-duty uniform answered that question. The top stopped at her mid-drift. Her pants sat low on her hips, exposing her belly button and those nice tight abs.

The skinny young woman he knew was gone.

He had been studying the way she interacted with the men constantly around her. In the beginning he thought she might have had several lovers, but now he wasn't sure. Storm, the Vespian she married, was her lover, of that, he was sure. Especially after that kiss when he slid his hands inside her clothing. Heather used to keep to herself. Being touched like that would make her uneasy and she had used her training to bring a few to their knees when they tried.

The other one, Fridon, who he had thought was another lover, treated her more like a sister. It looked like Storm was the only one she allowed in her bed.

He had wanted to speak to her, but there was always

someone around her. Her mate, Fridon, that doctor he had just seen, even Latimer, the man who had piloted the ship that brought them here. She was well protected. Perhaps it was better he couldn't get near her right now. He wouldn't know what to say to her.

The drink in his hand was warm, but he didn't want it anyway. It was more for show as he tried to learn as much as he could about Heather and these people. The few he had spoken to spoke of her with respect and love. It seemed she had captured a few more hearts along the way.

———

Storm wanted to know who the human was that was staring at his mate. After all they had been through, he didn't trust any stranger. Before he could move toward the man Skye had stepped up to him.

As tough as he was on Skye in the beginning, he was happy to have him on their side. Latimer would make sure the staring would stop and give him a briefing when he was done investigating the human.

His mate took his lack of attention to gather a group of Vespians around her. She might not have wanted the role of leader, but she had been doing a magnificent job so far. He worried she was pushing herself too much, which was her habit.

She gave the directions she wanted to give them before she came back to him, slipping her arm around his waist. She looked up at him. "Why are you frowning?"

"I felt this empty space beside me."

She laughed as she hugged him. It sounded like music to his ears.

"I promise not to do that too often, but you seemed to be preoccupied, and I needed to give directions to the chefs." The smile she gave him had his libido kicking into overdrive.

"And you have more you wish to speak with?"

"I need to speak to the head of each elite team and then our boards. Once that is done, I'm all yours."

He smiled back at that. Storm pulled her close and captured her lips with his. His tongue dipped into her mouth when she opened it for him. They clung to each other as he deepened the kiss. Their tongues danced together, causing their desire for each other to rise.

When he broke the kiss, they both sighed.

"I wish we were in our room." Storm brushed his fingers along her jaw.

"Soon, my heart."

———

Mark sensed someone step to his side and knew why they were there. He knew he could act like he didn't but refused to act stupid. "They have quite a passionate relationship, don't they?"

"They do." Skye was silent for a moment. "You realize you've made yourself a target by staring at Heather?"

"I haven't been staring, Commander, I have been observing. I read the dossier given to us by the Vespian council. I know what they've been through and that he's very protective of her. But I remember the young girl and can't help but compare them."

"You only knew her for a few weeks."

Mark smiled. Latimer had done his research as well.

"Heather Drexel is one of those people, Commander, that you never forget." He looked over at Skye Latimer. "And I wouldn't have been allowed to join the security contingent sent to help Vespia if I wasn't one of the best.

Her mate can focus on me all he wants. I'll prove I deserve to be here."

"Good, because you will be tested." Skye saw Heather signal him over. "And Mark? He is the best in any security so you will have to push yourself to make him respect you."

———

Heather was explaining how tomorrow would go when she noticed the chatter around her had died. She looked to see what caused everyone to quiet down. Toki was coming at them. The moment she spotted her mate's sister she bowed and everyone around her did the same thing.

Toki approached them with a smile. "This is your council." She stated more than was asked. "I believe it is incomplete."

Heather looked at Storm. They had filled every position properly. What was she talking about?

"I wish to be on your council."

"You do?" Heather realized her blunder too late. "Of course, Toki."

"Always curious." She pressed a kiss to Heather's cheek and whispered. "I was one of Storm's best security guards before I became religious leader."

Heather knew it to be true. Her friend was inside there; she just only came out when they were alone. "We would be honored to have you with us."

Toki smiled at her. Now Heather needed to introduce the staff of the War Council. Once that was done everyone would be free to do what they wanted.

———

Heather was happy that was over. Storm slipped his arm around her.

"Time to go, my heart," he whispered in her ear.

"I know." She sighed.

"What has you sighing like that?" He urged her toward the doors.

"I'm so used to being the last one to leave that this just feels strange."

"You have been my mate long enough to get used to leaving early," he reminded her.

"Yeah, well having Earth's security here has me remembering." She leaned into him. "And normally we left because your libido demanded it. Not because we had to."

"True, but if you had wanted to stay, I would have waited." He slipped his arm around her.

She laughed. "You would have pouted, and you knew it."

"I do enjoy our times alone." He gave her a squeeze. "And I have a wonderful surprise that will make you forget all about everything but us."

"Really?" She looked up at him with a spark in her eyes. "Let me deal with Arc first."

She gave him the same command as yesterday, with the exception of joining them in the training area. Arc had to be in place before the soldiers entered and started their warm-ups. Once she was done with him, she went back to Storm. "You said something about a surprise?"

"Yes." He handed her a bit of cloth. "But first you need to put this on."

"A blindfold?" She brushed a hand across the soft cloth. "I won't be able to see where I'm walking."

"You won't have to." Storm swept her up in his arms. "Now I'm not moving until you put it on."

She pressed the material against her eyes, allowing it to bond with her skin then looped her hands around his neck.

"That's my girl."

He carried her out of the main hall doors and down a corridor. He hadn't turned right, which was the way to their room, but left. Where was he taking her?

———

"Any hints?"

"That would spoil the fun." He pressed a kiss against her forehead. "And don't dispose of that blindfold. I have plans for it later."

He didn't carry her too far before he let her feet touch the ground. Storm turned her so she was facing him and took her hands. "Now I need you to be very careful. Take three steps back."

She held on as she did what he asked. Her feet banged against something hard.

"Now you need to lower yourself."

"You know you could let me remove the blindfold and make this easier on us." He didn't say a thing, but she knew by his silence he wasn't going to give in. She lowered herself to a soft seat.

"Good." Storm held onto her hands as he moved around her. "Now swing your right leg over. There you go."

He sat down, facing her. Pulling her close, he helped her wrap her arms around him. She felt him lean forward and activate whatever they were on. The hum was familiar.

"An airbike?" She could feel the bike lift off the ground before moving forward. What exactly did he plan on doing on the airbike?

"I need you to slide your legs over mine and lock them behind my back."

Heather hoped he knew what he was doing. Being intimate on a bike might be exhilarating to think about, but she did want to survive it. He wrapped one arm around her waist and steered the bike with the other. He maneuvered it so it would dip and shift from side to side so she couldn't tell when they were turning or entering a different cave that had a lower ceiling. Storm was doing a good job keeping their final destination a secret.

"You know holding you close like this has my mind on what I enjoy doing when it's just the two of us and I can hold you so intimately."

"I thought that was what you were up to."

"I know. I can smell your excitement at the thought." He pressed a kiss against her jawline. "It is a beautiful scent."

Hmm, he hadn't denied her comment, but he also hadn't made a move to undress her.

"That wonderful mind of yours is trying to figure this out, isn't it?"

She felt his voice next to her ear, his breath teasing the soft hairs there, and sending little frissons of desire through her.

"Too bad we've arrived, or I just might see how easy it is to be intimate on this airbike." He landed the bike then powered it down. She stood and found herself lifted off her feet. "Nope. You don't get to walk. I'm taking advantage of that blindfold."

She heard doors open then close again once Storm walked through them. He set her feet on the floor.

"Now I need you to kneel, my heart."

Now what was he up to? He helped her by holding her hands as she kneeled.

"You may remove the blindfold."

Heather pulled it off and found the twins grinning at her. She opened her arms. "My little hearts."

They ran to her, coming close to knocking her over in their excitement to hug her. She laughed at their enthusiasm. After there had been plenty of hugs and kisses Heather looked around the room. They were in their rooms at the palace. How did Storm do this?

"I spoke to Bert, and he offered a large section of his ship for the parents to use. There is enough space for all the parents to stay with their children in the evenings. Bert is setting up a common room so the children and their parents can mingle."

"My heart." She crawled over to him and pressed a kiss to his lips.

He pulled her toward him and soon they were joined by the twins. Storm laughed as a second round of hugs and kisses started. They played with the children until it was time for them to get ready for bed.

"I need to speak to Bert to get the final room assignments." Storm pressed a kiss to his daughter's cheek and then his son's. "I will be back in time to tuck you in."

"Okay, Daddy."

"See you in a few minutes." He wrapped his arms around Heather and pulled her close. His lips claimed hers. They clung to each other until the twins hugged their legs.

"Come on you two," said Heather. "Time to change."

"And then you'll tell us a story?"

"Of course."

They dressed quickly then curled up with her as she thought about what type of story to tell them.

Storm finished up with Bert as quickly as he could and headed back to their room. He found his mate curled up with the twins as she softly told them a story about a frightened young girl who had been left as a sacrifice for a fierce dragon. The dragon was enchanted and lived part of his time as a human. He needed someone to care for him, but the only way for him to break the enchantment was to have one of these women he demands from the village to fall in love with him.

Bubbles yawned and he knew it was time for him to interfere.

"Time for bed."

"But Mommy hasn't finished the story yet."

"You two can barely keep your eyes open." She kissed her son on the cheek then her daughter on the forehead.

Storm bent down and offered each child his forearm. Once they wrapped their hands around it and laced their fingers together the way their dad had shown them, he lifted them and carted them to their beds. "You two are going to be too big for this soon. Your feet can touch the ground."

"But we like this, Daddy," said Turrik. "We can scrunch up real small if that will help."

Storm chuckled as he deposited them in their beds. "Or maybe we can come up with something else that you will like just as much."

Heather gave her daughter and her son a kiss. Storm did the same thing. They clasped hands as they walked to the door and lowered the lights. "Sleep tight, my little hearts."

"Night, Mommy."

Storm pressed his palm against the pad to close the door to their room and put his arms around his mate. Normally the doors opened and closed when they triggered the censors, but the children running around their room as they played kept triggering the door and it drove him crazy, so he set it to be done manually. Once they got a little older and didn't trigger the door all the time, they would switch it back to the sensors.

"Thank you for this." She hugged him tightly.

"We have missed them, and I knew you wouldn't be able to focus knowing they were so close, yet you couldn't be with them as much as you wanted to." He returned her hug. "I would have the same problem."

"I knew you had a soft heart."

"I do when it comes to you and our children." He urged her toward their room. "Do you have that blindfold?"

Heather pulled it out of her pocket.

"I have a surprise for you and that blindfold will allow me to do this properly." He took the blindfold from her and gently pressed it against her brow. Once the bonds sealed on her face, he wrapped his left arm around her waist and took her right hand in his.

They stepped over the threshold and the doors closed behind them. "The one thing I missed was the power to remove our clothing with a thought."

"And now that you're close to Cim again?"

"I have that power once again." He smiled when his hand rested against her stomach and not her leisure outfit anymore.

They walked to the edge of the bed.

"I want you to climb into the middle of the bed and wait for me." With his help, she got on the bed and moved where he wanted her. She folded her legs under her and braced her hands on either side.

He found her beautiful. She sat there, naked, and so trusting. It took his breath away. Storm watched as her breasts gently swayed when he joined her on the bed. He wanted to show her how he now had the ability to program their room to look like any room they wanted. Three were already programmed in and that was what he wanted to show her, but he couldn't take his eyes off her.

"You're watching me again, aren't you?"

"Yes. Having you sit there with that blindfold on humbles me."

"Why?"

"The trust you have in me." He sat next to her and braced one arm behind her. "When I met you, you had these walls around you. You didn't trust anyone but yourself."

"True, but I had found it hard to rely on anyone. I was considered strange by my counterparts because of that device. They weren't sure they could trust me." She turned toward him and moved her hand until it rested on his heart. "Then you came along and accepted me as I was. Each time something has happened you've taken it in stride. I never saw the looks I would get from others when I developed a new 'talent' from you."

"My heart." He brushed his fingers along her jaw. "You have a wonderful ability."

"One that frightens me to death at times, but not you. Your faith in me and what I can do is humbling, too."

He pressed a kiss against her mark. "I also remember when you first learned I could shape-shift. It didn't frighten you. In fact, I believe you were mad at me for not telling you."

"Well. It was extenuating circumstances. I didn't have time to do anything but get angry."

Storm knew she was talking about the time she had been kidnapped by Ialog. That was when his talent developed. It allowed him to get close to her without Ialog knowing. He had some wonderful memories from that time.

"Your anger is a glorious thing to see." He ran his fingers against the edge of her blindfold then eased it off her face. "But so is your desire for me."

Heather laughed. "Until that anger is aimed at you."

"Which has happened from time to time, but then we always make up and that, my heart, is my favorite part." He pressed a kiss to her mark. "Now, what do you think?"

She looked around in awe. "This is the cave."

"I enjoyed our time here and I decided to program it into the system. I have two others." He wrapped his arms around her. "Loft."

Their surroundings changed. A high vaulted wood ceiling was above them. Heather hugged him. "This is your cabin from when you went back in time. I loved it here."

"And of course, I couldn't leave out one other place, but for our safety, we need to stand."

"I know what is coming." She looked at him. The smile she gave him told him she had pulled the word from his mind. Once they were safely standing, she uttered one word. "Wall."

The room changed once again, and they were on his ship where he had created a chair just for their intimacy. The wall was where he had added restraints for a mission simulation, and he used it to his advantage once the simulation was done.

"You were very proud of those screams," Heather murmured.

"Of course. It was the first time you gave up total control." He touched her face. "Of course, I didn't give you much of a chance, but we both enjoyed it immensely."

She tilted her face up and pressed her lips against his.

Storm wrapped his arms around her and pulled her closer as he deepened the kiss. His tongue dipped in and searched for hers, they swirled and stroked each other until he heard his mate sigh.

He broke the kiss and smiled down at her. "So which place would you like?"

"I was going to ask you the same thing."

"Oh, no you don't." He pressed a quick kiss against her lips. "I made this surprise for you. You get to pick."

"I don't know." She rested her hand against his heart. "I miss the palace and this whole scenario is a way to prove no matter what Reasta does we will win. But the other places have strong memories as well."

"This is our place now. We can utilize a different one each night until we get tired of them."

She laughed. "I doubt that will happen."

"No procrastinating, my heart."

"Do you mind if you use our room from the palace? I'd like to have familiar things around me for once."

"As long as I get to be intimate with you, I don't care what you choose."

She smiled as she touched his face. "Palace."

The room shifted to their room in the palace. Storm slipped his arms under her legs and lifted her before carrying her to their bed. He set her on the bed then joined her. His fingers caressed her skin as she settled back into the bed.

Tonight, he wanted to take it slowly and bring his mate to the heights he knew she could reach. Wild or sweet, he always looked forward to their intimacy. Heather's honest, open reaction to his touch was addictive.

"What?" Heather asked.

"I didn't say anything."

"No, but you're staring at me again."

"Not staring, my heart, anticipating." The smile she gave him had his heart racing. He brushed his fingers across her mark before sliding it down her collarbone to her breast.

Heather settled back on the bed once again and closed her eyes as she enjoyed his touch. Her hands hit the blindfold, and she looked at him with that beautiful smile of hers before pressing the blindfold against her eyes.

"Why the blindfold, my heart?"

"Because I don't want to know where you will touch me next. I remember when we were aboard ship and you used Fridon's invisibility cloak I didn't know where you were going to touch me, and it heightened my excitement. We're finally back in our rooms, even if it is a hologram, and I want to enjoy this."

"I promise you will, my heart." He brushed his fingers against the soft tissue of her breast. "We both will."

———

Heather let go of everything and allowed her mate to have what he wanted most. Time to play with her body the way he always wanted to, but she rarely let him. Her heart beat hard in her chest at the thought of what he might do. That was part of the problem. She knew what he was capable of and half the time just the thought of his hands on her body had her more than ready for him.

She fought the desire to pull his head down where she wanted it by curling her fingers into her palms. Storm must have seen her do that because his fingers started caressing the inside of the arm closest to him as he lifted it above her head. She felt something close around her wrist, and she knew he was using restraints on her.

"I'm not that bad."

"My heart, you are like me when it comes to our intimacy. You get overwhelmed and want to take control. This will allow you to just lay back and enjoy." He moved to her leg, still giving her the wonderful caresses that made her desire spiral up as he eased it into another restraint.

She felt the bed shift and knew he was going to the other side to restrict her movements. She opened her mouth to tell him she promised to behave and felt his finger on her lips.

"I know, you promise to behave, but I have found it's hard for you to keep that promise when your desire is high. You have enjoyed our intimacy a lot when I keep you still." He closed the last restraint then brushed his fingers along her jaw, down across her mark, through the valley between her breasts, and downward until he reached her toes. It was delicate and oh-so arousing.

She wanted to touch him, and her hands moved but were stopped by the restraints. Storm was right. His hands continued to travel her body, touching all the right places and igniting her need. He shifted and she felt the heat of his breath on her breast. Her nipples puckered in anticipation.

"You seem to be a bit over-sensitive. Did your mind expand again?"

"I don't think so." She licked her lips. "Perhaps it's the thought of being back in our rooms?"

"Whatever the reason will limit what I want to do to arouse you. If I'm not careful I'll end up in those restraints while you have your way with me, again."

"It only happened once." Heather laughed. "And you wanted to see if I could do it."

"And you could do it again."

"I doubt it. You always take my breath away and pull any focus I might muster up to what you do to me. I wouldn't be able to think about it let alone have a strong enough focus to even try to do it right now." She felt the bed shift again as he moved.

"And if I challenged you?" He placed his hands on her sides.

I'm not sure I can handle that."

"I know better."

She felt his tongue brush against the tip of her breast and held her breath. A sigh escaped her when his mouth closed over it. That was what she wanted. His tongue swirled against her tender tissue, and she sighed again. Her breath caught once again when he moved to her other breast.

His hands had stayed against her sides, but they started moving down her body as he focused on her other breast. The anticipation was driving her crazy. She felt his fingers move across her stomach before sliding down her hips. Then she felt them on the inside of her thighs, soft feather-like caresses that had her quivering. The gentle sucking motion doubled her need. She couldn't take much more.

"Storm."

"Easy, my heart." He placed a kiss on her abdomen, dipped his tongue into her belly button, then worked his way down to her core.

A sigh escaped her when she felt the heat of his mouth against her mound. Then gentle fingers entered her, stroking a very sensitive spot deep inside. She arched up when he brushed against it with perfect pressure. If she hadn't been retrained, she would have wrapped herself around him and probably flipped them over so she could be in control.

"You wish to be in control, don't you?" Storm rested his chin against her stomach.

"Yes." Her response was soft.

"Then I am glad I restrained you." He pressed another kiss against her abdomen. "You have been pushing yourself too hard and my job is to relax you until you become boneless."

"Everyone is depending on me."

"My heart, everyone is depending on your council. Don't forget you have us to help you." He brushed his hands across her ribs which drew a laugh from her.

Ever since she got pregnant with the twins, she had become ticklish, and Storm knew every spot and whenever she needed to relax, he would take advantage of it.

"I haven't forgotten."

"You still blame yourself for her being here."

She nodded. Words weren't needed.

"Then tonight I'm going to make you forget that. At least for a little while." He knew trying to convince her that Reasta could have come to Vespia without her presence was futile so tonight he wanted to take her breath away and send her to the stars. His fingers started to roam her body, gently caressing the soft skin they brushed against. She felt each touch deep inside.

"Storm." Her voice was close to a whisper. She was getting lost in the sensations.

Her mate knew she couldn't take much more. If she fought her restraints much longer, she just might hurt herself. He kissed his way up her body pausing at her breasts for a few moments. The moist heat of his mouth had her arching up against him, which had him slipping his arms around her so he could feast on her breasts more. His tongue circled her nipple, sending little currents of desire through her blood.

"Please."

"I can't deny you when you beg like that." He moved

up her body. His fingers laced with hers as he drove into her.

She moaned her pleasure as he filled her. Her body quaked. He started moving inside her, lighting her nerve endings on fire. Heather couldn't get enough. She met him thrust for thrust, pulling on her restraints as she lost herself in the sensations.

"So close," she murmured. There was a soft pressure on her wrists and then she was able to move. Storm had freed her hands and feet. Heather wrapped her legs around him and they raced toward their release. She felt hers start in the pit of her stomach flowing through her bloodstream until it enveloped her.

There was nothing but her, her mate, and that glorious climax.

FIVE

They had given Henry a smaller cavern to use for his crops. Heather knew he needed more space, but at the moment they just didn't have it. He had grumbled but understood. She would keep looking. Something would come along. She just didn't know how long it would take.

"Heather?"

She turned when she heard Fridon's voice. She caught a glimpse of Arc standing against one of the walls. True to her commands he had remained out of sight and watched. She had forgotten he was there most of the time.

"I think I found a solution for Henry and his crops." He held out a palm-size sphere. "I can put a shield over his seeds that will block out enough of our suns to mimic Earth's one sun."

"Really?" She took it from him. "He can use an empty field outside now?"

"Yes." He smiled. "I'll have a few more prototypes in a few days with the shield to protect our people when they are harvesting our fields."

"You are the best. It will give us some time to work with them so when the crops are ready to be moved, we'll have them perfected."

"I'll speak to some of the farmers to see who has space for him."

"We're also going to have to see who we can get to guard him when he's out there or Reasta could kidnap him." Heather paused. "He could get kidnapped!"

"Excuse me?"

"Gather the council. I'm going to join you after I get Henry." She knew where he was. He had planted anywhere he could in the beginning, and she knew every spot. Heather found Henry on his knees, working on one of his plants.

"What brings you here, Heather?" He sat back on his heels. "I would have thought you'd be busy with your men."

"My men?" She laughed. "They're not mine."

"Aren't you the leader of this council of yours?" He wiped his hands and stood.

Did he figure that out already? Oh boy. She wished she didn't have to have this conversation now.

"Never mind. I'm assuming this isn't a social visit. You must want something from me."

Was she that bad? "I was hoping you would join us in the board room."

"Of course. Anything for you, but it must be big if you want me with all your men." He winked at her as he followed her. "You going to tell me why?"

"Once we get to the council."

"You mean your men."

"Okay, my men." Heather smiled. "You make it sound like I have a harem."

"They are all good-looking men, except for Archie, of course."

Heather started laughing. No one called the admiral Archie either. And hearing Henry making a comment about his looks showed how close they were. They made it to the doors of the war council, which opened when they approached.

Toki was the only one not in attendance, but Heather knew her position as religious leader would supersede her role on the council at times. Everyone but Bear stood when she entered. When he saw what everyone else did, he stood as well.

Arc came in behind her and went to a dark corner to stay out of the way.

Heather knew Bear would be asking questions now. She had worked hard at making it look like she was just on the board, but this just showed she was in charge. She gestured to a chair for Henry as she sat in her chair.

"Now what was so secretive that you had to wait until I came here to talk to me?"

"Well, let me start with good news. We have found a place for you to plant the rest of your seeds." She looked at Fridon who sat his newest device on the table separating them. She picked it up and looked at Henry. "This will allow you to plant in our fields."

"But there is more to this."

"Yes. You'll have to plant them in one of the fields above ground where you run the risk of being captured."

"Then you're not going to let me, are you? Why tell me?"

"Because I have a huge favor to ask of you."

"You want me to get captured?"

"Reasta has tried to get information from us for a while,

but Vespians are too loyal. She knows she won't get much from them."

"You know I'd do anything for you, but you have your soldiers for that."

"I know and Bear has given me a list to use, and I will utilize them. I also know they will do their job, but they are soldiers, and she knows it." Heather paused for a moment, trying to find the right way to say her next comment. "If you are with them, I feel she'll be drawn to you. I promise to keep you safe. We have a way of putting what we want into your subconscious so if she questions you, your answers will come out naturally, but I must warn you if she does figure out you are not being honest with her it could be brutal."

"Will it help you?"

"Very much."

"Then I'll do whatever you want."

———

Her brother was a genius. He created some fake apparatus to make it look like the machine was what was putting the information they needed and wanted to give to Reasta deep in Henry's mind. She also added what was needed to the security guards assigned to guard him. Now everything was set up.

Bear approached her and she knew he was going to start questioning everything. She was amazed he hadn't questioned things before. He had a sixth sense that reviled her visions.

"Do you have a moment?" He didn't smile at her. That wasn't good.

"Of course." She gestured for him to walk with her.

"Perhaps we should go someplace quiet?"

She nodded. The safest place to have their conversation was the war room, but she knew they wouldn't have any privacy. "You know I'm never left alone."

"That has been brought to my attention." He clasped his hands behind his back. "I just want to know how you became the leader of this war."

"Noticed that, huh?"

"You know there's very little that gets by me."

"All too well." She pointed to the doors to their head-quarters. "It got me in more trouble."

The moment they entered the room, and the doors closed behind them Bear turned to face her. "So, Captain, how did a member of Earth's security become such a powerful person?"

She knew she could use half-truths and innuendoes to answer his questions, but this man had been her champion throughout her life, and she saw him as a father figure. Heather didn't want to lie to him.

"You remember that device in my back?"

"Of course."

"I found out what it was for. It was designed to hide my true race."

———

Storm watched as Heather and Bear walked off. What were they talking about? He went to Fridon and warned him that Heather might not want to be disturbed. He on the other hand was going to protect his mate.

"You are what?"

"I'm from Vespia. I found out I was genetically engi-neered and to keep me safe the Vespian council sent me to Earth." Heather heard the doors open and smiled when she saw her mate.

"My heart, are you sure this is wise?" He wrapped an arm around her waist.

"Bear has been there for me. He was the one I would run to when I was hurt, physically and mentally. I trust him with my life and my secrets." She looked up at him.

He wanted to stop her and protect her at all costs, but she knew this man best. If she felt it was safe to trust him, he had to support her.

"Then why didn't they know who you were when they came looking for a liaison?"

"It's a long story, but they had their memories wiped."

"All to protect you?"

Heather nodded. "Anyway, I am the daughter of one of the ruling families."

Storm noticed she didn't mention her ancient blood.

"And that is why you are the leader of this war?"

"That and the fact that Reasta is after me."

"And you never thought to tell me this?" Bear crossed his arms.

"There were several times I wanted to but was afraid the knowledge would put you in an awkward position with Earth security."

———

Once she had finished with Bear, Heather felt she had ignored Arc long enough. She had sent him to the main computer earlier and asked him to wait for her. She slipped away while the rest of the council was working on assignments so she could speak to him, of which Storm was unaware. Stepping into the computer's main room. "Arc, I have come to talk to you."

"I am here Heather." He stepped out of a shadowed corner.

"I want to talk about the day I found all those ordinances. Why did you lie to me?"

"I haven't lied to you."

"I asked you to go back to where I found you that first day and to return the next day when I needed you. You told me you couldn't." She jammed her hands on her hips. "Yet you were able to walk through a wall just like Mac does when I don't need her when I found the ordinances."

"I didn't do that, Heather. You did."

"What do you mean."

"I don't anticipate your needs like Mac and Sim. One moment I was working with Mac, the next I was in the cave with you and your mate. You called me there."

"Are you saying that all I need to do is call you and you'd be there? How is that different than the way Mac acts?"

"I do not have the data needed to answer that question."

Heather heard Storm asking for her. "You are to stay here until I call for you."

She needed to get back before her mate started looking for her.

———

Sam and Skye went over what would happen when they went through their mating ceremony with Toki. Sam found the whole thing made her nervous. Why, she wasn't sure. Maybe it was because she had rapidly aged and had really only lived a few years. What if this wasn't what she wanted? What if this wasn't what Skye wanted?

"Sam? You with us?" asked Skye. He watched her as she tried to remain calm.

"Oh, of course." She gave him her best smile.

"You were a million miles away, weren't you?" He took her hand in his.

He knew her too well. All she could do was shrug.

Her aunt had been taking everything in. "Skye, may I speak to Sam for a moment?"

Great, now she had drawn her aunt's attention as well.

"Sure." He looked at Sam. "There is something I want to speak to Heather about anyway."

Sam waited for the door to close behind him. "Aunt Toki."

"You are worried."

"A little." She sighed. Her aunt got right to the problem. Sam sat on a bench for two near the doors.

"Do you feel this is a mistake?" She worked her robes so she could sit next to Sam.

She shook her head. "No. I love him with all my heart."

"There is a but in there though."

"What if after we bond one of us decides this isn't what we want?"

"You are Vespian." She placed her hands on her knees. "Would you think about breaking a bond like this?"

Sam looked at her aunt. When she put it that way she knew the answer. "No."

"Then you're worried about Skye."

"I don't know. I know he loves me, but I don't want to pressure him into something he doesn't want."

"Yet, he was the one to ask you to bond. He is secure in this decision." Toki touched her arm. "You are the one questioning this."

"Skye was always in the background. He always hid what he was, where he came from, and his special talents. He trusted no one. I worry that the Vespian Way goes against his personal way."

"You worry too much. I have watched Skye. Once he

learned he was Vespian and mingled with our society he has relaxed. He has learned no one here would question his ability. No one here would try to use it to their advantage."

"But what if his true ability appears once we're mated? Dad's talent showed up once Mom became pregnant, but I've been told it could show up after bonding or mating."

"True, but Skye is more like your mother than a Vespian. Your mother's talent showed once her device dissolved. She had it all along. Her visions prove that. Your father didn't."

"And he fears my mother's talent. What if it frightens him to a point he leaves?"

"And that is what you fear." Toki smiled. "You have two choices. Speak to him and speak of this fear or keep it inside and see what he does."

"Neither choice is good."

"I will not mate you until you make the choice, Sam. I cannot until you two are sure this is what you want."

Great. Not what she wanted to hear.

Toki smiled as Skye walked back into the room and excused herself.

Skye watched her leave before he turned to Sam. "What's going on?"

"I guess we need to talk." She didn't want to do this, but Toki was right. They needed to work this out before the mating.

"Are you backing out on me?"

"Is that what you want?" She looked at him.

"What? No." He shook his head then he paused. "Is that what you want?"

"No."

"Then what is it?"

"There is something about the royal families that I

don't think you know." She took his hand and pulled him down to the small bench where she had been talking to Toki.

"You don't need to make this sound so ominous." He sat beside her.

"I don't mean to, but it could make you run for the hills."

"You do love those old Earth sayings." He brushed a few stray hairs behind her ears.

"I do." She grinned. "The royal families have more ancient in them than most."

"I know that, and your mother and I have more than anyone else. You do too."

"Not as much as you and Mom, but you're right." She ran one hand through her hair. "And having the ancient blood has given some a special talent. It's normally brought on by the bond, the mating, or the birth of children."

"You're talking about your father's ability to shift."

"You know about that?" She looked at him in shock. When did he figure that out?

"I spent a lot of time with your parents recently." Skye took one of her hands. "There is very little I miss and seeing a wolf on a planet that doesn't have them did catch my attention."

"Oh. Dad can shift into anything, but that is the most comfortable for him."

"That's how he was able to get close to Heather when she rescued you, correct?"

She nodded.

"And you want to warn me that you could develop something like that when we mate?"

"You could, too."

"I'm more like your mother who has had her power continue to grow on her."

"You don't talk too much about your ability with computers. Have you found any new things you can do now that you couldn't do before?"

He nodded as he looked at her. "Would you like to see?"

"Sure." She wondered what he would do. All of a sudden, her insert activated, and she could smell roses all around her. No one had ever hacked her insert before. Music filled the air next, as the lights dimmed. Skye hadn't moved or said a word to command the computers.

"So your mind is like Mom's."

"No. Heather's talent allows her to do so much more. I have a feeling it's because she was genetically engineered. I can control computers, and my reach is getting larger, but I won't be able to do what your mom can."

"Does she still frighten you?"

"I can't say frightened. Not anymore. What I don't want to have happen is for her to lose control and I have to fight all of you to keep everyone safe." He played with the palm of her hand in his. "I know she would never do anything to harm anyone so worrying about her trying to do something maniacal is gone, but the mind is a delicate thing and hers is so powerful if it ever expanded too fast on her she could do a lot of harm."

"But that has never happened."

"No, and as my abilities grow, I'm finding they don't go beyond what I can handle. Your mom seems to be the same way."

"I'm glad to hear you say that."

Her silence prompted Skye to find out what was on her mind. "Have you noticed something happening with you?"

"No." She shook her head.

"Then what's going on, Sam."

She shrugged.

Skye studied her. He knew her well enough to know better. Something was bothering her, and he needed to figure it out. "Are you afraid you won't get a special power?"

"A little. Anseri never developed any talent, and I do have that insert that could affect any special talent I could develop."

"Yeah, but it was inserted by an ancient. I would think he would have taken that into account." He knew this wasn't what was bothering her. Something else. Something that had to do with the mating ceremony. "You said you wanted to mate with me, but you're afraid of something. What is it, Sam?"

"Do you like living on Vespia?"

"It's the longest I've ever stayed in one place, so I really don't have anything to compare to, but it is growing on me." There was a flicker of some emotion on her face. "Are you afraid I'm going to get bored with you?"

"You have moved around a lot."

"I never had a place to call home before." He brushed his fingers against her cheek. "I never had anyone to come home to before. I want to be with you, Sam. All the time. I don't want to go on missions without you."

"What about Earth? They won't let you make such demands."

"I know. That is why I resigned my commission."

"What?" That wasn't what she expected to hear.

"Bear tried to talk me out of it. He even offered to allow me to pick my partner on any mission I would be given. He knew I didn't want to leave you behind. So, I pushed and now I've been assigned to work with Vespian security and the only time they can pull me is when they pull your mother."

"And Dad went along with that?"

"I actually told your mother first. I knew Bear would make her aware when they spoke next and didn't want her to be blindsided. I wanted to talk to you and make sure you were okay with it before I approached your father."

"When did you do this?"

"While we were on our way back with the troops." He could see she wanted to ask why but wasn't sure how he would react. "I love you, Sam. I guess I'm a bit like your mom. I went on missions that weren't expected to be successful. I didn't care. I had no family, no friends. No one I could trust. Now I have you, your family, and these Vespians have accepted me as I am. I have something to live for. Something I hold dear and want to protect with all my might."

———

"I'm not sure I can do this." Heather wiped her hands on her pant legs. A nervous habit she hadn't been able to stop yet.

"My heart. We're her parents."

"But do we have to watch their intimacy, Storm? That's not something I want to do."

"It is the Vespian way. You need to get over your shyness for Sam."

"I know." Heather couldn't look at Storm. This was hard for her. On Earth, the old stigmas of sex being very private and behind closed doors were still prevalent. That was the way she was trained.

"Look at me." Storm slipped his fingers under her chin and lifted her head, so she had to look him in the eyes. "I know you will do what is expected to keep your daughter happy. I also know our daughter will not push you to do something that upsets you."

———

He was right. Her desire to do the right thing would make her go. She would never do anything to upset Sam. There was still time for her to accept what she had to do. Sam and Skye were at the whim of Toki. She would decide when they would mate.

Right now, she needed to change the subject. "I'm going to introduce Arc to Mac."

Storm looked at her and waited. He knew what she was trying to do. Whether or not he allowed her to do it was the question.

"I'm hoping once they share their data Arc will understand us a little better." She continued when he remained quiet. "They are computers, but highly advanced, thinking computers."

"Yes, but Arc has no understanding of the social arts."

"I know, and I'm hoping interacting with Mac might help him develop some." She let out a pent-up breath. He was going to give her the time she needed to work through what was required of her for the mating ceremony. "If he is to work with us, he needs to meld in better."

"And not annoy you so much?"

She gave him a bright smile. Arc was following them at the moment.

"When do you plan on doing this?"

"This evening. We're due to meet with our staff later and we wanted to do a surprise inspection of a few of the elite teams before we meet with them."

"It's not a surprise inspection if you've scheduled it, my heart."

"Only for you and me. I knew if there wasn't something on our files someone would end up filling the slot and we wouldn't be able to make these supposed impromptu visits."

"How do you want to handle this?"

"We walk in unannounced and count to five. I want to see who notices us and reacts first."

They entered the area where the team they were inspecting was working out. Arc went and stood in a discreet spot. The team was on a break at the moment, milling about while they waited for their next challenge. Two of the three humans spotted her first and they looked at the rest of the team, but Heather could tell they didn't know what to say to get everyone's attention. The first two snapped to attention and saluted her, keeping their hand beside their forehead until she saluted back. The third one turned when he saw the other two and followed suit. The Vespians noticed them, but instead of looking at what caused them to stand there with their hand at their temple they poked each other and pointed.

Heather had been counting in her head the whole time she watched them. When she hit five, she said it out loud. Her voice rang in the cave, making everyone turn. The moment they saw her they fell in, dropping what they were doing.

Their commander stepped up in front of them and waited.

"How is it that Earth's three security members showed me proper respect when the rest of your team didn't?" She addressed the leader but looked at the whole team standing in front of her. "Is this the way you prove you deserve to lead this team? Perhaps I should put together an all-human team and let them show you how it is done."

"Mistress." He dropped his gaze.

"Has their translators been altered to understand the Vespian language?"

"No Mistress." He looked back up at her when he answered her.

"Why not?" This time she looked right at him. He swallowed. Good, she was making him sweat.

"The command hasn't come down yet."

"Really?" She looked at Storm. He was the one in control of that and never dragged his feet before.

"The command came down three hours ago, once all the teams were put together." Storm confirmed what she already knew.

"So why hasn't he gotten that command?"

"The command went out unilaterally."

Heather checked her system. "Hmm. Here's the command right here, with the timeline our future leader stated. Perhaps this branch of the caverns doesn't get the proper reception. Latimer, could you join me?"

Within seconds she heard him respond with how long it would take for him to get there.

"My system doesn't seem to have the problem yours does." She turned to Storm once again. "Can you contact anyone?"

And what would you like me to do, my heart?

How about have Fridon load this inspection into their systems. Showing all the team but the three humans with zero scores.

How high a score do you want the humans to have?

One hundred percent for this inspection. I'm sure they will make enough mistakes to bring that down.

Seconds later her vision filled with the data she asked

for. She could tell the rest of the team saw it too because of the slight reaction before they snapped back to attention.

"How about that. There is nothing wrong with your system." She stepped up to him. "Now I ask again. Why haven't they received the insert that was ordered hours ago?"

He took a moment before answering. "I have no excuse, Mistress. I was so focused on doing a good job and training the men to act like a unit that I didn't pay attention to the notice."

"And you didn't think to teach them the Vespian word for my presence while you worked with them just in case I might show up?"

"No, Mistress."

"I expected better." Heather let her words hang between them for a few moments. "You will have a code phrase. It is get strong. Every time you hear it from me or any of my staff you and your team are to drop what you are doing and do twenty push-ups. Since you didn't do what was expected you will double everything everyone else will be tasked to do for the next two days. If I tell another team to do twenty sit-ups you will do forty, if we tell the other teams to run five miles you will run ten. Get me?"

"Yes, Mistress."

She glared at the rest of the team and raised her voice. "Get me?"

"Yes, Mistress," they said in unison.

"Get Strong!"

They dropped to the floor and started counting off.

"We are on our way to the communication lab. I expect you to beat me there." Heather turned on her heel and headed in the direction of the lab she mentioned. She heard the team counting off quicker so they could beat her to the lab.

"Am I to stay with you for the next few inspections or are you going to call me each time?" asked Skye.

"I'm going to call you if I get the same excuse, but hopefully the next two inspections will go better."

Skye nodded as he headed back to what he was working on.

"I truly enjoyed that." Storm slipped his arm around her shoulders. "The sarcastic tone was different."

"I've had people scream in my face most of my career and like most soldiers I have learned to tune it out, but the commander who taught me the most didn't scream. He taught me to own up to my mistakes and fix them. That's what I want from our soldiers." She looked up at him and smiled. "You can still do all the screaming you want."

"I'm glad to hear that. I do have a reputation to uphold." He dipped his head down to whisper in her ear. "But I know one scream I want to hear over and over."

The heat of a blush filled her cheeks. "And you hope to hear one of those screams soon."

"Oh, yes." He brushed his knuckles along her jaw. "I also want to see that lovely flush that fills your skin when you orgasm."

"You make it hard to function when you say things like that."

"And you make it hard, my heart." He wrapped his arms around her and pulled her into a small alcove. Lifting her and pinning her to the wall, he captured her lips with his. His tongue begged for entrance. Heather opened her mouth and wrapped her legs around his waist as she shielded them from view.

Desire raced through her as their tongues met. She

wondered how Earth security would react to their relationship. They weren't allowed to show any emotion while in uniform. Storm must have picked up her thoughts because he broke the kiss and looked at her.

"You worry about how these humans will take our relationship?"

"My heart. I love how you show your affection for me. It thrills me when you pull me aside like this."

"Like I can't control myself?" he gave her one of his bone-melting smiles.

"Exactly." She brushed her fingers along his jaw. "I'm just trying to figure out the best way to explain it to Earth's security. It goes back to how their society handles the show of emotions while in uniform. Men still see women as the weaker sex, no matter how hard they have worked to prove otherwise."

"Are you going to ask me to refrain from touching you when we're around them?"

"No. Our people have gotten used to the way we behave around each other. I don't want them to think something is wrong if we stop. I will not allow Earth's lifestyle to dictate ours. I'm just trying to figure out how to stop our people from fighting any human who might make a comment that they might consider rude."

"Like me dragging you into an alcove like this?"

"Maybe I should be the one dragging you into one once."

"Now that might be fun, my heart. Will you throw me over your shoulder as well?"

Heather laughed. "Not sure if I can manage that, but I know how to get your attention when I want to."

"Are you planning on wearing your lingerie for everyone to see?"

She shook her head. "Not sure I'm that brave yet."

"Why? You have used the public showers with our people. They've seen you change your clothes in front of them as well."

"I know but to me that's different. I block out who's around me. Other people were doing the same thing I was. I'm not sure I can do that when everyone is watching me."

"You would definitely have my attention." He dipped his head to her mark.

The heat of his mouth brushing against her mark had her wanting to give him whatever he wanted. She smiled. Heather knew what she needed to do. She started with soft brushes against his mind. Once he gave her access, she created the hall they had just walked through.

Where are you, my heart? Storm stood close to the alcove they occupied.

Heather made sure she had everything just the way he wanted it. The stilettos she wore tapped against the stone floor, his favorite red bra and panty outfit encased her body. He couldn't see her yet, but she could feel his excitement coursing through him. People milled about, but because she created all this with her mind no one paid any attention to her. As she got closer to Storm, she felt the same excitement he did. Maybe she had a bit of that exhibitionist in her too. Using the images of other people, she kept them in front of her until she was close enough to reveal herself.

She stopped about three feet in front of him then moved the people out of her way. One by one they stepped aside until nothing stood between them.

You are so beautiful.

You make me that way.

Storm moved to touch her.

Not yet, my heart I still have a few things to take care of. She brushed her hands along his waist, erasing his uniform with a sweep of her hands. She caressed his mark and watched him shudder.

It isn't fair that I can't touch you when you can touch me.

You'll get your turn. This is your fantasy after all.

She released him and felt the heat of his hands sliding over the lace resting against her lower stomach then her hips as he pulled her closer. His mouth claimed hers. The brush of his tongue inside her mouth made her sigh. He lifted her and she hung in the air. Creating this in her mind allowed them to do things that gravity would have made difficult. Storm's hands slid down her back to cup her derriere as he slid in deep, allowing her heat to surround him.

I love these crotchless panties you are wearing.

You like the convenience of the lack of material there.

You have me there, but you know I don't care what you wear. Our intimacy is special, and I always look forward to it.

He dipped his head to her mark, pulling the delicate tissue into his mouth. In the alcove they were hiding in she could feel his hands working on the seals of her uniform. His hands moved against her skin, igniting a flame that had her breathless. In her mind and in the alcove, she could feel his mouth on her mark, his hands on her body, what she wanted was to feel him inside her.

Now that I can do, my heart. He centered himself, driving deep inside her physically.

She moaned.

My heart.

Heather was always quiet when they were intimate. The sensations he caused in her made her focus on what she was feeling, and it took her breath away.

They moved together as they raced toward a mutual goal. Storm kept hitting a sensitive spot inside her, making her body shake as she pushed to reach her climax. It was close. She could feel it. Her body started to quiver.

"So close." The soft words flowed out of her.

Storm shifted the pace, slowing things down which frustrated her, but he made the strokes deeper and she found her all elusive orgasm racing toward her once again. Her muscles tightened against him, drawing a moan out of her mate. She wanted to push him to have his release first, but she wasn't sure she could hold out long enough to make it happen. She could feel her release moving toward her. It started in her stomach, building inside her until it consumed her, filling her with euphoria. Heather relaxed against Storm just as he hit his climax. They clung to each other, neither speaking as they worked to control their breathing.

"Oh, my heart, that was beautiful."

She could only nod.

"Still a little boneless?"

She nodded again.

Storm chuckled as he eased himself out of her. The gentle way he held her while he waited for her mind and body to start obeying her again was so sweet. It made her a little misty-eyed.

"My heart, are you crying again?"

"I have been a bit emotional, haven't I?"

"We're under a lot of pressure which can make your emotions run high." He pressed a kiss against her forehead. "You may cry in my arms any time you wish."

She laughed.

They dressed quietly.

"I have a request."

"You wish to do this again?" He gave her another bone-melting smile as he brushed his knuckles along her jaw.

"With you? Always. I would like to alter one of the programs you set for our room."

"Have you already tried?" She smiled and he returned the smile. "You found I locked it."

"I'm not going to do more than alter one just a little bit."

"You can have access." He shifted so she could move past him and leave the alcove. "What do you want to do?"

"It wouldn't be much of a surprise if I tell you." She looked up and saw the spark of excitement enter his eyes. "Now let's get back to our inspections. We should be able to do three or four more before we need to be back in the war room."

The rest of the inspections went well. News traveled fast so no one got caught the way the first team did. They headed back to the war room to meet up with Fridon and Bear. They had been doing inspections as well. After directing Arc to where she wanted him to stand, Heather had made Toki aware of the meeting, but she declined. It made Heather wonder why she wanted to be on the council. She hadn't made any of the meetings or inspections so far.

"Time to see how fast the leaders can get here." Heather sent out a message telling the leaders of each elite squad to be at the doors in fifteen minutes. Anyone late would find the doors locked.

"How did they look Fridon?"

"The humans looked a little lost. I had two teams who hadn't had our language downloaded yet, but at least they were working with their new recruits. One team was using our modified hand signals which the humans picked up quickly. I sent them to the lab after I let them know that was unsatisfactory. They have been given the same punishment you doled out earlier."

Heather grinned. News really did travel fast.

At the appointed time the doors opened, and the elite leaders marched in. They lined up in front of the table the council sat behind. Heather was happy to see no one was missing. The doors swung closed, and silence hung in the air as she watched them. She waited several beats before she spoke. "I called you here because you need to be aware that our human brethren could make some comments about me that might offend."

No one spoke, but she could feel their protectiveness of her grow.

"They mean no offense. It is the way they were raised. Humans still don't understand that a woman can be strong yet feminine at the same time. They feel if they have to protect it, they consider it weaker than them. Human women have worked hard to be seen as equals, and for the most part, have gotten the men to see them as their counterparts but the sight of tears, or allowing their mate to make decisions for them and the men revert back to the protector of weaker things." She stood up and walked around to the front of the desk. "I want you to see this attitude as a chance to teach. Teach them the Vespian way, the way we teach our children. Show them why their attitude doesn't belong here. That is all."

"Permission to speak?"

"Yes."

"Why would they think less of you?"

"I'd like to answer that one," said Bear.

Heather nodded.

"The passion between Heather and Storm is something

you're used to, but not my soldiers. There are some who believe that the way Heather and Storm show their affection toward each other is something that should be kept behind closed doors. In the bedroom in other words. They could make a few comments when they see it for the first time."

"Most of what they might say will be a gut-shot reaction. They don't mean anything by it," added Heather. "They just don't know how to handle what they might see."

"We will make sure they understand."

Heather smiled.

———

Heather sat on the floor with the twins. Storm wanted to join her, but they had to make the evening meeting. This was the newest group of humans' first one and they needed to see why it was important. He hated interrupting her, but he had to.

"My heart, you need to change so we can get to the evening gathering."

She sat there in her uniform after having dinner with their children.

"But Daddy, Mommy is going to tell us more about the princess and the dragon," said Bubbles.

"I thought she was from the village."

"We all know she's a princess in disguise." She looked up at her mother. "Just a little more?"

When Heather looked at Storm so did both of the children, crying please in unison. The look on their little faces had him laughing.

"All right. I will give you while I change my clothes and wait for Dian to come here to be with you while your mother and I work, but when she gets here you have to get to your studies."

"Oh, we're already done with those."

Storm shook his head. If they were finishing their schoolwork that fast, he might have to give them something more challenging.

SIX

"So where did I leave off?" asked Heather.

"You don't remember?" Bubbles sounded shocked. "You never forget anything."

"I want to be sure you remember where I left off."

"Our princess had been picked to be one of the maidens for the dragon. The girls picked had been tied to a stake and left behind. Then the dragon came and chose her. Her scream was the last thing you told us."

"Well, as you figured, she passed out from fear."

"Mommy, why?"

"How would you feel if a giant fire-breathing dragon grabbed you out of all the other girls? I'd be scared so much I think I would pass out too." She brushed her fingers through her daughter's hair. "Anyway, when she woke up, she found herself in her bedroom. She sat up and looked around. Laughing at herself, she thought it was nothing but a dream."

"Was it a dream, Mommy?"

"She got dressed and opened her door." Heather smiled at her son, who had asked the question. "She stepped out into a massive cavern. Our princess realized she hadn't dreamed a thing, and her heart started to pound in her chest."

"Was she afraid of the dragon, Mommy?"

"Yes." She ruffled her daughter's hair. "The stories she had heard growing up were designed to frighten the children so they would behave. She looked around but didn't see any sign of the dragon."

"She's going to try to escape, isn't she, Mommy."

"That was her thought. If she could get out of the cave, she might be able to go back home, but she had no idea where the mouth of the cave was. Terrik, what would you do to find the opening?"

He stuck his finger in his mouth then pulled it out and held it up. "The draft should lead her in the right direction."

"Very good. That is what she did. Once she was sure of the direction, she moved down the wall closest to her, heading in the direction of the entrance. She inched along, being careful not to make a lot of noise. The air she breathed became fresher and she knew she was getting close."

"Where is the dragon, Mommy?" asked Terrik.

"That was her question. Was he at the mouth of the cavern, waiting for her to try to escape so he could gobble her up in one bite? If he was there, she knew she couldn't escape easily. Her father had told her they normally made their home in the cliffs of the big mountain, and she wasn't sure how she would climb down."

"Too bad she didn't have Terrik to help her," said Bubbles. "He can climb anything."

"It's time children." Storm leaned against the door like he had been waiting for a few moments.

"Oh, and Mommy was just getting to the good part." Terrik stood and gave his mother a hug.

"And we'll pick up from that part tomorrow." She took the hand Storm offered her and dashed into their room. Heather changed her clothes quickly and walked out into the main room where Storm waited.

The moment Storm saw her outfit he smiled. "I'm glad to see you're not letting the humans here change the way you want to dress."

"They never would have. We've had humans here for several weeks and I didn't change the way I dressed then. Why would I do it now?" Her top was a no-sleeved cropped top with a deep V in the front. Her pants sat low on her hips.

"You have your pad?"

She patted a pocket on her hip.

"Let's go." He slipped a hand around her and rested it on her side. "I do like the fact that I get to touch your skin when you wear this outfit."

"Why do you think I wore this?"

"My heart." He gave her waist a light squeeze. "So how do you plan on handling so many people at one time?"

"Break them into their elite squads for now. Then we'll move amongst the different groups and listen in. As time goes on, we'll go back to having the groups together for the evening meeting. I want to see how they work together in their groups first."

"We're going to be very busy."

"All of the council will be helping, including Toki. I thought I'd see who worked best with the groups. I know the humans will gravitate to Bear or Skye."

"And you. They still believe you are human."

"I'm also the leader of this. If I work with any group other than the ones our council puts together, I'm afraid they will see it as favoritism." They reached the doors to the area where everyone was waiting.

"You realize that everyone will honor you tonight so that the humans will know how important you are."

"Because of my comment earlier?"

He nodded.

The doors opened.

Heather paused for a moment. This would be the first time anyone from Earth would see how the people of Vespia saw her. She still hadn't gotten used to it and as the head of the war council, it had blossomed to a point that made her feel like Anseri when she walked amongst the people. The bows, stopping to let her pass. It humbled her. She brushed her hands against the legs of her pants then took Storm's hand. They stepped through the doors.

All the Vespians there turned to face them. The humans followed suit. Smiles filled the faces of their people as they bowed to her and Storm. The way they turned in unison made Heather wonder if she had mentally alerted them.

No, my heart. Our people just seem to have an innate way of knowing where their leaders are. We've always been behind my mother, but this is how she is greeted all the time.

"Good evening, everyone." Heather inclined her head when they all stood back up. *Yet we caught them earlier.*

"Good evening, Heather," they said in unison. "Good evening, Storm."

He dipped his head and returned the greeting then guided her to where the rest of their council stood. Everyone went back to what they were doing before Heather and Storm showed up.

"That was quite a welcome," commented Bear.

Heather felt the heat of a blush fill her cheeks.

"It is like the way your men salute you when you enter any room, Admiral. They are showing respect to our leaders," Fridon informed him. "We will get the same treatment once the war council is complete."

"I thought it was complete."

"Each council member has yet to pick all of their elite team members." Fridon looked at him. "It's one of the reasons for these evening meetings."

"How many teams do you plan on having?"

"As many as it takes."

———

Storm watched as his mate spoke to his sister. Toki had shown up in her robes but was taking an active interest in what the council was doing. He knew it was hard for her to be the religious leader and a soldier, but it was her choice to join the council. If he focused, he could hear what they were saying, but he wanted to turn his attention to the humans. He noticed they were migrating toward each other instead of keeping to their groups. Heather told him that was to be expected and that they would not leave their teams once they felt comfortable. Right now, they were sharing stories and getting pointers from each other.

He felt they should be getting that from their leaders. Some had spoken in depth with their leaders before heading toward other humans. They were the ones to watch for their teams.

One voice caught his hyper-hearing.

"Damn, the Captain sure is exposing a lot of skin."

Several humans tried to silence him.

"They don't like it when you talk about the Captain that way."

"What? Is she some sort of saint? She puts her pants on the same way we do. One luscious leg at a time."

Storm wanted to rush over there and grab the man by

the throat. He used his insert to ping his information. This one would have to be watched.

———

The evening went well. Heather was happy with how everything worked out. Their team, as she liked to think about the war council, worked their way through all the other teams, making notes and marking the contenders for their elite teams. They stood together, going over the data as the squads mingled. She had found a few that caught her attention and would speak to Skye about them later.

"There are a few strong candidates in these squads," commented Storm. He marked the ones that had caught his attention. So did Fridon and Heather. She studied the data on her handheld.

"My heart." The sound of her mate's voice next to her ear and the feel of his hand sliding across her abdomen had her desire for him climb. "There is a young man staring at you. Wait. He stopped the moment he realized I caught him."

"Where?"

"To your left. Skye just stepped up to his side."

Heather looked where Storm suggested and saw the young man Skye was now talking to. "It looks like our daughter's mate is explaining things, my heart."

"Do you know him?" asked Storm.

Her insert pinged his uniform. Heather pulled up the data on him. His name seemed familiar, but she didn't recognize him. As she worked through his file, she found a younger picture of the young man. "I do know him!"

"You do?"

"Yes. He is the one who befriended me just before I left

school. The one you saw in one of my memories when I confronted Susan because she kept changing the timeline."

"The one who bowed to peer pressure?"

"It is the right name." She took a couple of steps toward the man before her mate stopped her.

"I wish to go with you."

"Want to mark your territory?" She smiled up at him.

He gave her a heart-stopping smile. "I just wish to meet this man who was crazy enough to walk away from you."

"We were very young, Storm, and he wasn't you. It never would have worked out." She grabbed his hand and made her way through the crowd. His record showed he was one of Earth's best. How did she miss his name before this?

"Mark."

"Captain Drexel." He snapped to attention.

"Hmm." Storm circled him. "You knew my mate while she was at the academy."

"Yes, sir."

Heather knew he was trying to intimidate the man.

"Captain, I want to apologize."

"Apologize?" Her brow crinkled. "For what?"

"The way I treated you when we were at the academy. It was wrong and I had felt bad about it since it happened."

"That was a long time ago."

"I know and I should have searched you out and apologized way back when, but I didn't know where you were, and to be honest I didn't have the guts. Then I heard you went to Vespia."

"And you thought you'd come all the way to this planet to apologize?"

"I am here to fight for your planet, being able to apologize and offer my services will help me atone for what I did is a bonus."

"I don't need people who are trying to clear their conscience. Go home."

———

"No ma'am." He kept looking forward. "I have worked hard as a soldier. I was one of the first of security to be picked for an elite team."

"You think you are one of Admiral Barrington's better soldiers?"

"No, Ma'am. I know I am."

"You know we're picking the best of the best to be on three elite teams headed by myself, Storm and Fridon." She pulled out her pad. "Now you can show us how good you are."

"Is there a problem here?"

"No." Heather turned to Bear who had just spoken. "You will be part of the testing for our elite teams to help with those from Earth security who make it. He is your first recruit." With that Heather wrapped an arm around her mate's waist and led him away.

"His apology bothered you?" Storm ran a hand up and down her back. "I thought it would make you happy."

"That he has carried this around with him all this time?" She looked at her mate. "What if that was what drove him into security and kept him safe all this time? Now that he's been able to apologize, he won't be as careful and will make costly mistakes."

"You are worrying about something you're not sure will even happen." He wrapped his arm around her shoulders as he led her out of the meeting area and to their rooms.

"I can't help it. There is so much at stake." She sighed as she leaned into him.

"If things had been different between the two of you, do you think he would have been a lover?"

"I don't know. Maybe?" She looked up at him, worried he might be jealous of an imaginary lover. "I left the academy about two weeks after I met him, and he wasn't studying security when I met him. He was in the sciences."

"That is why you are worried about his skill."

"Yes."

"But he has been in security after he tried the sciences for one year. His training is only one year behind yours."

"True, but he is also human, so I wonder if he has passed his prime."

"You worry too much and there is only one thing I know that will take your focus away." He crowded her up against the nearest wall.

Heather felt his lips on her throat, pulling the delicate tissue into his mouth. Desire spiked inside her. "Storm, my heart, I had plans."

He released her neck so he could speak softly in her ear. "I know, my heart, I'm just priming my favorite playground."

She felt the heat of one of his hands against her stomach as it inched its way down, slipping inside her pants and moving to her core. With gentle strokes he caressed her, making her knees weak. All thoughts of what she had planned left her as she got caught up in the sensations he was causing. He brought her to the brink then stopped.

He slipped one arm around her shoulders and the other under her knees before lifting her. His long strides brought them to Bert's ship and their rooms quickly.

"I will put you in our room and relieve Dian so we can

have some privacy." The doors opened and he strode in. He entered their room, sat her on the bed, and kissed her forehead. "I will be right back."

———

The doors closed behind him. Storm wanted to stay in the room with his mate, but he promised her a few minutes, and he needed to say goodnight to Dian for the two of them.

"You're back." Dian set the computer pad she was working on the table. "They just went to bed a few minutes ago."

"Thank you for staying with them for us."

"Of course." She stood. "When you and Heather get a chance, I would like to talk about developing Zunni's art talent. I would like to teach her more mediums to use."

"I will make Heather aware. We realize both of them need to be challenged more when they told us they had all their work done earlier."

"We have noticed that too." Dian gathered her things. "I can program Cim to give them things to do until you can meet with me."

"That sounds good."

Dian smiled and headed out of their rooms.

Storm thought she'd never leave. He turned toward their bedroom door and hoped he had given his mate enough time because he wasn't going to wait anymore. Stepping up to the door he took a deep breath and touched the panel. The door opened to reveal the cave scenario he had programmed. A fire danced in the fireplace to the left. The bed was covered with fur. Something he had thought of doing but wasn't sure how his mate would feel about it.

Heather was lying on her side, waiting for him. She

wore the silk nylons he loved so much, but nothing else. He was so grateful that they now had access to Cim. One thought and his clothes disappeared.

"My heart."

"I didn't do much." She looked at him with eyes filled with so much promise.

"You didn't have to, and you know that. Just the thought that you wanted to please me fills me with joy." He smiled as he climbed onto the bed with her. "Seeing you like this fills me with desire."

"And that was my goal." She smiled back as she shifted so she was lying on her back.

He brushed his hand against her mark before sliding it down her body. She followed his motions by brushing her hand against his mark before moving it across his chest and waist. They continued touching each other, soft gentle caresses in just the right places to heighten their need for each other.

Storm captured her lips with his. He wrapped his arms around her and pulled her against his body. She, in turn, wrapped those silk-covered legs around his waist, trapping his erection against her heat. He wanted to move away. The screams he could get from her when he aroused her properly were goals he always wanted to reach, but she had a habit of stopping him before he could arouse her the way he wanted. He would never complain. Their sex life was always good. He just loved to hear those screams of joy.

———

Heather shifted her weight so she could slide down his length. This was what she wanted. He had started that fire in her out in the hall. She knew by the look in his eyes he had planned on doing the same thing to her now to see if he could get one of those elusive screams out of her. They both knew that her screams only showed up when they wanted to, but he loved trying anyway and she couldn't complain because the sex was always explosive.

Storm wrapped his arms around her to help her keep her balance. She rode him the way she liked. She slid up and down his length, enjoying the way he filled her each time she descended on him. Each time he filled her she felt the delicious tendrils of desire fill her. Heather knew she was losing control.

Storm must have noticed it too because he eased himself backwards until she was lying on top of him before he flipped them over so he could take control. He started with a nice strong pace, filling her completely with each stroke. Need filled her. Heather tilted her hips to give her mate better access, and he started hitting the sensitive spot that gave her the most intense orgasms. Just a few strokes had her shaking. A few more had her orgasm racing toward her. It filled her blood and flung her out to the stars. She lost touch with everything but her mate.

She felt his fingers gliding along her jaw.

"Glorious."

"That's about your favorite word for our intimacy."

"And it's the truth." He shifted his weight so he could lie on his back and drew her with him.

Heather rested her head on his chest as she snuggled against him and settled down for sleep. "I guess I need to find a word for it too."

"Why, my heart?" He wrapped his arms around her. "You becoming boneless every time shows me how much you enjoy it. Words aren't necessary."

"Still, I feel I could come up with something." She

smiled, knowing that what she said next could get her pinned to the bed again. "I could say how sweet."

"Sweet?" She heard the shock in his voice as he flipped them, so she was on her back once again with his face only inches from hers. "Our intimacy is many things, but sweet?"

"Really? What would you suggest?" She slid a leg up his.

"Passionate." He pressed a kiss against one temple. "Mind-blowing."

"True." She ran her hands over the muscles in his back.

"Or you could use the word you've used in the past." He pressed a kiss to her other temple. "Wow."

"Is that enough?"

He captured her lips with his. His tongue dipped into her mouth, swirling with hers and drawing a sigh out of her when he ended the kiss. "For me it is."

And that was all that really mattered.

———

The next morning, before their staff arrived, Heather and Storm walked into the war room. Heather had gone back and forth on allowing the two androids to meet.

"Arc, I give you permission to come to the war room." She paused for a moment. "Mac, will you join us?"

"If you're still not sure, perhaps you should wait," said Storm.

"I need to bring them together sooner or later and Arc might learn how not to annoy me so much with Mac's influence."

"Hmm, an annoying android is worse than an annoying Vespian. Good to know."

Heather laughed as she slipped her arms around his

waist. "My heart, you can be annoying. There's no denying that. So can I, but Arc doesn't understand, and that bothers me. He doesn't know how to interact with us properly."

The doors opened and Mac came in. "You wish to speak to me, Heather?"

"I do, Mac. I am waiting for one more to join us then I will explain everything."

The doors opened a second time to allow Arc to enter.

"I am here."

The two androids were so different. Heather looked from one to the other. "Mac, explain to me what will happen if I allow you two to interact."

"We will share data and be linked to each other."

"Does that mean you will absorb each other's memories?"

"Yes. Although Arc has been aware of everything since your people began to live in the caves his data has been limited to what would pertain to his programming."

"Will he be able to access the way our people interact with each other and learn from it?"

"If that is part of his programming, then yes."

"And what about you? Will you become more like Arc?"

"Our personalities are programmed in. They can't be overwritten."

"Wonderful." Not what she wanted to hear. "Is there a way to adjust his personality?"

"Adjust?"

"It seems like his has not activated."

"Has he run a diagnostic?" asked Mac.

"He tells me everything is running within the proper parameters."

Mac was quiet for a moment. "My system shows

nothing out of the ordinary. Have you asked him why he behaves the way he does?"

"I have but have not been happy with his response."

"And you think if he could access my files, he would understand you better and behave appropriately?"

"Yes." Heather crossed her arms over her chest. "If he is to interact with our soldiers, he must fit in. No one except a select few are to know you two are androids. The less our people know the safer they are."

"You don't want them to know about us?" asked Arc. It was the first time he spoke since he had come into the room. "But in the beginning, you showed me off."

"There are key people who know I am looking for these systems." The door opened and Skye and Sam entered. "My daughter and her mate are two. My brother and his mate also know. Fridon also knows and of course Storm."

Arc looked at Heather. "Then why did you bring me in front of your Vespian soldiers?"

"Because I thought you would behave the same way Mac did when she had to interact with others. I was excited to find you and wanted my mate to meet you."

"Why?"

"Here we go again." She dropped her hands to her side. "Why do you question everything I say?"

"It is part of my programming."

"Even when we're not using your specific function?"

Arc didn't answer her.

"Is that why you want us to connect?"

"I know that sooner or later this needs to happen." Heather looked at Mac. "I deliberated on this for days and decided that allowing you to merge now will allow me to be better prepared when I find the rest of the computers."

"Shall we proceed then?"

Heather nodded.

The two androids faced each other, held up their palms then touched them together. They stood like that for a few seconds before turning back to her.

The door opened once again and Fridon entered. Bear came in right behind him.

"You're dismissed." Heather acknowledged the two men before she turned her attention back to her androids. "Arc, you are to work with Mac today."

"Understood." They turned together and headed out the door.

"So did you have a problem with your androids?" asked Bear.

Heather smiled. The man's sixth sense had kicked in again. It was time to explain what they were.

———

Storm entered the war room with every intention to force his mate to lunch if he found her in there. He found her sitting on the massive table that dominated the room in the lotus position. She had her eyes closed and her head slightly tilted back. Heather was meditating. Good. He knew she wasn't doing it enough.

The doors opened behind him to allow Sam and Skye to come in carrying a tray from their dining hall. He smiled. It didn't matter whose idea this was as long as Heather was taking care of herself properly. She opened her eyes at the sound of the tray clacking against the table. Heather smiled when she spotted him.

"I am happy to see you meditating and eating properly."

"I have too many people watching me, my heart."

"She also had a headache earlier and Sam knew they

only showed up when she hasn't been meditating enough," commented Skye.

Heather shot him a glare before she smiled at Storm again. "I have been meditating as much as possible."

"Perhaps you should go and see your brother before we make rounds." He stepped up to her and touched her jaw.

"Skye has already called him."

"Good." He placed his hands on the table she still sat on and leaned in to kiss his mate. Just as she wrapped her arms around his neck and brought her face close enough for him to capture her lips with his, her brother walked in.

"I think I might just faint if I ever find you two more than a few feet apart." Kuarto stepped up to Storm and ran his scanner over him. "Hmm."

"What?" Storm wanted to get a look at Kuarto's scanner, but the man kept moving. He scanned his mate then Sam and Skye.

"Just as I thought."

"What?" Heather asked this time.

"They are making sure you are taking care of yourself, Sis, but they're not doing that for themselves." He worked on his pad, pointing it toward Heather, then Storm, Skye and Sam.

Heather grinned.

"Since your council has assigned me as the main medical director and my job is to help you make sure each team is healthy as well as have a strong medical tech, I can also order anyone I want to get a physical. I have been working on upgrading your medical inserts and in order for me to get the readings to sync with the new system. You six are the first." He waited until Fridon and Bear came in. "Okay, let's go."

"Go where?" asked Bear as he fell into step with everyone else.

"The medlab. The doc here has a new toy he wants to try out on us." Heather linked arms with Storm. "He wants to have accurate readings to activate the new system."

"And we need to go to the lab?"

"I want a full scan of each of you." He gestured for Storm to step through the machine. "It is easier to tie the systems together using this. This new system will pick up the minute details of where your health is at any given time."

Bear went next.

"Thank you." Kuarto looked at Fridon. "You're next."

Storm signaled for Bear to walk with him. He had a feeling Kuarto went through all of this because of Heather's mental ability. Her mind kept expanding and none of his instruments could keep up. His main scanner could, but in order to keep her from being singled out he asked the whole team. Her secret needed to be kept safe, and Storm knew the data on her would appear on the main screens. That's why the good doctor always cleared the room when he needed to scan her. He just needed to get Bear out so Kuarto could do his work.

"You want to scan everyone because of me, don't you?"

"Actually, I want to scan all three of you. With Sam and Skye getting ready to go through the mating ceremony I need a starting point to work with."

"You've scanned us a hundred times," said Skye.

"Not like this. I just got an upgrade from Bert." He gestured for Skye to step through.

"What sort of starting point are you talking about?" Skye looked at the machine but didn't move toward it.

"You and Heather have the same ratio of ancient and

Vespian blood. Her abilities activated when she met Storm and that device started to disintegrate. The device was designed to hide her race, but according to Bert that was all it was designed to do, so her bonding with Storm activated her abilities. You and Sam have already bonded, and you haven't had any outward signs of a special ability."

Skye frowned. "I'm not going to be some sort of guinea pig."

"Yet my sister has been one for you and Sam."

"What are you talking about?" Skye ground out.

"From the time she was a child Heather has been poked and prodded. When she joined Vespian society you would have thought that would have ended, but her mind started to expand. Never having someone with as much ancient blood as she has, we had no idea how to treat her if something went wrong. If it hadn't been for her, I wouldn't know how to treat you." Kuarto glared at him. "She met Storm before I met her and no one else knew of her heritage until after she became pregnant. None of us knows what happens when you mate. This isn't for you but the twins and the children you and Sam might have."

"I'll go," said Sam. She waited for her uncle to give her a nod before she stepped through the machine.

He then pointedly looked at Skye.

"Fine. I'll do it." He stepped up to the machine and stepped through once Kuarto gave him permission.

Kuarto tapped a few keys before a frown appeared on his forehead. "You've already experienced some sort of ability, haven't you?"

"What makes you say that?" Skye narrowed his eyes at him.

"Because you tried to skew my readings." Kuarto pointed to the main screen where he had sent all his data. "This is what I recorded."

The computer showed several spikes in different categories just before they flatlined then went to normal readings.

"You don't have the device my sister had, or the minerals still in her body, so I'm assuming you did that yourself."

"Okay, so I seem to have a way with computers."

"Something you've been able to do all your life?"

Skye nodded.

"Like my sister, whose mind has always warned her when she would be in danger. You've always been able to manipulate computers with your mind?"

"No. When I was young, I found I had the ability to retain any data I saw on a computer screen. Once I started working with Earth security, I realized I could change their readings to see me as human."

"And you worked hard at keeping it that way." Kuarto made a few more notes.

"Sam? Have you noticed anything happening with you?"

"Nope. I'm pretty ordinary."

"You, my dear niece, are much more than ordinary, but I understand what you mean. Your readings show no spikes in any category."

"Do you think my computer insert could be affecting me?"

"Knowing an ancient put that in you I have to say no." He looked at her. "Ialog wouldn't have done anything to block your natural abilities. Rapid aging you has probably changed a few things. Your mom told me the dreams she had didn't start until she was about six or seven. Skye pretty much said the same thing."

"You think whatever my talent might be should start appearing in the next year or so?"

"Very possible. It could also start when you mate with Skye."

"One of the reasons you want to keep up-to-date records?"

Kuarto smiled at her. He then turned to Heather. "Your turn, my dear."

Heather nodded and approached the machine. She really hated these things but knowing her brother understood made her go along with anything he asked of her. He gave her a nod, and she stepped through.

"Thank you." He worked his pad for a moment. "Everything looks good, Heather. You are showing a little more fatigue than I like but meditating or getting a little more sleep will fix that. I know as head of the war council you feel obligated to oversee everything, but that is why you have a council. If you need a break, take it, don't push yourself too much."

"I try not to, but you know it doesn't always work out that way."

"I know, but I also know you feel responsible so will take on more than you should."

"Kuarto."

"Am I wrong?"

"No," said Sam. She put an arm around her mother. "But we all keep an eye on her, so she doesn't push herself too hard."

"I can tell. Of the six of you, she is the healthiest." He made some notations on his pad. "I will be by in a little while to give each of you a shot to help the deficiencies I'm finding. Warn your mate, Heather. I don't want him growling at me."

"I will."

———

Mac worked on a computation Heather asked her to complete. Arc stood nearby, doing nothing.

"Heather asked you to work with me."

"That is not part of my program."

"Yet you must fit in if you don't want to be sent back to your computer." Mac added a few notes to the data in front of her before moving on to the next assignment.

"I must test her."

"I know. All of us do. She has passed mine." Mac turned from the computer and faced Arc. "You have been following her, and she has shown leadership qualities. Can you extrapolate from the way she handles her soldiers?"

"No. My parameters were preset, but she is always with her mate or another member of this war council." He looked at the information on the screen, made a few changes then looked at Mac. "You were able to use the situation to your advantage. If I can't separate them, I am not sure I will be able to do that."

"You could be honest with her."

"It would skew the results. I need an honest reaction."

"And the situation must be life-threatening?"

"I need to be sure she can control herself and the power she will have at her disposal once the test is finished."

"Her bond with her mate is very strong. She trusts him in everything. Asks for his input regularly."

"I have seen."

"You must do it in a way that doesn't affect that bond." Mac sent the assignment Arc just worked on to Heather and opened the next one. "He is as important as she is."

"I do not plan on interfering with any of her relationships." Arc worked on the next assignment. "I will let you know when I have completed this task."

SEVEN

"So tell me about this Collins," Storm asked Bear.

"He's caught your attention, has he?" At Storm's nod, he continued. "He's a good soldier. He just doesn't know when to keep his mouth shut and that should work in our favor."

"He is one of your mole soldiers?"

"He's creating his cover with our soldiers so they will believe it when he turns traitor."

"Does he have to do it the way he is?" Storm growled. "I do not like the way he has spoken about my mate."

"It is the one thing that will alienate him from the rest of the soldiers. If it upsets you that much, I will talk to him and ask him to try a different tactic."

"No. As long as he knows he will have my attention every time he says something I don't approve of, and I will throw him in the brig if he steps over the line."

———

Heather held the comb she had gotten from Dian in one of the other timelines Susan had created because she thought being married to Storm meant a soft life. If it hadn't been for Skye and Sam, who had been protected by their ship, no one would have known about the timeline change. She had left it on the ship during one of the timelines. Heather had been nervous about talking to her, which was why she had put it off for so long. This wouldn't be happening now if she hadn't found the comb sitting in the middle of her bed. Storm must have put it there, reminding her she needed to do this. How did she talk about a past Dian wouldn't remember?

She stepped up to Dian's door. It opened for her. "Dian?"

"Come in, Heather. I was expecting you."

She stepped into Dian's main room, not sure how to start this conversation.

"Your daughter is quite the artist." Dian gestured for her to sit on her couch.

"She has shown me some of her work." Heather smiled as she sat down. "It is beautiful."

"And prophetic."

"I noticed that too." Heather pulled the comb out of her pocket and sat it on the coffee table near where they sat.

"She drew this while you all were in limbo." Dian handed her a picture. Dian picked the comb up and turned it over in her hands. "Where did you get this?"

"I got it from you in another timeline."

"Bert explained what had happened. He said I raised you in some of the alternate timelines."

"You did." Heather shifted in her seat. "And I remember those years together. You were wonderful and taught me so much. You have this place in my heart no one else could ever fill."

"I wish I could remember, my dear. I know how I felt when I couldn't be there for you like we planned. Seeing you that first time when you were searching for Storm took my breath away. You had grown into a beautiful woman who showed no fear."

"Yeah, well, if my mate hadn't been a shapeshifter then I might have had a different reaction to seeing you change into a human." Heather laughed. "He had no clue you were a shifter too, but somehow deep inside I think I did."

"If I remember right, you thought I was interested in your mate."

"In the beginning, but it didn't take me long to figure out you were protecting him." Heather smiled. "You never tried to mark your territory or fight me for him."

"True." She sat the comb back down. "If you have questions about our time together, I'm not sure I'll have the answers."

"I figured that. To be honest I'm not sure what I want. We had a strong bond in those timelines. Something I only have with Storm and my children. It was nice to have someone to talk to; confide in."

"And you want that again?"

"Yes. I guess. I mean we have a good friendship now, but what we had then went beyond what we have now, and even though ultimately it wasn't real it sure feels it in here." Heather touched her heart.

"Would you be willing to share the memories with me?"

"Are you sure? It is only what I saw and how I felt."

"Heather, I was supposed to raise you and couldn't. This would give me what I missed. I see you and am so proud of how you turned out, but there is a part of me that wonders what if. Your memories would give me that."

"How about I bury the memories to come out in dreams?"

Dian smiled. "That would be perfect."

―――――

Heather sighed as she relaxed in the hot tub. Storm had gone to speak to Bert about challenging their children a bit more while she got a chance to relax and meditate. Zunnie and Terrik were in bed. Or they were supposed to be, but her mental connection told her they were still awake. Zunnie was drawing in her bed and Terrik had one of his favorite toys and was pretending he was a space captain chasing bad guys. She had her eyes closed. Her body felt like it was floating. This was what she needed. Even though she had tried to meditate as often as possible her chances had been few and far between lately and she could feel the pressure building in her because of her lack of meditation. She had set stones of different sizes to lift with her mind. Once she was done with that, she would try her hand at lighting the candles she had placed around the hot tub as well.

She wished she could use some sort of incendiary device, but Bert told her she should be able to make the wick hot enough for it to burst into flames. Heather hadn't mastered it yet but had been able to get one candle to smoke recently so she would keep trying. First, though, she would work with her stones.

―――――

Storm stepped into their rooms and headed straight to the twin's bedroom. The door opened to reveal his son playing with his favorite toy and his daughter drawing.

"What are you two doing?" He used that stern voice that set his soldiers scrambling, but it had no effect on his children or his mate.

"Daddy!" His daughter set her pad down and turned in her bed so she could get up and hug him. His son was right behind his sister.

Those hugs melted any anger he might have felt toward them staying up past their bedtime. He lifted them up in his arms. "Why are you still up?"

"We didn't get to say goodnight to you."

"That will happen from time to time. You need your rest."

"We know, but Mommy said you wouldn't be that long, and she knew we were waiting for you."

"Oh, so I need to punish your mother and not you?"

"Oh, Daddy." Zunnie rested her head on his shoulder. "You would never hurt Mommy. She means too much to you."

"True, but a little discipline is good for everyone."

"Oh, you mean *that* kind of discipline. Mommy does seem to like that."

Storm had to grin. Even their children knew. If Heather knew she would probably turn a bright red. "Time for bed you two."

"Yes, Daddy," they said in unison.

He carried Zunnie to her bed and tucked her in, then turned to his son who had hopped up on his bed when Storm sat him down to put Zunnie in her bed, waiting for his turn. Storm hugged his son and tucked him in as well before giving him a kiss on the forehead. "Now. The lights are going off and you will close your eyes."

"Yes, Daddy," they said again. Zunnie's words came out as a sigh. She was already falling asleep. Terrik yawned right after he answered his father.

Storm knew it wouldn't take long for the two of them to fall asleep. He programmed the lights to dim as sleep overtook them and closed the doors. Entering the living area, he knew his mate was meditating. Where was the question. He walked into the room they shared and found it empty. Removing his uniform, he went to find his mate.

Storm knew he hadn't shifted in a while. He kept pushing his mate to use her mind because of the issues that could crop up when she didn't, but he was being a bit of a hypocrite if he didn't do the same thing. It would also make him keep his hands to himself if he found his mate meditating in the hot tub, which is where he thought she might be. He shifted easily. It felt good to be in this shape again. Something he needed to do more often. In their rooms, he was safe from people finding out about his special ability. Besides, the twins loved to play with him in his wolf form.

He didn't want to disturb his mate, but he couldn't stop the clicking sound of his nails against the floor as he entered their bathing area. She sat in the tub without the jets on, leaning against the pillow he had specially made for her to use when she meditated in the hot tub.

His heart swelled as he took on her beauty. To know she was his took his breath away. He knew she was aware of his presence. Storm sat, then lowered himself to the ground and waited until she was finished.

She had stacked the stones she had been working with off to the side of the tub and was now working on lighting the candles. He knew this because one of them started to smolder.

My heart, you need to relax more. You can do this. I have faith.

You are distracting me.

Not yet, but I could if that is what you wish me to do.

———

Heather opened her eyes and smiled. "I have missed this."

What? Me being in wolf form?

She nodded. "When I see you like this, I feel protected. I'm not saying you don't protect me all the time, but there is something about your wolf that relaxes me more than anything else."

This form was there when you needed it most.

True, but it is you I need, no matter what the form. Heather patted her shoulder.

He blew out a breath as he walked around and rested his head on her shoulder. He heard Heather sigh as she ran her fingers through his fur. He had missed this as well. Slowly, as his mate continued to play with his fur each of the candles lit.

Look.

Heather lifted her head. "All the candles are lit."

I knew you could do it.

She buried her face in his fur.

———

Heather couldn't believe it. She had done it without trying. Her mate was so good for her. She lifted her head and smiled at him.

Storm got up and shifted beside her then walked to the controls of the hot tub. Turning up the temperature and the jets, he walked back to the tub and climbed in. He offered her his hand as he sat on his legs in the middle of the water.

Her smile brightened as she took his hand. Straddling him, she climbed on his lap and wrapped her legs around him. She sighed as she rested her head on his shoulders.

"Let's see you do that again."

She lifted her head and looked at him. "You realize I have no idea how I did that."

"You stopped trying too hard. Now you need to do it again and remember how you did it."

"Alright." She shifted on his lap to move toward the candles.

"You aren't moving." He tightened his hold on her. "You need to snuff them out then relight them with your mind."

"Are you crazy? I don't know how to do any of that."

"Yes, you do." He brushed the knuckles from one hand along her jaw. "You fight your ability every step of the way and you need to embrace it. You've been given this glorious gift."

"That could kill if I'm not careful."

"And you think being a shapeshifter doesn't have its risks?"

The power she could wield frightened her and that fear blinded her to anything else.

"Any ability can be used for good or evil. You threatened to pop Susan out of an airlock when you found out she was the one who kept altering the timeline not too long ago, but you didn't, and that wouldn't have taken any special talent to do that to her." He pressed his hand on her heart. "You are just and would never harm anyone just to be spiteful. You are Vespian and you protect what is yours."

Heather didn't know what to say.

"When you showed Susan your memories of your missions you always allowed her to feel the shame you felt when you got into trouble. You were reprimanded for taking matters into your own hands."

"They didn't like it when I broke the rules."

"You were following your heart. Your Vespian heart. We don't blindly make you follow the rules. That doesn't make sense to us. When I saw how you handled each of those situations, pride swelled inside of me. Without realizing it you were acting like a Vespian. If you had done that here you would have been praised, not reprimanded." He stroked a cheek. "Seeing the look on your face I should have said something before this. I was very proud of how you handled every mission. I would have done exactly the same thing."

"Wait, is that why I'm leading this war council? Because of what you saw?"

"The elders made the decision. You spoke to them, just like Fridon and I did, but I didn't have any input on their choice of you."

"Where you surprised?" She had wondered how he felt when they chose her instead of him.

"At their choice? No. You are the best choice. You have the training, and that wonderful mind of yours looks at things differently so you catch flaws and come up with ideas a lot faster than the rest of us."

"Plus, I'm the one she wants. They knew I have a personal stake and would want to have a hand in the final mission where we take her out."

"The confidence you have at being successful is why they chose you."

"I can't let her win."

"Which is why you need to work on this." He gestured toward the candles, which were now lit. "Imagine how you could use this ability when we face Reasta."

Heather knew he was right. She took a deep breath and focused her thoughts on the candles. Making the candles go out took a few tries, but she smiled when they finally snuffed themselves out. Now she had to relight them.

Focusing, she saw the candle in her mind and applied what she had learned. Heather watched as the first candle on her right burst into flames. Maybe she was on the right track. The second candle took a little longer, but she caught a glimpse of it lighting as well. "You're going to have to watch the other candles and let me know when they light."

"Why don't you try without my input first."

"Why?"

"Because I know you can do this." He smiled as he looked into her eyes. "I saw you do it while we were talking earlier."

He was right. She had done it without thinking about it. The question was how?

"Try."

She nodded. Each candle floated in her mind for a few seconds before she moved on to the next one. Her peripheral vision saw the last candle catch fire. Then she waited.

Storm stood with her in his arms, turned her around and sat back down again. Once he sat on his legs and eased her legs around his. "Look."

"Damn." The only candles lit were the three she watched light up.

"Do you have to see to move things?"

"Um, I think I have faced them each time but have never really tried to do it with my back to anything."

"Then that is what you need to work on next."

She nodded. He was right again. "It's a matter of knowing where everything is."

"That explains how you were able to light the first two and the last candle. You could see them, yet when we were talking about Reasta earlier you lit everyone, several times." He spoke next to her ear. "What were you thinking when we were talking earlier?"

"How much you love me to put up with my lack of confidence."

He laughed. "Your lack of confidence is your own doing. I have every confidence in you."

"You said I did it before with my back to the candles so that proves I don't need to see them." She looked at the six candles that weren't lit. So how did she do the last time?

"I think you need to relax a little." Storm's breath brushed against her neck. His hands moved down her arms to her waist then continued down until she felt his fingers in her folds. Soft gentle caresses had her melting against him. These stupid candles better light quickly because his hands were making her think of what she'd rather be doing.

One by one the candles lit. Heather smiled. She had it.

She leaned her head back against Storm's shoulder. Allowing the wonderful sensations her mate was causing to wash over her she continued to snuff out the candles then light them again.

"Now you're just showing off."

"I didn't want you to think I wasn't trying."

Storm claimed her lips as he continued to stroke her, swallowing a moan as she got close to her release.

Heather broke the kiss first then moved so she could get what she wanted. She smiled as she slid down his length. A sigh escaped her as she settled around him.

"Decided to take matters into your own hands?" He wrapped his arms around her.

"I love your hands. You know that, but I needed more, wanted more."

"You have no patience, my heart. We would have gotten there."

She started moving against him. It felt so good. Each time she slid down his length she could feel him fill her completely. Her body tightened against him, increasing the friction between them. Heather started to move faster. Storm's strong hands helped her keep up the pace as she got lost in the sensations.

Her head dropped back as she felt her orgasm get closer and closer. One of Storm's hands started to wander. Keeping one hand on her hips to help her keep her balance, his other hand slowly inched its way to her folds. She sucked her breath in when she felt him caressing her once again. Her muscles clinched against him with each stroke.

She felt Storm shudder and knew he was as close as she was.

"My heart, I can't take anymore."

"So close." She continued to move, and his fingers continued to glide against her. It raced toward her, consuming her in a white-hot flame that roared through her blood and shot her out to the stars. Heather collapsed against him.

"That was glorious."

All she could do was nod. Each time took her breath away.

———

Heather slipped into another bizarre dream. She was standing in the main hall of the palace, surrounded by her friends. They were getting ready to battle Reasta, but she wasn't sure what their goal was yet. She looked around to see if her mate made it into this dream. Sometimes he did, but not always.

Oh great, it was one of those dreams where she didn't recognize anyone.

She heard a voice. "How do you plan on using the weapons you found?"

Weapons? The ones she got from Arc? Was she that worried about them that it was seeping into her dreams? This was the strangest dream ever because she felt like she was awake. Heather sifted against Storm. His hand brushed along her spine. Yep. She was still awake. Snuggling against her mate she did her relaxing exercises to make her mind shut down. The dream though didn't go away.

"Where are the weapons?"

Heather stared at the man. "What weapons?"

"The ones you said you had so we could defeat Reasta."

A pile of weapons appeared to her right. She pointed. The man just stared at her. Great now he wanted her to figure out who should use what. Was Storm here? He always helped her make decisions like this.

The man she had been talking to had disappeared, and so did the pile of weapons. Heather headed down a long hallway, looking for her mate. She passed through several large rooms where someone would stop her and ask about the weapons again.

She had no answer. Heather had an idea but didn't want to verbalize it until she had spoken to Storm. Opening doors along the way, she continued her search. Finding herself outside she saw a large blue tent not too far away. As she walked up to the entrance, she asked the guards there if they had seen Storm. They point inside.

When she entered, she found Storm in bed with two women. "What the hell?"

"Heather. Did you need something? I'm going to be busy for a while. If you like I can bring in one of my guards to take care of you while you wait." He smiled down at the woman who was beneath him.

"Oh, hell no!" She tried to run forward. She wanted to grab the woman by the hair and pull her away from her mate, but she found her legs wouldn't move. When she tried to use her arms, they were restricted as well.

———

Storm's eyes opened when his mate stiffened beside him. She was struggling with the covers and mumbling to herself.

"Oh, hell no!"

He moved quickly and pinned her to the bed. He had learned before whenever she had one of her visions or just a nightmare, she could get a few good punches in before she woke up. He reached up and retrained one of her hands with a soft cuff and he held her other hand so she couldn't move.

"My heart, you're dreaming."

"Let me go!" Her eyes snapped open, revealing a very angry mate.

"Sorry, you get quite violent when you have a nightmare, and I didn't want to go through that again. Now, what did you dream?"

"Storm, how could you?" Tears filled her eyes.

"What did I do?" He kissed the soft skin near one of her eyes, stopping the tears from sliding down.

"You were with a woman. Two actually."

"It was nothing but a dream." He kissed the other side of her face, stopping that tear as well.

"It seemed so real."

"My heart, how long have we been mated?" He needed her to let go of her anger.

"Six years now."

"And who has always been in my bed?"

"Me."

"Have I ever given you reason to think I would want another partner? As often as we're intimate?"

"No, but you could have kept it from me?"

"How? We share our thoughts. You know what is in my heart." He brushed his free hand along her jaw. "What do I do when my men tease me about the wild night they had?"

"Tell them that those women don't hold a candle to me, make me blush then normally try to drag me somewhere to prove that you are quite happy with your mate."

"Exactly."

Heather had relaxed enough to allow him to release her wrist so he could reach for the other restraint. He would have to prove to his mate that he didn't need any other woman, and he wouldn't be able to do that if she had free reign. "You are all that I want, my heart."

———

"She pulled right out of the scenario I set up for her." Arc looked at Mac.

"Why did you set up the dream so she would find her mate with another woman? That goes against your protocol."

"Using dreams isn't against my protocol. I need to test her alone and she kept focusing on finding her mate. I thought I could use the dream to make her think for herself."

"The way you are trying to do it isn't going to work. Heather has always relied on Storm's tactical ability to make decisions."

"And I need her to make the right choices on her own." Arc paused for a moment. "You were able to do it."

"Because the situation allowed me to test them all at the same time. I still had to be careful because Heather's mind would figure out the test quickly." Mac watched several people walk by them. "She has links with most of her board and as powerful as her mind is you might not be able to get only her input. You will never be able to tell if she is tapping into someone else's mind."

"You're right but I must follow my parameters."

"Part of your parameters is not disrupting the war council. You cannot take Heather out of the equation to get your test done."

"I know. I will try to continue the way I have started, but if it doesn't work then I will have to try something else."

———

The dream still filled her thoughts and made her grumpy.

"How do you stand doing all these inspections?" Heather asked Bear. "I'm finding this a bit tedious."

"All part of the job." Bear gave her a bright smile. "Something that comes with rank."

Heather had all of the council with her. She would break them into groups once they entered the hall where the new elite teams would be training, but right now they were going for an effect. Let them know the heads of the council had entered the area. How everyone was going to react to Toki on the council was the question. She wore a security uniform and not her robes, which was what she normally wore when walking amongst the people.

They stepped in and Heather saw red. Two of Earth's

security were fighting with each other. Vespians would never fight amongst themselves because they knew the punishment. Humans weren't as smart because the laws were so different.

She moved quickly toward the two, pushing against the fisted hand aimed at the other man's jaw. It figured that one of the men was Mark. She shifted it just enough to block any contact then followed the hand around until she could control it and wrenched it up behind the shoulder. Using pressure, she drove him to his knees.

"Let go of me." He struggled against her.

"I don't think so."

The moment Mark heard her voice he stopped fighting. "Captain…"

Storm had grabbed the other man and had lifted him from the floor. It took him two moves to get him on his knees in front of him.

"We don't fight amongst ourselves. If you have aggression, take it out when you're being trained or exercising. Not each other. Not like this." She looked at the Vespians surrounding them. The moment they saw her they dropped to one knee, showing her proper respect. That was what was missing from Earth's culture. Most didn't understand what real respect was. "You see these men? They are showing proper respect because they know they should have stopped you two before I got here. Why would you two be stupid enough to do this?"

"I—" Mark started to answer her.

"I didn't give you permission to speak." She pressed her knee into his back and put some of her weight into it. He groaned as she pressed him down harder so his face smashed against the floor. "It's obvious you have too much time on your hands. I could just ship you back to Earth like

I threatened before, but I fear it may be too dangerous. I could also pull you from your elite squad."

She felt his body sag. Heather knew he wouldn't have come here if he didn't want to help.

"But I'm going to try a different tactic. You need to learn the Vespian way so you are now going to be buddied with one of our best." She looked at the man in question. "You are to know where he is at all times. I don't want to hear he's working on the assignment I or another council member gave him. If he is sitting on the toilet picking his nose that is what I want you to tell me."

The man nodded.

"I am also going to take a personal interest in you." She turned her attention back to Mark, the man she had pinned to the ground. "You will be at the doors of the war council before we get there tomorrow morning, and you will do whatever any of the council needs done. If that is getting us coffee, you will do it without question. I will also give you an assignment every day that must be done before you retire for the evening. I will make sure you don't have any time to even contemplate something like this again.

"Do you understand?" She eased the pressure off his back.

"Yes."

"Yes, what?" She pulled on his arm a little more.

"Yes, Ma'am," he mumbled.

"I can't hear you."

"Yes, ma'am." He said that nice and clear.

She released him and waited. His head tilted up as he looked at his Vespian counterpart. It was slight, but she saw him shake his head once. If Mark was smart, he would stay right where he was until she released him. Now she wanted to see if he listened to his new partner.

He dropped his head back down and remained on the floor the way she left him.

"I wish to take a personal interest in this one." Storm gestured his head down toward the one in front of him.

Heather had other plans for him, but the glint in her mate's eyes showed he would argue with her if she denied him this. She gave him a slight nod of her head.

Storm smiled as he pulled the man to his feet.

Heather looked around at the teams who had gathered around them. "We're going to have to start doing mock missions to keep them busy. Most have adjusted to the atmosphere and have mastered the training."

"We do have grain on the surface close to harvest," suggested Toki. "We could use them to draw Reasta's attention away from the farms so we can get it safely underground before she can highjack it from us."

Heather nodded. That was a problem they had with the woman. Most of Vespia was underground now, but the farmers had remained above ground because of their crops. If they could reap all of it, they'd be able to feed the population for almost a year, and it would leave Reasta without the grain she used to control her troops.

"Put that at the top of our agenda, Skye."

They split up then and check on the rest of the elite teams. Toki was with her. The Vespians all shifted so they gave her the proper distance as they passed by.

Heather was glad when it was all done. The teams were starting to work together beautifully. She was happy with the results so far. Her brother had sent her two messages to remind her to stop by so he could make the final adjustments to her upgraded insert. With all the things that had to be done she didn't want to, but she promised.

Skye followed her. He hadn't been by the medlab either.

157

"Glad to see you two. You're the last of the council."

"Is that a dig?"

"Just a comment." He ran his scans on Heather first.

She saw Micali nearby and headed toward her the moment her brother released her.

"Heather!" Micali hugged her.

"You okay?" Heather could see a shadow in her eyes. Something was bothering her friend.

"Yes." She looked away as she answered her.

Heather knew better.

"It's nothing." Micali sighed.

"It has to be something to have you so sad."

"I haven't gotten pregnant."

"Oh, Micali, you know it is hard for Vespians to have children."

"But I'm not Vespian. My people always have large families. I thought it would be easier because of this. Fridon—" Her voice broke. "He says it's alright, but I know he is disappointed in me."

Heather knew from having been to her planet several times that Micali feared Fridon would reject her as time went on if she didn't produce children. That was what would have happened on her planet. "Fridon has mated with you. That's forever. This planet doesn't cast aside their mates because they can't produce children."

Micali started crying. Heather embraced her, allowing her to get the grief she felt out. Micali wiped the tears from her cheeks and stepped away from Heather when Kuarto stepped up to them.

"Why the tears?"

"It's nothing," Micali said again.

"She's upset because she hasn't been able to conceive." Heather looked at her brother. "Have you finished it yet?"

"Yes." His eyes had that spark of excitement when he

turned to Micali. "I've been working on a formula to help Vespians get pregnant, and I have just finished my first batch of serums. If you'd like I can use you and Fridon as my test subjects."

"Really?" She pressed her hands to her heart. "We must check with Fridon first."

"I'll have him join us."

EIGHT

"**M**y heart, are you alright?"

She had been deep in thought. She had wanted to assign the second man in the fight to work with Henry. It would come across as a punishment but would put him right where she wanted him. The fight would have been a perfect ruse to give him the assignment to work with Henry as he worked his crops and she could have buried what she wanted Resta to know into his subconscious like she had done with the others if she went after Henry. Heather looked at her mate. "I am."

"You seem distracted."

"There is something I wish to speak to you about." They had retired for the evening and had just tucked the twins in bed.

"What, my heart?" he slipped his arm around her as they headed for their room.

"Why did you want to take a special interest in the human?"

He stiffened beside her. She had brought up a sensitive subject.

"He was one of the ones fighting."

"I know there is more to it. You know he was setting up his cover as a mole. What did you hear?"

The doors to their room closed behind them.

"He said things he had no right to."

"Storm, human males can make comments that aren't proper. They've done it for ages. It's part of that dominant male of the species." She started working on her braided hair. "And he said it to alienate himself from everyone else."

"You defend him?"

"No. I'm defending the reason. You have been around humans enough to know that they constantly say inappropriate things."

"This was different." He stepped up behind her and took over her hair.

"Why? Because it was about me?" She loved the feel of his fingers working their way through her hair after he had released the braids.

"Yes."

"Storm." She turned to face him.

"You are my mate, and I'm supposed to protect you."

"I am your mate." Heather grabbed his hand, spun him, and twisted his arm up behind his back. "And I can take care of myself."

He turned and got out of her hold only to wrap her in one of his. "I know, but it's not going to stop something that is inbred in me."

She slipped out of his hold.

"I don't need this. I already feel like something is trying to distract me." She backed away and he advanced on her. "Having Earth security here. Then finding the second computer. And of all people to show up from my past I have the one person I happened to show you in a memory. Plus worrying about Earth security fighting with Vespian soldiers and finally Micali wanting to get pregnant."

"I agree that is a lot to contend, and with your soft heart you take it all personally, but I must ask why you think all this happened to distract you." He smiled at her stance.

"I'm going to sound crazy." She didn't always win their matches, but it was fun to try.

"My heart." He said one word after that. "Wall."

"Okay." She watched as the room turned into the bridge of his ship and the wall he added restraints to that made her scream twice when he used it during their intimacy a while ago. "Small edit. Padded floor and walls."

"Agreed." Storm took a stance as well. "What about clothing?"

"Doesn't matter to me." She knew he was calculating how he could get her to the wall and undressed.

"Good." With a thought he removed their clothes. "Nice to have Cim back."

"So what are the rules?"

"If I get you to the wall, I get to arouse you at my pace. Bring you to the heights I know you can reach."

"And if I win?"

"I will still bring you to the heights I know you can reach."

"So it's a win-win for me."

His smile was less predatory and more natural. Either one, when aimed at her personally, made her heart flutter. They circled each other, looking for an opening.

"Why do you want to protect the humans? Most of them didn't treat you very nicely."

"I know, but they left their homes to help us."

"You and your soft heart." Storm grabbed her hand,

spun her, and wrapped her in his embrace. "It is their job. Just like it was yours."

She slipped out of the hold he was trying to trap her in. "Yet you won't trust them. They're here to help, Storm."

"I know that, but when one of them decides to act like an imbecile you take it personally."

Heather knew he was right. She also knew he was no longer angry over the situation. Now she really had to be careful because her mate's libido would be in control. "I don't take it personally, but I'm the one who allowed them to join us. I do feel responsible when they act like idiots."

"Like a mother watching over their children?" Storm circled her.

"I see what you're trying to do." She dodged his attack. "I'm not Anseri."

"I didn't say you were." This time he swooped in and was able to grab her and take her to the ground.

"This isn't the wall."

"I know." He lowered his mouth to her mark and drew the soft tissue into his mouth for a moment. "But we don't have to make it to the wall the first time."

The thought of them spending the night being intimate sent a little thrill down her spine. Storm gave her his heart-stopping smile, and she knew she needed to fight back. Leveraging her hands in the right spot she used her legs and threw him off, hopping to her feet before he could regain his.

"You were right where you wanted to be, my heart. Why did you move me?"

"I was promised you would work hard to get me against the wall and I'm going to keep you to your promise."

His smile widened. His strikes became more sensual. Soft brushes against the area he knew aroused her. Heather did the same thing, whenever she could she would brush his mark, the nape of his neck, any spot she knew affected him.

She smiled when she heard him growl. The glow in his eyes brightened as he gave her a calculating smile. Now it would just be a move or two before she'd find her back against that wall and her mate having his way with her.

Heather was able to dodge the first attack by sprinting past him when he tried to grab her, but not the second one. He wrapped her in a bear hug that brought their bodies together. Her breasts were pressed up against his chest and she could feel his erection trapped between them.

"I believe you gave in," he murmured as he pressed his lips against her mark.

"I can fight longer if you need me to," she responded softly. It was something she didn't want to do, but if Storm wanted it she would.

"Maybe later." He pressed her against the wall. "Right now, I want to see if I can get a scream or two out of you again."

He lifted one of her arms and pressed it into the restraints. Not wanting her to hang by one arm for too long he made short work of placing her other arm in the second restraint. Her legs he decided to press kisses all along each one as he eased them into the restraints. Once he had her secured, he stepped back and studied her.

"What?"

"I just want to be sure that I haven't harmed my favorite playground in our sparring." He studied her for a few more moments before he stepped up to her. "Still as beautiful as ever."

She felt his fingers brush along her waist, then her hip before he stepped back.

"I think there is something missing."

What was he up to now? Her vision was suddenly blocked when a blindfold covered her eyes. "A blindfold? Really?"

"I love your honest reaction to my touch during our intimacy, and I know I'll get it when you have no idea where or how I'm going to touch you."

She knew she could use her mind to gain the upper hand, but this was something she was going to allow her mate to do to her. The joy they had shared when she allowed him to do things like this filled her with excitement. He just might get his scream tonight.

She was happy the twins had already gone to bed and their door was sealed. It made the room soundproof.

Something soft brushed against her nipples, then she felt it against her inner thigh. It wasn't Storm's hand. She knew his touch. So what was it? Then she smiled. "A feather."

"Very good, my heart." He brushed it against the underside of her breasts. "I knew if I used my fingers, I wouldn't be able to do it for very long before I'd want to feel your heat except me in."

"And the feather will extend that out?" She sucked in her breath when she felt it against her skin.

"I'm hoping." The heat of his breath against her mark proved he was close. "The scent of your arousal is hard to ignore, my heart. Your mark calls to me, begging for me to taste it once again."

She sighed when his mouth dipped to her mark. The gentle tug of his mouth compounded by the feather continuing to brush against her sensitive skin had her pulling against her restraints. Heather moaned when he dropped the feather and started using his hands. They slid across her stomach and gripped her hips.

Storm started kissing his way down her throat, taking a

nip on her collarbone. He surprised her when he moved back up her neck to her mouth. His lips claimed hers as his fingers found her core and slid in to caress her. Her body tightened as each stroke of his tongue was timed with the caresses of his fingers. She started to shake as her orgasm raced toward her.

Storm knew she was close. She felt his fingers glide to her hips, frustrating her. He pressed soft wet kisses down her throat, across her collarbone, and then down to one breast. The heat of his breath against the delicate tissue had her sucking in her breath. It made her forget her frustration from seconds ago.

A moan escaped her when his mouth closed over one nipple. His teeth captured the tip, holding it still as his tongue brushed against the tip.

"Storm." She couldn't take much more.

"Yes, you can, my heart. We've proven that before." His voice was deep and soft. He pressed a kiss against her breast. "The real problem is I don't know if I can take any more. Your desire is high, and the scent of your need is overpowering."

"I can't help it."

"And I don't want you to. I love it when you are so ready for me you can't control yourself."

"And I love it when you can't control yourself either."

She felt his erection pressing against her and wished she could maneuver her body to get him inside her.

"My heart, you aren't making this any easier." He spoke softly next to her ear as he released her legs. Storm gently pulled off her blindfold as he drove into her.

She screamed her pleasure.

"That is the most beautiful sound in the galaxy to me." He set a strong pace. "Do you have any more in there?"

"It's possible, but I never know until we're done."

Heather wrapped her legs around him, giving him a better angle.

"All that does is push me to try." He dipped his head down to capture her lips for a quick kiss before he worked his way to her mark.

The heat of his mouth on the delicate tissue had her arching against him. He released her hands as well so they could wrap around him.

She met him thrust for thrust as she felt the beginning tendrils of her orgasm take hold. His hands moved over her body, at least what he could reach as they worked toward their mutual release. Each time he filled her she quaked a little. Soon he was doing the same thing. They were racing toward their orgasms. When she started to lose control, Storm helped by pressing his mouth against her mark as they continued to move together. Everything inside tightened as she continued on her quest.

A moan escaped her lips as she felt her body clench around Storm. He returned it when her muscles clamped down on him.

"My heart."

She wanted to respond but couldn't. She was too close. Every fiber in her being wanted this release. It was so close but seemed so elusive. Then it started. It filled her and exploded inside her, filling her with a euphoria that made her boneless.

"Beautiful."

———

Heather curled against her mate. Their intimacy always amazed her. She rested her head against his chest and listened to his heart. They had been working hard on getting the teams ready to clear the fields.

"Now, why would I think you were crazy?" He spoke quietly as he went back to their conversation.

"I keep having the same dream. We're at the palace and being attacked by Reasta." She lifted her head so she could look at him. "People keep asking me what to do and about the cache of weapons we found."

"The ones that belong to Arc?"

She nodded.

"And how do you think this ties to the other things you mentioned?"

"Just a feeling." She slid a leg against his. "I guess I'm feeling I'm being pulled in about twenty directions right now and my focus should be on getting rid of Reasta."

"We're still moving toward that. Building the council is our first step. This does take time."

"I know, and we're getting closer to having all of the elite teams done." Heather rested her head against his chest once again.

"These dreams bother you."

"I don't understand them. How am I to know who will get what weapon? I won't share them with all the soldiers. I need to pick and choose the proper weapon for the right person."

"So you don't plan on mass producing any of the weapons?" He brushed his fingers through her hair.

"Not yet. First the council needs to work with each of them and see what they are capable of. Once we are sure our people and the humans can handle any of the weapons, we will make that decision." She brushed her fingers against his ribs.

"Have you said that in the dream?"

"No. I have no idea who to say it to. I'm bombarded with the same question from several people."

"I'd try saying it to the first one who asks you." He

rolled so he had her beneath him. "Maybe the dreams will stop once you answer that question."

"All I can do is try." She wrapped her legs around his waist.

"Good. Now I want to help relax you so you can sleep."

"By making me boneless again?"

"Exactly."

———

The week had been hard, but they had made it through it. The teams were very close to being ready. A few more simulations and they would be. They had tucked the children in and were ready to retire for the evening.

"What do you think of our newest addition, Mark? He's been with us, what? Two weeks? And he has been a great asset," said Storm.

"I'm glad you see it that way." Heather stretched to loosen her muscles. "He's filled in the blanks while we build our teams."

"And we will get there. We only need a few more members and we will have that done." Storm brushed his fingers across her cheek. "But I don't think we should be talking about work. I think you need to relax."

"And you want to help?" She sat on the bed and smiled up at him.

"Of course." He joined her on the bed. "Our days are filled with elite teams and saving our crops."

"The teams did very well with our simulations. But I fear it won't be as easy because Reasta will figure out what we were up to when we do this for real."

"True." He nibbled on her throat. "But we will be ready for that."

He was right it was time to forget about work for a little while. "I have a surprise for you."

That got his attention. "You do?"

Heather smiled. She pulled him to his feet. "Scenario five."

The room changed into the grotto Storm liked to use when his desire was so strong, that they couldn't make it back to their rooms.

Heather used her mind and made an alteration inside her uniform, while doing the same adjustment to the program. Now part of this scenario was the little outfit she hid under her clothes. She hoped her mate liked it. He normally loved any of her lingerie, but she hadn't been able to beat his favorite red one. Several had come close, and she enjoyed trying. Of course, Storm enjoyed it as much as she did.

He smiled as he removed his uniform. Then he started working on hers. Storm caressed a strap. "What is this?"

"A present for you."

He took his time undoing her seals, not wanting to ruin the gift she had created for him. Storm sucked in his breath when he finally revealed what she was wearing. "This is beautiful."

Heather had a hard time trying to figure out the color then settled on an emerald green. Demi cups covered her breasts, and the slight panties were held together with three straps from the front panel to the back one. Then there were straps that crisscrossed between the top and the bottom.

"I'm glad you like it."

"Very much." His fingers slid along the straps, making sure they touched her skin at the same time. The soft delicate brushes caused her to want him more. Something so small, yet he knew just how to touch her to get the reaction he desired. The grotto beckoned so she took his hand and led him to it.

She took her time drawing him with her. She knew if she hesitated Storm would take over and she didn't want that. Coming up with this hadn't been easy. Storm was constantly around. Whenever she found a moment to herself, she worked on it, slipping away when she could to make sure the programing was the way she wanted it.

Once they entered the grotto Storm found a few changes. He pointed to the change she made to the bench. "What is that?"

"I thought you'd like some padding?"

"My heart, the material the bench is made of is quite comfortable."

"I know." She shrugged.

"I appreciate you doing this." He wrapped his arms around her and pulled her against him.

"We could change the bench back," she suggested.

"It is fine."

"You sure?" Heather looked at him with a soft smile. "Chair."

It was a smaller version, but she did her best to duplicate the chair they had enjoyed many times on the ship. She had to if she wanted it to fit in the grotto.

"You did this for me?" He gave her his bone-melting smile and lifted her in his arms. "We must try it out."

That was the reaction she hoped for. The glow in his eyes was so bright they didn't need any lighting. He sat her down in the chair, then brushed his fingers along her jaw. Storm knelt in front of her.

"This is a wonderful gift." He captured her lips for a quick kiss. "Now I know why you kept disappearing."

"Was I that obvious?" She had tried to be as discreet as

she could. It figured her mate would know when she was sneaking off. His hyper senses didn't miss much.

"You are my heart." He lifted her up and sat on the soft leather she had just occupied, bringing her with him. Her braid dropped forward and brushed Storm's forearm. He lifted it and undid the clasp. With slow deliberation he released her hair, undoing the braid then running his fingers through it to loosen the waves so her tresses flowed all around her shoulders.

He loved her hair and now that it was long, he enjoyed playing with it. The feel of his fingers sliding through her tresses relaxed her. Took the stress of the day away for her. She could melt from something so simple and sweet.

"You have that look in your eye."

She had been caught. "What look?"

"The one you have when you're totally relaxed. If you had that satisfied smile, I know so well I'd swear you had an orgasm."

She did smile then. Wrapping her arms around him, she pressed herself against him. "You are very good at getting that smile."

"I hope so. It is the most beautiful thing I've seen." He brushed his fingers against her jaw. "I strive to see it all the time."

"And I can't thank you enough." She braced her knees on either side of his hips and pressed him back against the chair. His strong arms wrapped around her and brought her with him.

"So am I to add unbraiding your hair to my list of acceptable foreplay?"

She started laughing then. Storm knew she enjoyed it when he released her hair, but so did he. It was one of those elusive quite moments they wished they had more of. He undid her hair every chance he got. "You are my heart."

He pulled her head down so he could capture her lips with his. His tongue delved into her mouth when she opened for him. Their tongues swirled and danced together, arousing them as their kiss continued. Storm's arms tightened around her, and he ended the kiss.

"If you want to flip us over, you're going to find this chair a little harder to do that in."

He gave her a bone-melting smile, and he brought her with him to one edge of the chair then rolled them so she was beneath him. "My heart, you know I love a challenge."

"And you always succeed at any challenge I seem to give you."

"When it comes to our intimacy I'm driven." He brushed his fingers along her sides, from her ribs to her hips. "I need to arouse you more and the best way is to have you here, with you back against the chair."

"Storm."

He pressed a finger against her lips and shushed her. "I know you think you're ready, but my nose knows best."

———

Heather sat in the war room trying to figure out how they were going to use Henry. She didn't want him in real danger. Reasta needed to know what he meant to her. Heather knew she would treat him differently if she saw them interacting with each other. How to do it without making it look like it was staged was the question.

Fridon came into the room and sat in his chair. "We found another clone amongst our ranks."

"Why does she keep trying? We always find them

before they can enter our compound." Heather rubbed her hands against her face.

"I think she does it to annoy you. You do like to do the same thing to her."

Heather grinned. "I do, don't I."

"I guess I need to find out if that was her way of contacting me." Heather stood.

"She always contacts you when she wants to talk."

"I know and normally I wait until she does, but I think I'm going to beat her to it." She headed out the door and toward the command center.

She walked up to their main screen and placed her hand on the chair of the soldier on duty. "I wish to speak to Reasta."

"Yes, Mistress." He worked his control board and sat back. "Um, Mistress, she has requested you contact her later. She says she's busy."

Heather laughed. "She's doing to me what I do to her all the time."

"Heather, you are a hard one to keep up with," said her brother. "I need to make a few more alterations to your scanner."

"We can go back to the war room."

"No need." He tapped on a pad then touched a stylus against her chest. "That should do it."

"Thanks, Kuarto."

"She's ready to talk to you, Mistress."

Heather turned to the large screen Reasta's head floated on.

"You wished to speak to me?"

"It's not that important. I'll call you back." Heather stepped forward and placed her hand on the control panel.

"I have no time for your games!"

"Fine. I'm curious about something." Someone handed

her a cup of coffee. She took a sip before she continued. "Why do you keep cloning your people and make them look Vespian when you know we can detect them? Doesn't that waste your meager supplies?"

"I don't know what you're talking about." Her gaze flicked to someone behind Heather.

Heather turned to find Henry offering coffee to anyone who wanted some, which was a lot of the warriors now. As Vespians got a taste of coffee they found they liked it. Heather frowned. What was he doing here anyway? As she turned back to the screen, she noticed Arc standing there watching. That made her frown more.

Reasta noticed her frown. "What's wrong, Heather?"

"Nothing." She schooled her features. She just got what she wanted. Reasta noticed Henry. Now she needed to draw her attention away so Reasta would question what Henry was to her.

———

A few hours later, Heather found herself in the same dream. She stood in the main halls of the palace with people rushing all around her.

"Where are the weapons?" This time it was Fridon asking the question.

"Why is this such a focal point of this dream?"

"What dream? Heather, you need to make a decision."

She shook her head and moved away. The ground moved under her. "We're under attack!"

Whatever they were hit with was powerful enough to knock more than half the people around her off their feet. The weird thing was she felt it more against her back than through her feet. A second blast told her this was for real, not in her dream.

She tried to claw her way out of the dream. The palace faded away and she found herself in the white room she had created when Reasta had first arrived. Why was she here? And why hadn't her exit shown up so she could wake up?

A door appeared in front of her. It wasn't her normal door but hopefully, it would allow her to wake up. She reached for the door and found she couldn't connect with it. Each time she moved toward it; it moved out of reach. What was going on?

"I'm not going to chase you, you stupid thing. I need to get to the command center and see what is going on. I know we're under attack and whatever is keeping me here is stopping me from helping my people." She stepped up to the door and this time it didn't move. Grabbing the knob, she twisted it, but the door refused to open.

"Damn it!" She banged against it. "Let me out of here!"

———

Storm shot up in bed when he felt the ground move. Heather rolled off him. The second shift in the ground had him up and climbing into his uniform.

"My heart, do you want me to get the children to Bert while you head to the command center?" He knew she always wanted to be sure of the safety of the twins before joining any battle to fight off one of Reasta's attacks, but as leader she needed to be the one to go to the command center first. When she didn't answer him, he turned around and noticed she was still sleeping. "Heather?"

She hadn't moved.

He climbed on the bed and patted her cheek. Nothing. What the hell was wrong with his mate? Storm felt for a pulse. It was nice and strong. He lifted a lid, and her eyes were rolled into the back of her head. That couldn't be good.

"Daddy?"

He turned to see Terrik standing at the door.

"Is Mommy okay?"

"She's fine, son." Storm climbed off the bed and crouched in front of him. "I'm going to take you and your sister to Bert and when we're done, we'll come back to get you."

His daughter came up to him and handed him one of her drawings.

"Mommy is in trouble. She can't get out."

Storm looked at the picture. It showed Heather banging on a large white door. He looked at his daughter. "Did you just draw this?"

She nodded.

"Did you hear your mommy say anything?"

"She was screaming let me out of here and then I saw lightning."

"Lightning? Like a bolt hitting the ground?"

"Not really. It was more across my vision. Like an arch."

"Arch?" He lifted his daughter. "Like an arc?"

"Yes. Do you understand what I saw, Daddy?"

"I do." He smiled at his daughter. "Now I need to get you two to Bert."

Just as he scooped up his son and headed to the door, he heard the door chime. He allowed his son to open the door. Dian stood in the doorway.

"I thought I'd come for the children so you and Heather could head to the command center."

"Thank you, Dian." Storm sat his son and daughter down. Although he had no trouble carrying them, it wasn't as easy for others. They had enough of his blood to grow larger than a human or ancient. Heather struggled to hold them at the same time, even though she kept trying.

As she walked away with the children, he turned around and tried to wake his mate up once more. When he was sure he couldn't do it, he grabbed her uniform, placed it on her stomach then wrapped her in the cover on the bed. This wasn't going to look good but he needed to get her to Kuarto so he could track down that damned android. Zunni's lightning had to be Arc and he was going to tear the damn thing apart.

Taking as many shortcuts as he could, he walked in with Heather in his arms and laid her on a medical bed.

"What happened?"

"I can't wake her up."

Kuarto hooked her up to the bed to see what type of readings he could find. The one thing Storm wanted to see was her active brain patterns. It gave his hunch power.

"I'll do what I can, Storm."

"And I will do what I can." He stepped out of the med lab and walked to where Mac was assigned. Right beside her was Arc. He moved behind the android, found the coupling for his right arm, and pulled it off. After dropping it to the floor he did the same to the other arm.

"What are you doing?"

"Making sure you can't fight back." He felt the coupling at his waist and pulled his torso free. Sitting it on a counter he turned it so he could remove his head. "Now that I have you the way I want you, you will release my mate from whatever simulation you have her trapped in."

"I don't understand."

"We are under attack and my mate is the leader. She needs to be telling people what to do not fulfill some crazy program you have to follow." Storm opened the chamber where the android's on/off switch resided. "If you don't release her, I will continue to disassemble you. If that doesn't work, I will shut you down and wipe your hard drive. Whatever it takes to get Heather back."

"In order for her to be able to access my system she needs to prove what she can do."

"And if you release her, you will see what she is capable of while she deals with the attack we're under. Which would prove her more. Some insipid test or a true challenge?"

"I will release her."

"Good." Storm tucked his head under his arm and walked away.

"Why are you taking my head with you."

"I need to see my mate free before I even think of allowing you to reassemble. Mac will know where to find your head when I give her permission to put you back together."

NINE

Heather opened her eyes and found herself restrained. She fought with her bonds.

"Hey, hey." Her brother came over to her and placed his hand on her chest to stop her from struggling. "Storm brought you here, unconscious."

"Did he have to make this so tight?"

"I think he was thinking of your modesty when he brought you in."

She sat up and peeked inside her blanket. Great, she couldn't go to the command center like this, but then she spied a bit of gray and realized her mate sent her uniform with her. With Kuarto's help, she hopped off the bed.

"I can't move in this."

He helped her unwrap enough for her to change inside the cover. "I still don't get how sometimes you hide like this and other times you don't seem to care who sees you naked."

"Vespians don't gawk and stare the way humans do, and you have a few humans here in the lab." She kept her voice soft as she pulled her uniform up her body then sealed it. "I had enough of that when I was in Earth's security."

"I guess I see everyone as a patient, but I see what you are saying." He looked around and found several of the human males looking a little disappointed when she dropped the cover and they realized she had already donned her uniform.

Slipping into her boots, she sealed them into the uniform as well. She gave him a quick kiss on the cheek, and she was gone. Heather raced down the halls to the main command. Storm turned toward her when she entered the room. Like everyone else, he gave her the proper bow before he stepped up to her and pulled her into his embrace.

"I am happy to see you." He brushed his knuckles along her jaw.

"Thank you." She caressed his cheek. "How did you figure it out?'

"Our daughter, she drew a picture of you. I'll explain more later."

She pressed a quick kiss to his lips.

"Now what was that?" He pulled her closer. "That is not a proper kiss for your mate."

"That?" She kissed him again. "That was just a bit of a tease."

"You know what happens when you tease me."

"I do, and I love it."

He captured her lips with his, dipping his tongue into her mouth when she opened for him. They swirled together, touching and dancing as they moved together. When Storm released her, she wished he hadn't. He must have seen something in her eyes.

"There's more where that came from." He smiled at her.

"I hope so since that's all I'm going to get from you."

Storm laughed. "I have created a monster."

Heather gave him a soft smile before she turned her attention to the screens dominating the room. "What do we know?"

"Reasta has destroyed three fields. She has three ships above the farm they have attacked, and they are remaining stationary for the moment."

"Then we should be hearing from her soon." She studied the screens. "We have twelve farms left with about twenty fields each?"

"Yes, Mistress. It will take all our elite teams to clear them in time, but we need to start now. It will take us about an hour to complete the mission. Those ships could take out three-fourths of our crops in that amount of time."

Heather wanted to kick something. "Where is Arc?"

Storm smiled and gestured for her to follow him. They entered the war room and in the center of their table sat his head.

"You took him apart?"

"I had to make him know I was serious."

Heather couldn't help but grin. Her mate had his way of doing things. She might not always agree with them but today she did.

"I might need him in one piece."

"And that is up to you, my heart. I didn't need that to achieve my goal." He pressed a kiss against the side of her head. "Mac has the rest of him and is waiting for your instructions."

"Thank you." Arc watched her as she approached him. "Now is the time for you to be useful."

"That has been my goal the whole time, Heather."

"Yet you have been more of an annoyance than anything. Something I haven't cared for." Heather crossed her arms over her chest. "I need a particle or de-atomizing weapon. Something that can be held and has a range of several thousand feet. I also want no collateral damage."

"Which is why you don't want to use any of the Vespian weapons. They will cause a lot of damage if you use them."

"Correct."

"There are three weapons that will fit your needs the most." Three images appeared between them. "They are among the weapons you found when I first appeared."

"Can these be combined?"

"Yes."

"Thank you." She studied each weapon before she pressed the com button on her collar. "Sam, you're needed in the war room."

"Our daughter?"

"She is the best and has the ability to download all the data on the weapons. She is my first choice."

"And why not Skye? He has the ability to download the same data."

"True, but our daughter has the training I need to do this. Skye would be better suited in the fields helping us. If I thought someone else could do what I want she would be joining us in the fields."

"May I ask why we will be in the fields as well?" asked Storm. "What is your plan?"

"I'm going to send most of the teams to the outermost fields, having them work their way in, while the war council with the members we have been considering for our elite teams will go out and work the fields near where those ships are."

"You must be protected." Storm frowned at her.

"One of the reasons Sam will be manning the weapon instead of me. I also need a black uniform. This one would be a dead giveaway." She touched his heart. "I will go out surrounded by guards and will not put myself in a position where I might be in jeopardy."

The doors opened and Sam walked in.

Heather touched his face. "We will speak about this later."

"You wanted me?"

"Yes." Heather looked at Storm, giving him a chance to speak his piece.

He backed away from her and allowed her to speak to Sam.

"I've done my research on the ships attacking and have found some weapons to do what we need." She brought Sam to the images floating in front of Arc.

"And you want me to fire it?"

"You always question when we pass you over. This time there will be no question. You are perfect for this."

Sam gave her mother a brilliant smile.

"This is the schematics for the ships. Study it before you try using the weapon. It is ancient in design."

"I will do you proud, Mom."

"I am already proud of you."

"And what is my goal?"

"To take out those ships within thirty seconds, with little to no collateral."

"Save as much of the farms as possible. Get the farmers to safety and remove those ships from the equation. Sounds like a normal day for you, Mom." Sam pressed a kiss against Heather's cheek before turning her attention back to the weapons. "Can they be combined?"

"According to Arc yes." Heather smiled.

Sam pulled the images up so she had them floating in front of her. Tilting them this way and that, she removed the parts she didn't want, then rearranged the parts to her satisfaction. "Okay, ready."

Storm walked over to the cabinet where they had put the weapons they had found and opened the door.

"Wow." Sam pulled out several smaller weapons and checked them over before she grabbed the three she needed. Turning them over in her hands a few times before she found the seals holding them together, she separated the weapons and attached the pieces she wanted to use and put the unneeded parts back in the slots they came from. "I'm ready when you are."

It didn't take long to have everyone armed and ready. Heather pulled the people they wanted to go with the council and rearranged the elite teams so all the teams were full, then sent them out to rescue their crops.

Heather and her team waited behind Sam as she prepared to take the shots.

"One." Sam aimed and struck the first ship. She hit the engines, and it lit up before the ship folded in on itself and winked out of sight. They took off running.

"Two," murmured Heather as they dashed out and started setting up the safety grid. The second ship did the same thing when Sam hit the same spot. They started lifting and moving the crops as Sam aimed at the third ship.

"Three." They continued to move as quickly as they could, moving from one cleared field to another.

"The other teams have cleared three farms now," said a voice in her ear.

"Good. Save the newest plants for last. They might not survive the move, and I want to give them the most time in the suns as possible." Data streamed across her helmet. They had incoming.

Guards moved all around her.

"Stand down. If I'm surrounded, Reasta will be able to figure out which soldier I am. As long as we have the security grid, they shouldn't be able to hit any of us."

The soldiers around her kept moving like they had gotten an order to move toward their attackers.

"We are close to having this field completed."

"Then start moving to the next. Teams of eight, four with the shields and four of the field hands." Their temporary security grid was just a small handheld device in the shape of a ball. The four members carrying the balls could move with four others and as long as they were a certain distance apart the grid would still be active and keep them protected.

Heather shifted to the new field with the second group. They knew Reasta would be looking for her in the crowd of soldiers and would expect her to stay to make sure everything was done the way she wanted it to be done, so she was moved to the new fields in the first few groups to keep Reasta from figuring out which soldier she was.

"We have three more ships coming your way."

"Understood," said Heather.

"On it," said Sam. The weapon Heather had given her was strapped to her back. She headed back to the cave opening with some of the crops and prepared to fire the weapon again.

They continued to move crops as quickly as they could.

"I'm getting intel on injuries," said Fridon. "They are getting a few stray shots through the grid when it thins."

"We expected that," said Heather. "Any casualties?"

"No. Our uniform shields have protected those hit so far, but the shots have knocked out their electronics. Anyone hit has had to be carried back into the cave until the suit can be repowered."

One of the second group of ships got close enough for

Sam to take out, but the other two stayed just out of her range and continued to pummel everyone's shields.

"We've gotten about forty-five percent moved to the caves."

"Good. We should have this done within the hour then." Heather focused on the task at hand. Her visor flashed an alert, and she looked up to see a blast coming right at her. She started to move when she felt something slam into her side, shoving her to the left and into the ground. "What the hell?"

"You okay? I saw that blast coming and wasn't sure you knew it was coming right at you."

"I'm fine. A little heads up would have been nice though." Heather brushed her uniform. Anger filled her and she knew where it was coming from. *My heart?*

We will speak of this later. Storm was upset with her.

Something she would have to face once they returned to the cave.

Everything continued to move until they hit the plants that weren't quite ready for the move. Those they had to handle delicately. They needed to stay in the Vespian suns a little longer, but Heather knew if they left them Reasta would find a way to get them so they decided to take the risk of moving them. Hopefully, they would survive. This plant had so many uses but it was fragile. That was why they had to ship it instead of teleport it and it had to be removed by hand instead of using harvesters.

Storm stepped up to her side. *We are close to being finished. Perhaps you should head for the safety of the caves now.*

She was grateful he spoke to her mentally. Part of her wanted to wait until every last soldier was safe, but she knew that her safety was what everyone wanted.

"I need to get back in and wait for Reasta's call. Fridon, make sure everyone makes it inside safely."

"Of course."

Each person paused as she passed them. Nothing Reasta should pick up, but she noticed. They would have bowed if it wouldn't have put her in jeopardy. Storm walked behind her. He kept the proper distance between them, but she knew in his mind he wanted to sweep her up and dash inside with her.

Once they entered the cave she released the seal on her helmet, then gloves. Storm did the same. Someone standing nearby stepped up to take them and put them in their proper place.

"Where do you wish to speak?"

"Some place private." His voice was deeper. She knew he was fighting to keep his anger at bay.

That meant he didn't want anyone to record them. About the only place they weren't recorded was their rooms and it would probably be hours before they could get away.

They entered the war room so Heather could switch into her gray suit once again. Just as she sealed it she was called to the command center.

"We have gotten eighty percent of the crops. Reasta destroyed ten percent, and the rest are the newer crops that probably won't make it."

"I'm happy with eighty percent."

"Reasta is asking to speak to you."

Heather rubbed her eyes, before giving the nod to put her on screen. Storm stepped up behind her and wrapped his arms around her.

"You never go anywhere without him, do you?"

"Does it bother you, Reasta?" Heather leaned back into Storm's chest. Reasta didn't respond, but the twitch in her jaw told Heather what she wanted to know. "Why have you called me again?"

"I wanted to congratulate you on your little endeavor."

"You mean getting to the crops before you could?" Fridon stood next to the screen and gave her a thumbs up. That meant everyone made it back to safety. Heather smiled. "Why, thank you. We're quite happy to have gotten most of the crops before you could destroy them, but I have to ask why would you want to destroy something you need so desperately."

"What are you talking about, Heather?"

"You use that plant to control your soldiers. I'm sure the last supply you received must be getting pretty low by now."

Reasta cut their connection.

"Well, that went well." She turned to look at Storm. His anger was still just below the surface. She needed to address it soon. She knew all would go to their assignments in a few hours if she didn't release them even though no one really got any sleep.

She was surprised to see Toki standing there in a security uniform. Heather knew she was in the command center but figured she would be wearing her robes.

"I am glad you were successful." Her smile was genuine.

"Thank you, Toki."

"May I suggest you give everyone the day off."

Storm arched a brow at her.

"They deserve it after tonight." Toki arched her brow back at her brother. "You should celebrate their hard work."

"I agree," said Storm.

"I'll see that it is done," said Fridon.

"You need your rest as well," said Heather.

"And I promise I will get it." Fridon smiled. "I will

delegate the assignment out to the right people then join my mate."

Heather pressed her collar. "Everyone involved in saving our crops have already done their shift for the day. I will expect you to be ready for inspection this evening. The time will be released an hour before you are needed. Good rest everyone."

Storm put his arm around her and escorted her toward their rooms. Now she would face his anger. Something she wasn't looking forward to.

―――――

Storm was grateful everything went well, but his mate was taking too many chances. He tucked the twins in then went to talk to his mate. He stepped into a darkened room. Heather must have lowered the lights. It took a second for his eyes to adjust.

She sat in the middle of the bed, naked. Heather sat on her legs, with her hands on her thighs. Her gaze was down. Being with his society had taught her a lot. She was showing him she realized she had been wrong by taking the submissive position a Vespian woman would when she angered her mate. Seeing her like this melted any anger he had.

He removed his uniform and kneeled next to the bed. He wanted her to know he wasn't angry at her. "I see you've been learning from our people."

"A few of the women explained the right way to deal with an angry mate since I've been interacting with them."

"Deal?" Her head dipped a little lower when she realized she chose a wrong word. "Heather, look at me."

"Okay, so I'm new at this." She lifted her head and found him on his knees. Her shocked look told him she knew what his position meant too. She scooted a little closer to the edge of the bed. "What are you shamed about?"

"I worry about your safety and take it out on you. I think that you still don't see yourself as a leader or a Vespian, then you do something like this. It humbles my heart."

"I do see myself as a leader, but I also believe a good leader gets out there with their people. I can't see making others put their life on the line when I'm not willing to." She paused for a moment. "It is what you would do."

"You're right." He got up and sat next to her. "But I don't have a maniacal woman after me."

"Storm, we ran the numbers. The chances of me being a target were negligible. I wouldn't have gone if I thought I was in danger."

"I know. I think the anger I felt started when I couldn't wake you up because of that damn android. Then seeing that blast heading straight for you made my heart stop." He pulled her onto his lap.

"But that blast would have only damaged the suit. I was in no mortal danger."

"You don't know. If Mark hadn't knocked you out of the way, it could have been the one in a million that could have done more than damage the suit."

"Storm." Heather shifted in his lap so she was straddling him and so she could look him in the eye. "No one can predict something like that. I could trip on a rock, bash my head, and hemorrhage out."

He wrapped his arms around her and pulled her close. "I don't even want to think about something like that."

"Then don't worry about these small things. I have the same fear every time you join me on any of these missions."

"We are a pair, aren't we?" He lay back on the bed and brought her with him. "Did you know you have a title as leader, but no one will use it because they don't want to upset you?"

"Is that why everyone keeps calling me mistress instead of using my name? I haven't heard that since we mated." Heather brushed a few strands of hair out of his face. "What is my title?"

"Ansira, very close to my mother's title." He rubbed his knuckles along her jaw. "Would you allow them to call you that?"

"It would show that I have embraced my position and will make them feel more relaxed, won't it?" She braced her hands against his chest and pushed herself up into a sitting position. "I'm still a soldier, Storm, and I want to be treated that way."

"You will not be treated any differently. Our people want to show you proper respect. That is all. This will allow them that opportunity."

"And when this is all said and done, and we're rid of Reasta can we go back to normal?"

"You mean where you can hide in the shadows like you did when you first got here?" Storm ran his hands up her waist to cup her breasts.

"I miss our alone time."

"I do too, my heart, but you have now made too many friends for us to hide away the way we used to. They will want some of your time as well."

"And they will also understand that there will be times when we want to be alone. Whether it is with each other or to spend time with our family." She shifted herself so she had his erection trapped beneath her.

"You are being very distracting and haven't answered my question."

"Distracting?" She smiled down at him. "Is there a problem?"

He wrapped his arms around her and flipped them over. Now he was pressing his weight into her. "Never, but you have a tendency to change the subject or distract me when you don't want to talk about something."

"I'm not that bad."

"Yes, you are." He pressed a soft kiss against her mark. "But luckily I know how to keep you focused."

Heather sighed.

"I need an answer." This time he drew the soft tissue into his mouth.

"Yes."

"Yes, what, my heart?"

"They can use my title." Her words came out soft.

"That is my wonderful mate." He shifted so he could move down her body a little. "I'll pass the word."

"No. I think the right thing to do is to have you call me by my title at the gathering this evening."

"See? That is why I mated you." He captured a nipple in his mouth.

"You mated with me because of the great sex we have."

He lifted his head and gave her one of his bone-melting smiles. "I mated with you because you're my heart. The great sex we have is a glorious bonus."

"You are incorrigible."

"I am your heart." When she remained quiet, he focused back on her body. As much as he wanted to take his time with her, he knew they were needed for the evening meeting and Heather should be the first to arrive. He brushed his fingers against all her sensitive spots that he knew aroused her. It wasn't long before she was moving beneath him, trying to will him to fill her. He moved back up her body, pausing to press a kiss between her breasts and again to press his lips against her mark. Storm brushed his fingers along her cheek as he entered her and smiled when she sucked in her breath and arched against him.

He set a nice slow pace, watching his mate for the subtle signs that told him she was close. The vise-like grip she had on him was exquisite. Storm continued to move, reveling in the joy he always felt in Heather's arms. They moved together, reaching for that bliss they always felt. Their minds became one. Their desires became one. Heather's breath hitched. He switched the pace slightly, hitting the spot that brought her more powerful orgasms. He could feel her orgasm blossom like it was his own. His started as well, intensifying everything. They soared through their releases together as one.

This he would never be tired of.

———

Fridon outdid himself. The hall was ready for them. Heather hoped they could fit everyone in there. Even though some of security still needed to man their stations, they would rotate so all would be there. This would be a nice respite for everyone. Arches stood in front of the main hall they were using so anyone who needed it could fabricate an outfit.

He had also done a wonderful job of keeping it a secret. She had told everyone to be ready for inspection. No one had a clue to the real reason she wanted everyone together.

The room was quiet when their council walked in. It made her feel uncomfortable. Heather wondered if this was how Anseri felt when she entered a major function. What if she tripped and fell on her face? She took a deep calming breath. Standing in front of their troops she addressed them. "We were successful in gathering our crops before Reasta could destroy or steal them. Now everyone who stayed to help with crops can join us here, and we can start our battle outright.

"We have been training and fighting hard for months. I'm proud of what we have accomplished." She stepped amongst the first row of soldiers. The rest of her council followed her lead, and they started their inspection. Faces blank they walked among the teams. Each would pause for a moment or longer and stare at the person they were evaluating. Heather walked around several, studying their uniforms, hair, and posture.

Once everyone was done, they all headed back up to where they had stood before. They spoke quietly to each other.

"So, you noticed it too?" Heather said it loud enough that the perfect acoustics of the room would allow everyone to hear her.

"Yes, Ansira. No one is dressed properly," said Storm.

"I thought the same thing." Heather turned toward the crowd again. "We had special plans for this evening, but your dress uniform is the wrong apparel. Dismissing everyone to change your clothing will take too long."

"Ansira, I think this would be a good time to try the arches we just completed," Fridon answered. "You could show everyone the proper attire and we could get to the next phase of this evening without too much time lost."

Heather headed toward the main hall where the arches stood. She wondered how everyone would react when she stepped through. Her garment was loaded and the moment it read her DNA it would transform her uniform to the gown she had picked.

The moment the last soldier left the other hall workers

hurried in to convert it into another area for people to mingle.

She stepped up to the arch then turned to face the people behind her. "This arch has been programmed based on your personal data. All you need to do is step in and the system will read your DNA. Now understand I have already programmed my outfit into it."

Heather turned and stepped into the arch. Her uniform was replaced with a beautiful form-fitting gown. She loved the design. The dress was backless with a beautiful drape that went from one shoulder to another. The bodice dipped just low enough to show off a little cleavage. It was modest enough for Earth's security, yet very Vespian. It was a soft beige and mostly see-through, except for key areas of her body. It had an outer sheath that was made of a net material that looked invisible against the dress. The only thing that could be seen was a simple pattern in a deep maroon. It was the mark her mate gave her, and the design of the outer layer made it look like a hologram dancing around her body when she moved.

No one reacted when they saw her outfit, but she could feel their surprise in their thoughts. She smiled. "Outfits have been programmed for each of you. If you wish to pick something else that isn't a problem. All I ask is that you wait until everyone has had a chance to change."

Storm was the next person through the arch. He wore a typical Vespian outfit with dark trousers and a long coat. He made one change in his choice and changed his shirt to match her dress which was expected amongst mates. Once his clothing had changed, he stepped up to her and took her hand.

"You look beautiful, and I am humbled by the design." He kissed her cheek.

"I thought you'd like it." She linked arms with him. "Ready to see what Fridon has prepared for us?"

"You have my undivided attention." He smiled at her. "Especially in that dress."

They walked into the room to find it had been converted into the palace ballroom, or as close as it could be. Heather hugged his arm as she looked around.

"I'm going to have to give him a kiss for this."

"Only on the cheek, my heart." He wrapped his arm around her waist. "Micali might get jealous."

"Oh, I don't think she's the one who would be jealous." Heather turned toward him so he could wrap his arms around her. "You don't like it at all when someone pays me a little too much attention whether it is male or female."

"I am much better at sharing now."

She laughed as she wrapped her arms around his neck. "You are my heart."

"Hmm, I see I need to work on that a little more." He dipped his head down to capture her lips for a moment.

"I have no problem with your jealousy or over-protectiveness, most of the time. If you didn't behave that way, then I'd fear you didn't care."

"You know how I feel about you, my heart. I show it as often as I can."

"Yes, you do." She smiled at him.

Fridon joined them and soon the whole council stood around them.

"Bear had a good idea to help speed up time with the reception line."

"And what did he suggest?" Heather had hoped they could bypass that altogether.

"We line everyone up and walk amongst them."

Even though they just did that the reception line was a way for the people to thank and honor their leaders. She knew it would be better than standing in one place as everyone filed in front of them. It would take hours the normal way and she knew she couldn't get out of it.

"Then we need to get them lined up as soon as possible."

———

They lined up in perfect rows, making Heather proud. She wanted to race through the rows of people as quickly as possible, but having them standing at attention, waiting for some tidbit from her she knew she couldn't cut it short.

Heather stepped between the first and second rows of soldiers, placing her hand on the shoulder of the people on both sides of her. As she walked, she talked to them, telling them how the council couldn't have been successful without them. That their success was due to everyone's hard work. She worked her way through row after row. Heather also made sure the humans knew how to handle Vespian protocol. "If you wish to speak to anyone on the council make your squad leader aware. They will either have an answer for you or know who to speak to get you an answer. We want you to enjoy tonight because tomorrow could be another fight with Reasta."

Once she had touched each of her soldiers, she stepped up on the dais set aside for her and the rest of the council. Storm joined her.

"Thank goodness that is over."

"You were wonderful, my heart. You showed them how much they meant to you, and I know each of them appreciated that." He wrapped his arms around her.

Each of the council finished walking and talking amongst their soldiers and joined Heather. She knew the protocol wasn't over. She still had a few more things she had to do so everyone would have a good time. When the head chef signaled her, she touched Storm's arm and allowed him to escort her to the tables laden with food.

She wasn't that hungry so only picked up a few things.

"My heart, you need to take more than that," Storm spoke next to her ear as he took her plate and added a few things to it.

"Storm."

"If you only put a few things on your plate everyone else will do the same thing." He kept his voice low. "You don't have to eat it all."

He saw one of her favorite foods and picked one up and offered it to her.

She smiled as she arched a brow. "You know this always gets us in trouble."

"And our people love it." He continued to hold it out for her.

Heather took his offering into her mouth; her tongue swirled around his fingers just long enough to cause his eyes to glow in arousal. She knew he wanted her to do the same thing for him. When she spotted his favorite bite, she handed him her plate.

"Can you carry this for me?"

"Why?" He took the plate and watched her with curiosity.

She picked up three pieces and placed them on another plate, then turned and headed back to the dais.

"Where are you going with that?"

"We shouldn't hold up the line." She turned back and smiled at him. He picked up his pace and caught up with her just as she placed the plate on their table. "I thought we could move to our table."

Storm placed their plates on the table as well. "I see you grabbed three pieces."

"I knew one wouldn't be enough but was afraid we'd run out."

"We never have that problem, and you know that." He wrapped his arms around her. "Our chefs would just make more."

"True." She picked up one piece. "But you know there are three on that plate. I'm offering you one now, but you won't know when I'll offer the other two."

"You're going to have my undivided attention all night."

"My heart, I'm pretty sure I have that anyway. But this will add a little something to you watching me all night."

"I enjoy watching you." He brushed his knuckles along her jaw.

"I can put them back." She reached for the plate.

"Oh, no you don't." He placed his hand on top of hers and pushed the plate back to the table. "I know you love to tease me, and this will allow me to tease you as well."

"We never need a reason to tease each other." She placed the first piece between her teeth and offered it to him.

"True, but to have one just makes it that much more fun." He lowered his mouth to hers and snagged the morsel she offered. After a quick bite and swallow his lips covered hers and he drew her against his body as he deepened the kiss. Their tongues danced with each other. Storm tightened his hold on her as the kiss aroused him. When he broke it, he rested his forehead against hers. "I wish we were in our rooms."

"Soon, my heart but tonight is for our people."

He kissed her again. This one was soft, quick, and took her breath away.

TEN

Skye filled his plate and turned to find Heather and Storm locked in an intimate embrace. Bear was beside him. He heard the man sigh.

"Is there a problem, Admiral?"

"Are they always like this?" He paused for a moment. "Don't get me wrong, Skye, I'm happy Heather has found someone who makes her happy. She's like my daughter and I couldn't have picked a better man for her, but this is a little unprofessional."

"Let me ask you two questions, sir."

The admiral looked at him.

"Whose standard are you using?" Skye popped a bite into his mouth.

He didn't answer.

"And what planet are you on?" He gave the Admiral a moment to answer. When he didn't, Skye continued. "The Vespian people want to see Heather and Storm like this. It gives them hope."

"Hope?"

"Yes. Heather and Storm are soldiers. Two of the best on Vespia and the people know it. They would never do anything to jeopardize the welfare of their people and as long as Heather and Storm can forget about everything but each other they know things aren't so dire."

"I never thought of it that way."

"That's because you haven't lived here long enough to understand how these people see things. I've never wanted to call any place home before, but these people make me feel welcome. I get why they never let anyone on their planet. It is to protect the people. They don't lie, don't have hangups. No one shirks their duty or feels the need to be better than their neighbor. The best part, they don't care about your past, or where you came from. They take you at face value and believe in the good of everyone."

"The Vespians don't strike me as being naive."

"I never said they were naïve, just honest, and have no reason not to trust people on their own planet." Skye paused for a moment. "That's why they don't allow outsiders here. They want to keep their way of life and now that I live here, I don't blame them."

"Then why did they allow us here? I thought you had to be Vespian to set foot on this planet."

"You do. Heather went to the council and vouched for you. In human terms, she adopted all of you to make you Vespian. She is responsible for any issues your people make. If anyone does anything that will cause the use of Vespian justice she will pay the price. You might want to tell your people that."

———

Music played softly in the background as everyone nibbled. Storm stepped up, turned to face her, and bowed.

She was grateful for his timing because he always knew the right time to do things. Now they would dance. Just the two of them expressing their life through the steps they had created together. Their dance wasn't very long, but Heather felt what they had created was beautiful.

Once she finished her dance with Storm she walked up to Bear and bowed. They would waltz to show everyone they were allowed to dance with human or Vespian. Bear was an excellent dancer, and they glided across the floor. The song ended and she only had one more dance to do.

She walked up to her assistant, Mark. He might have gotten the job as a punishment, but he saved her life today and she wanted to honor him. Skye had already warned him. He looked nervous but gave her the proper bow before he stepped up so they could waltz.

"Captain Latimer says you're dancing with me because I saved your life."

"Vespians show thanks a little differently than humans do. You won't get a medal, not until you go back home, but I wanted you to know I appreciate what you did."

"Thank you, Ma'am."

"I've been very happy with your performance as our assistant. I know it started as a punishment, but I would like to make it your permanent position. No more watcher, no more having to tell us your every move."

"I would like that a lot, Captain. I never knew I had a knack for the small details, but I've enjoyed helping you and your council."

"Good. I'll make it official tomorrow."

"She has done it again," Fridon spoke softly next to Storm.

"I know. They seem to migrate to her."

"And here you are, watching her instead of doing the same thing."

"You see that smile on her face? I will stand here all the time if I know I can see that smile." Storm continued to watch his mate. "I stand here because I want to be sure she is safe."

"You think someone would hurt her? Here?"

"I trust our people, but we have humans here."

"I think they would be too afraid to anger you."

"Maybe." Storm also kept an eye on his mate because she carried the plate with the two other bites on it. He knew she could offer it at any moment, and he wasn't going to miss his chance to kiss his mate. Of course, he didn't need that as an excuse, but it was one of the games they liked to play to heighten their intimacy. She called it teasing him.

Heather looked up at him at the moment and her smile brightened.

He decided not to wait for her to offer the treat. He needed to feel her soft lips against his now.

"I'll be back." Storm handed Fridon a drink he had been holding and headed to his mate. The women talking to her stepped aside when they saw him coming. He smiled at the curious look she gave him. Wrapping his arms around her, he pulled her close, lifted her off her feet, and pressed his lips to hers. He brushed his tongue against her lips, and she opened for him. When she did, he swept in, taking her breath away as his tongue searched for hers. They moved together, intertwining as he demanded more.

The sweet taste of wine clung to her mouth, making him want to drink from her lips forever. The scent of her arousal filled his senses. Storm broke the kiss and whispered in her ear. "I think tonight we should use the wall again." It was slight but he heard her breath hitch for a second. He smiled at her. "My heart."

She smiled back, a beautiful sexy smile that made him want to sweep her off her feet and drag her back to their rooms. He also knew if he let her remain the teasing would continue, and their intimacy would be mind-blowing.

"And you are my heart." She touched his cheek. The soft caress increased his desire for her. He didn't want to leave but knew she enjoyed the time she spent with the women.

"I'll be watching."

She looked at the plate. "You didn't need it this time."

"Yet you still have them." He stole another quick kiss before leaving. He heard her sigh as he walked away.

———

"He really loves you, doesn't he?" asked one of the Earth women.

"As much as I love him." Heather watched her mate leave. The man knew how to make her blood boil.

"What is it like?" asked another.

"What?" Heather looked at the woman.

"Being with a Vespian. They're all so big."

Heather heard some of the Vespian women chuckle. She found the comment a little funny too but understood why it was asked.

"Let me tell you something. If you're interested in any of the men you will find any of the Vespian men gentle, caring, and willing to make sure you enjoy your time with them."

"But there are rumors of Vespians putting humans into hospitals after having sex with them."

At that, Heather did laugh. "That was my husband

who did that and that was because he wanted it all the time. The human women he had been with just couldn't keep up with his libido."

"Are they are pretty average in size?"

Heather felt her cheeks heat up a little. "Let me put it this way. You will have no complaints on size. In fact, you will have no complaints at all. Vespian males have this belief that their partners must orgasm before they do. They strive to accomplish that."

"Really?"

"Oh yes, why do you think we want to keep them to ourselves?" asked one of the other Vespian women.

Heather heard laughter as she noticed Toki enter the room. Her sister-in-law looked at her before heading to the dais.

"Ladies, please excuse me." She worked her way through the crowd so she could reach Storm's side before Toki reached the dais. Thank goodness Toki took her time, but she might have done that so Heather could get there before she arrived.

She bowed to Heather and her brother before turning and facing the people gathered around the dais. "Tonight, we are celebrating something precious. Two of our people are mating. I felt tonight, after all we have been through, would be perfect for this couple to join as one."

Two of her assistants stepped up with cloaks. Heather wanted to know where these two hid until needed. She never saw them on the sidelines waiting for their cue.

"Sam, Skye, will you join me?"

Sam grabbed Skye's hand, and they walked up to Toki.

"This is your night. When you are ready, I will be waiting to create the bond that will last your lifetimes." She took one of the cloaks her assistants were holding and handed it to Sam. "This was the cloak Heather wore when she mated to Storm."

Sam bowed and took the cloak, glancing at her mother with a smile.

"Skye, this is the cloak Storm wore when he mated with Heather." She handed the other cloak to him.

He bowed as well and took his cloak.

She kissed Sam then Skye on the cheek before she turned to Heather and Storm. She gave her brother a quick peck on the cheek then turned to Heather. As she kissed her cheek she spoke softly. "I know they are anxious to be mated, but I do not want to spoil the fun. I'll be meditating for several hours. Alert me when you leave, and I will be ready for them."

Heather gave her a slight nod. Great, now she would have to be aware of the time, so Sam and Skye made it to their mating ceremony.

————

Skye kept an eye on Heather and Storm. He knew he and Sam would have to leave right after them to meet with Toki.

One of the elite leaders came up to his side. They normally went straight to Heather and Storm with questions and concerns. Why was he approaching him? "Is there a problem?"

"I am not sure. That human that Storm has been working with keeps making inappropriate comments about Ansira. I know that humans sometimes speak this way after a battle, but it is upsetting me and my team."

"What is he saying?" Skye knew the difference between blowing off steam and trying to cause trouble.

"He started with questions about Heather's sexual

prowess. Then asked if she has taken on any other partners." He paused as someone walked nearby. "Recently he boasted he would be the first to be her next partner."

"Several of our men laughed at him, warning him he had to get through Storm first, but this evening he has been watching our future leader and his mate a little too closely."

"Like he's trying to figure out how to separate them?"

He nodded.

"Some humans have been known to speak in such a manner to burn off energy."

"Which is why I hope you could observe us without his knowledge. Perhaps he is harmless. Storm has made sure he remains focused. He is a very good soldier and while training he follows orders and shows strong leadership qualities."

"I'll need to check his records. If this is something he does all the time it might be in there. But I will make sure we get to the bottom of this."

———

Storm had his arm around her waist when he let out a low growl.

"My heart?"

"I just heard something I didn't like."

"Your sensitive ears pick up a lot more than the rest of us." Heather placed a hand on his chest. "What did you hear?"

He wrapped his arms around his mate and pulled her close. "Skye is making plans for tomorrow even though tonight is his mating ceremony."

"And you think he should spend it with Sam?"

"Of course. Most couples aren't seen for a week or more when they first mate."

"Your sister was in our room the next morning." Heather looked up at him.

"That was extenuating circumstances. We didn't know we had mated, remember? We thought it was a trail run."

"True."

"I only want to let him know that he doesn't have to work."

"I'll come with you."

"You still have two more pieces of fruit to offer me, and I know you won't do that if you're at my side. Go and mingle. I'm pretty sure it won't take long before you're surrounded by a bunch of women again."

———

"I wish to speak with you."

Skye turned at the sound of Storm's voice. What did he want now?

"I overhead your conversation about the human."

"Just how good is your hearing?"

Storm just smiled at him. Once Sam told them that Skye knew about her father's ability to shift Heather and Storm had sat them down and explained about the special talents the ruling families had. Most Vespians didn't have that much ancient blood in them but every once in a while there were a few born in the general population that did. Those that had twenty percent or more could develop some sort of ability. It was never a guarantee. Anseri had thirty percent but never developed anything unique.

Since he and Sam had more, they wanted to prepare them in case it showed up after they mated. Skye already had a talent with computers and Heather told him it could get stronger after the ceremony. Sam hadn't shown any ability yet, but the twins had. Storm wondered if her rapid aging had something to do with that.

"What do you want, Storm?"

"Two things. One is that I join you on the inspection. I know why he's doing what he's doing but our soldiers aren't supposed to. If I don't join you, they will figure out why. They know I have been training this man and our soldiers espected him to stop his comments about my mate."

"So you want to put on a good face."

It took Storm a second to figure out what he meant. "Yes."

"And the second?"

"You do not need to assume your duties right after mating."

"We're at war, Storm."

"True, but the mating ceremony is a sacred thing. No one would think less of you for wanting to be with your mate."

"Sam and I have talked about it, and we will celebrate our mating, but not until we defeat Reasta."

Storm nodded. He understood. He noticed people near them. Time to help spread those rumors. "And this man making comments about my mate?"

"Some humans are all talk. It's a way for them to burn off access energy. That's why I need to look at his record. It will reveal his behavior."

"Bear gave me his file when I first took him to train. I will send it to you now. It shows he is a good soldier but a bit mouthy."

"Has he been reprimanded?"

"Yes, but I didn't go into the details of each reprimand."

"I will. What do you want to do if he is serious about his comments about Heather?"

Storm just smiled.

————

Heather wondered what Storm and Skye were talking about.

"You're deep in thought."

Heather looked at her daughter, who had joined her. "Storm excused himself to speak to Skye."

"What do you think he is up to?"

"I don't know and that is what has me worried."

Sam smiled. "I know they don't see eye to eye a lot, but tonight is our mating ceremony, perhaps he is giving Skye some pointers."

"He has grilled both of you on every angle on the ceremony for the last week or so. I doubt seriously that he suddenly came up with something new. I could also tell he was angry. He overheard something that upset him."

"Something Skye said?"

"I don't think so. He was speaking to one of the elite leaders when Storm reacted."

"So you think it was a human."

Heather didn't need to respond. She looked at her mate before she looked at her daughter again. "Are you ready to get going? Toki said she would be meditating until you were ready."

"Um, did she sound like she expected us right away?"

"She said she would be ready when you are. Her meditating can take several hours so there is no rush."

"Good." Sam nodded as she brushed a stray hair from her face. "I know everyone is enjoying themselves and I would hate to be the cause of this ending."

"I know, but everyone needs to rest too so I don't think they would be that upset if we were to say our goodbyes now."

"Just a little longer." Sam touched her arm.

"Whatever you wish."

"Can I ask why you are carrying that plate?"

"It's for your father."

"You're teasing him?"

Heather just smiled.

"No wonder he's watching you like a hawk."

"You see him?"

"Not right at the moment but if you have that I'm sure he is close."

"Let's see." Heather picked up one of the two pieces and held it in her hand for a moment before she popped it in her mouth.

Sam stepped back as Storm came up behind his mate and wrapped his arms around her, he turned her to face him and smiled when he saw the small fruit between her teeth. He covered her lips with his, sucking the small piece of fruit into his mouth. One bite freed him to deepen the kiss.

His tongue swept into her mouth, searching for hers. They slid and danced together, spiking their desire for each other. Heather didn't want him to stop. When he did, she couldn't stop the sigh that escaped her.

Storm rested his forehead against hers. "And think, we have one more."

"We do." She smiled up at him.

"Unless you want to offer it to me now." He smiled back.

Heather pretended to be shocked. "Now that would spoil all the fun."

"Had to try." He brushed his fingers along her jaw. "But I don't need those to have a reason to kiss you."

She laughed. "Admit it, you enjoy it as much as I do."

"When it deals with you?" he pressed a kiss against her lips. "I enjoy everything."

"You are my heart."

"And you're mine."

"You two either need to mingle a little more or go to your quarters." Fridon stepped up to their side.

"I don't think Sam is quite ready." Heather rested her hand on Storm's chest. "I've been keeping an eye on her and she's still talking to several women."

"Do you think she is afraid to go through with the ceremony?"

"No." Heather shook her head. "She doesn't want to ruin the festivities. There is an underlying excitement within her that I can feel. Sam is more than ready."

"They shouldn't keep Toki waiting."

"Toki is meditating right now and said she be going to for hours. When Toki is ready so will Sam and Skye."

Storm pressed his hand against the small of her back and got her walking. "Then let's spend a little more time with our people."

———

Sam clutched at Skye's hand as they stood together in front of Toki. A jumble of emotions filled her, fear, excitement, desire, and raw nerves ran inside her. They stood in the large cave that they had used to simulate Reasta's ship when they rescued the elders. It had been converted into a beautiful garden for their mating ceremony.

"Tonight is when you two become one. Your hearts will

join together as your bodies will join together. This is your night."

Sam turned to look at Skye. Was this what he really wanted? The smile he gave her answered her question. Love shined in his gaze.

"I place my blessing on this union."

Skye turned toward her, taking her other hand in his as he drew her close to him. He let go so he could brush a few strands of hair out of her face as he wrapped his cloak around hers. She opened hers so their bodies could touch. The heat from his body had her wishing she could just snuggle up against him.

Sam had refused to admit it, but she was scared. Not of getting mated but whether or not she would finally get a power like the rest of her family. Out of all of them she was the only one who hadn't gotten any sort of power yet, and she was worried that she wouldn't get one now.

"What is on your mind?" asked Toki.

Her aunt could pick up on anything.

She felt embarrassed being caught.

"Sam?"

"It's not you, Skye, or our mating. It's something stupid I shouldn't be worried about."

"What?"

"I'm just wondering if I'll get my abilities soon."

Toki laughed. "Your power will come to you at the right time. Your father didn't get his until after your mom became pregnant with your brother and sister. You can't rush something like this."

"I know." She knew her aunt was right but couldn't stop the way she felt.

"Yet it worries you."

"What if I don't develop an ability?" Her honest answer slipped out before she could stop it.

"Are you afraid of what others will think of you?"

Sam wasn't sure how to answer the question. It sounded juvenile and a bit ridiculous after it was said out loud. She nodded her head. It wouldn't be very wise to lie to the woman who knew things she shouldn't.

"There is no one here who would fault you for how you feel." Toki placed her hand on Sam's cloaked arm. "You also need to think about this. Being religious leader is my gift, and I have it for only fifty years."

Sam looked at her. Now she had to ask the question that had been nagging her. "Do you know who your successor is?"

"Are you asking me if it is you?" Toki laughed. "It has not been revealed to me yet. I have a feeling I have not met her or him."

"Why is it so important to you, Sam?" asked Skye.

"I'm going to sound like my mother." She paused for a moment. "I'm feeling a little bit like a freak right now. I've been rapidly aged, have a computer inside me to teach me the things I should have learned naturally as I grew up, am half ancient, yet have no noticeable power."

"It will come, Sam. You just need to be patient." Toki took a deep breath. "Now we are here to celebrate a very joyous occasion. Your mating."

Sam and Skye smiled at each other.

The ancient words Toki said flowed around them as they focused on each other. As she spoke, Skye eased Sam down to the grass.

"You know I don't care if you have any special power," said Skye. "My heart knows you're special."

"Skye." Sam brushed her fingers against his cheek. His words made her heart soar. He was right. Tonight was all about them, not what she could or couldn't do. He didn't care about that. He cared about her.

"You ready?" She nodded then felt him enter her. No words were needed as they focused on each other. Each touch. Each caress heightened their desire for each other. They moved together as one. As they grew closer to their release Sam smiled up at Skye. He needed to say the words first.

"You are my heart, my soul." He touched her face. "There will be no other. I will protect you, care for you, give you the passion you deserve. Make you as happy as I can for the rest of my days."

Tears entered Sam's eyes when she repeated the words back. Skye's invisible mark became visible as he said the words. This was real. He was now hers and she couldn't be happier.

Storm felt his mate's agitation at watching her daughter be intimate with her mate, but it was part of their society, and she needed to be there to witness the mating.

"My heart." He spoke softly to her.

"I know." She leaned back against him. "I need to stop acting like I'm living on Earth."

Storm wrapped his arms around his mate. "This reminds me of our mating ceremony."

"You mean the one we thought was a practice run?" She smiled up at him. "Your uncle sure was sneaky."

"You feel you were tricked?"

"Of course not." She turned to face him and wrapped her arms around him. "We belong together. But Uncle knew a lot about me before I met either of you. The real ceremony would have made me so nervous I would have tried to find a way around it. He knew that. Why else did he put the capes in your room?"

"You think he did it on purpose?"

"I do." She nodded as she smiled. "He could have had us do the ceremony the way it should have been done, but he planted those cloaks, followed us to the garden, and did the mating ceremony, knowing it would work."

"Do you remember the words?"

"I do." She placed her hand on his heart. "You are my heart, my soul. There will be no other. I will protect you, care for you, give you the passion you deserve. Make you as happy as I can for the rest of my days."

"And you have."

"You have as well my heart." Heather rested her head against Storm's chest. This really wasn't much different from a human wedding. Her friends used to tell her how they would remember their own wedding when they attended a friend's. That was what she and Storm were doing.

"My sister is signaling us." He guided her to a spot that blocked them from view.

"Normally we would just walk off but having the ceremony in the creation room we need to leave by the doors. Can you shield them, Heather? They don't need to hear the sounds or see the lights from the hall."

Heather nodded. She brought Storm and Toki to the door then built a shield behind them. It would disintegrate behind them once they left.

———

Sam felt boneless. She smiled up at Skye who looked a little boneless himself. He shifted his weight and propped his hand under his head so he could look down at her. "My mate."

She touched his face. "It looks like we're alone now."

"It would have been nice if they would have programed this place to give us a little comfort."

Sam laughed when a large bed and a table filled with food and drink appeared to their left. "Looks like Mom thought of that."

"Perhaps we should take advantage of this then." He got to his feet and helped her to hers. "She did think of everything."

Sam filled a plate with their favorites, which was everything there. That's how she knew this was her mom's doing. Skye carried two glasses to the bed and sat them on the small table that appeared with the bed.

"I don't think we need these anymore." He removed his cape, then helped Sam with hers.

"Do you feel any different?" asked Sam as she sat on the bed.

"A little." He sat beside her. "You?"

"Yeah. I feel more comfortable." She shrugged. "Your mark is more pronounced."

"Too bad I can't see it."

A mirror materialized in front of them. Sam laughed.

Skye turned his head so he could see where he knew the bumps had been. When Sam had marked him, it had no color. Kuarto said it was because of the race his ancestors had merged with. He turned this way and that to see.

"I'm not getting much, Sam."

"It seemed darker a few moments ago." She brushed her hand against it and watch in amazement as it bloomed from her touch. It stood out against his skin for a few moments before fading again. "Now that's new."

"Yours is here." He touched the top of her shoulder blade.

Sam had to turn her back to the mirror and had to bend

a bit before she could see hers as well. Her father had told her it could show up anywhere.

"It's beautiful."

"And quite intricate." Skye stepped up behind her and slid his hand over her new mark. "Is yours as sensitive as your parents?"

"Was it for you?"

"A little." He turned her so they were face to face. "But I have had mine longer."

"True…"

———

Heather was watching the teams work out when she noticed Henry walking toward her. She hoped Reasta had taken the bait and was waiting for a chance to grab him. It just couldn't look planned. Reasta had her ways, and Heather knew better than to let too many people know about her plan, including Henry. She had told him she needed time to think about how to keep him safe so he would play into what she needed. She sure hoped it worked. She hated tricking one of the men who had a hand in raising her.

"Have you had enough time to think about how you're going to let me plant my crops?" Henry had a hard edge to his voice.

"I know I said you could plant outside, but that was before Reasta attacked our farmland." She looked at him.

"You have all these people here trained in security. Assign me a few." Henry pointed to a few of the people paying attention to their conversation. "And you have those new shields."

"I don't want you to get hurt, Henry."

"If I get hurt it's on my shoulders. I know the danger.

I've seen how you work around that woman and know you will only allow me to go out there when you feel it's safe."

"And you'll listen to me? If I say you can't go outside the safety of the caves? I'm not going to hear 'but I need to water them or weed them or harvest them?'"

"I trust you to keep me safe."

"Good because I want you to start working out with the war council. Storm will make sure you can protect yourself."

ELEVEN

Heather stepped into the medlab to speak to her brother. She might want Storm to help train Henry, but she wanted to be sure he was healthy enough to keep up with their intense workouts.

"Ansira."

She smiled at her brother. Everyone had started using her title and she was getting used to it. "Henry will be joining our workouts, and I want to be sure he can handle it."

"He'll be fine. I've been through everyone's record and found all of them healthy enough to withstand any rigorous training we might put them through."

"Good to hear." She spotted Micali working nearby. "How is she doing?"

He shook his head. "It's a long process and it's weighing heavily on her."

"Will it work?"

"I don't know yet." He looked at her. "I've gone through the notes you brought back from the timeline switches. I gave you several injections during that timeline before I could get one of your eggs to fertilize. It's the waiting that's getting to her."

"Her planet is very fertile. I would think it would help."

"Just like with any race some of her people are more fertile than others. Micali is fertile, but when you mix two different races, sometimes they aren't compatible no matter how fertile the races might be."

"Even with your serum?"

I won't know until she gets all the shots. I'm just worried about her morale. She is so depressed, and it shows. Perhaps you should go and talk to her. Let her know it will all work out."

"I can do that." The patient Micali was working with left the lab. Heather touched her arm. "I have missed talking to you."

"And I have missed you." She hugged Heather. "You've been so busy."

"I know."

"Fridon has said you're doing a good job as a leader."

"He's always been a strong supporter of me."

"He has, but he has told me some of the things you have done that he never would have thought to do."

How many times had she heard she always looked at things differently? Time to change the subject. "Kuarto said he has started the shots."

"Yes." She nodded. "He says I need to take a few more before Fridon and I can try to get pregnant."

"You are still being intimate with him, right?" Heather knew Vespians couldn't go very long without having sex.

"Of course. He is my mate, and I want to keep him happy." She looked around and lowered her voice. "He calls it practice. Something he learned from you."

Heather laughed.

"He's excited about the chance."

"You two will make such great parents. I can't wait to see our children play together." Heather hugged her again.

———

Heather needed to speak to Arc now. That stupid android annoyed her so much. She needed to get it on her side, but she wasn't sure how to do that. He had been observing her for several weeks now and she had hoped he would change his attitude, but as far as she could tell he still didn't see her as the woman he thought she should be.

She walked into the war room to find it empty. That surprised her. Checking her insert, she learned Storm, Fridon and Bear were working out with the teams while Sam and Skye were working with Henry and the guards she assigned him.

"Arc, I wish to see you." She waited until he walked into the room.

"Yes, Heather."

"Have I passed your test yet?"

"No."

"Right." That was what she figured since she got shot at. "What is it going to take?"

"Allow me to test you properly."

"When? This war is what I need to focus on. As much as I need all seven of you, I don't have the time."

Arc didn't say anything which didn't surprise her.

"I would have thought after allowing you to follow me and see what we're trying to accomplish you would see that I am the leader here."

"I know you are a leader, Heather. That isn't the question. I need to prove that you can handle the weapons I can release to you."

"There's more than we found?" That surprised her.

"You have only found a small part of what is available. My goal is to release all of them to you, but those weapons are more advanced than what you have found. The power they could give you is what I need to be sure you can control."

"You've shadowed me and the council. Didn't that give you what you want?"

"I have seen some of your qualities, but I need more time."

"How much?"

"I don't know right now. As long as I can continue to follow you, I feel confident that you will pass my tests."

She wished she could turn a switch and have that done but she did understand. No matter how much this android annoyed her she knew it was to make sure she could handle the power she'd have at her fingertips. She learned that much in their conversation. It made her appreciate him a little.

Storm entered the room. "My heart."

"How are our soldiers?"

He looked at Arc who now stood behind her then looked at her.

"Arc and I have come to an agreement. He will continue to accompany us on any council meetings and inspections. He explained what he was looking for a little more." She clasped her hands in front of her. "I didn't pass his test."

"I can take him apart again."

Heather laughed. "I need to pass his test. We know that."

"And how do you plan on explaining him to Bear and your new assistant."

"Arc is observing. I shouldn't have to say anything else."

———

Heather was happy to be back in their rooms. She had been spending so much time dealing with this war and felt she was neglecting her children. They came running out of their room when they heard the doors open.

"Mommy!" They cried when they saw her.

"How are my little hearts?" She knelt to give them hugs.

"Better now that you're here." Her daughter tucked her head into Heather's neck as she returned her hug.

"And you have behaved for Dian?"

"They have," Dian said as she entered the main room. "And I love being with them."

"My parents have asked to spend time with them tomorrow."

"I know. They stopped by earlier today and mentioned it." Dian touched Terrick on the head and smiled. "Once they are done with their schoolwork tomorrow, I will release them to your parents."

"Good." She touched her daughter's cheek. "And today?"

"We're finished, Mommy."

"Yeah, Bert gave us a special assignment," said Terrik. "We get to simulate the battles you have had. See if we can predict others like it."

"And Bert is having me create artwork showing how to make your responses to these attacks more precise."

"Really?" Heather looked up at Dian. She didn't want her children involved in their battles. What was Bert thinking?

"They constantly ask questions about what is going on. Bert felt it would help distract the children by having them look at your past encounters with Reasta," Dian said. "He has them at the most advanced level of learning right now and they are finding it too easy. He plans on adding new subjects for them to study but they need to know the basics before he can increase the level."

The doors opened and Storm stepped in. He would have entered with her except his mother asked him to stop by their room before they had to make the evening meeting.

He didn't say anything, just dropped to one knee and opened his arms. The twins ran to him and wrapped themselves around him. Heather couldn't help but smile at the sight. The man so many feared knelt there, hugging and kissing his children with such tenderness that her heart skipped a beat.

He looked up at her and smiled—the smile that had a tendency to take her breath away. "You're next."

That made her smile back. She loved his attention.

"Why don't you two say bye to Dian while I say hello to your mother."

In the beginning, they used to question why since they knew he had spent the whole day with her, but now they understood that their parents had a strong relationship and being apart for even a few minutes had them acting like they had been apart too long.

Storm swept her up in his arms as he claimed her lips. His tongue brushed along the seam of her mouth, wanting entrance. She opened for him, and he swept in, drawing her tongue into the personal dance they shared every time they touched.

Heather wished she was a little bit taller. Each time Storm kissed her like this her feet couldn't touch the floor. She felt something develop below her feet. What the hell?

It disappeared as quickly as it appeared, but something happened.

Storm broke the kiss and looked into her eyes. "You okay?"

Since she didn't know what was going on she just smiled and nodded. "Guess I'm just a little overwhelmed with it all."

"You're doing a wonderful job, Heather. You have to stop second-guessing yourself." He lowered her to the floor.

"How did your talk with your mother go?"

"Well, we've been invited to dinner this evening. Since we have access to Burt's ship Mother wants to utilize that so she and my father can see the twins."

"I bet she wants an update." Heather reached for her pad.

"You've been giving her those."

"I know, but she hasn't responded with questions the way she did with yours."

"You were very thorough."

Heather wasn't sure.

Dian left and they got ready to go to Anseri's quarters. Bert had given the council rooms in his compound as well. She answered the door and was swarmed by the twins.

"Anseri!" They spoke in unison as they gave her hugs.

"How are you, my darlings?" She hugged them back.

The fact they called her Anseri instead of grandma caught Heather's attention. Who else was joining them? They stepped into the doorway and her question was answered. There sat her parents as well, and the other family that was part of the council. Here everyone would remember that Heather and Storm had children.

Iresna came up and took the children by the hand then brought them to a playroom they had set up just for the twins.

"Are we having a council meeting?" Heather kissed her on the cheek.

"My dear, we are no longer the council. They wanted to come over and see the twins."

Heather knew better. "Well, since we're all here do you have any questions?"

"No." She shook her head as she looked at the other council members. "Your updates are quite thorough."

There was that word again.

"My training with Earth security forced me to be thorough. My mission files were seen by lots of people and the more thorough you were the less trouble you got in."

"My son liked to leave things out he didn't think we needed to know and as the ruling council we did need certain data he tried to omit, but you are the leader now Heather. You don't have to report to us as a subordinate but as an equal. Just tell us what is going on. You don't have to do these elaborate missives."

Heather nodded. That would be a lot easier for her. She spent hours on those stupid updates. "How do you want it then?"

"How do you wish to do it?"

"We could come by each night, and I update you or I could do a recording."

"Then I will leave it up to you. You know we love to have you visit, but I know there will be times when you will not be able to do any update in person."

"Thank you, Anseri."

"I was surprised to see you have given your friend Henry permission to farm outside. I wouldn't have thought you would put him in harm's way like that."

"I would never put anyone I hold dear in unnecessary danger."

Anseri dipped her head.

———

Heather sat with her children on the floor and continued with her story. Their evening meeting went smoothly and ended a little early. "So, our heroine is trying to find a way home."

"How is she going to do it, Mommy?"

"That is the question, isn't it?" She touched her daughter's head. "She continued to inch her way along the cavern wall until she started to notice a change in the light. She was close to the entrance. Of course, she wondered what she would find when she got there."

"Was the dragon there?"

"That's what she wanted to know." Heather smiled. "She inched her way along the wall until she could see out the opening. Do you know what she saw?"

"A dragon!"

"A man." Heather tussled her son's hair. "It surprised her. She stepped out of the cave and confronted him. 'Who are you?' she asked. 'Can you help me get home?' The man shook his head. 'You're safer here,' he told her."

"Why, Mommy?"

"Because the dragon protected her village. When she looked out over the valley the dragon's nest sat above her village. She could see where the other villages had been attacked when hers was still intact. The smell of burnt-out buildings filled the air around them. Their destroyed fields would take years to repair."

"Wow."

"I know. The man told her that her village would only

be safe if she stayed there. He would be there to help her when she needed it, but she needed to find a way to work with the dragon for one year." Heather paused to let her words sink in. "That made our heroine think. 'One year? What happens at the end of one year? Will he eat me?'"

"'No.' He found her comment funny. 'The dragon only asks for a year of your life. After that, you can go anywhere you want.'"

"'Even home?' she asked."

"Mommy, if she could go home then why haven't any of the other girls gone home?" asked Bubbles.

"Very good question." Heather smiled as she brushed her hand along her daughter's jawline. "She asked the man the same question and he told her she could go anywhere but home. The people in her village wouldn't understand if she were to go back after a year. They wouldn't fear the dragon and wouldn't offer their daughters. If that happened the village would no longer be protected."

"Why not?"

"Because the dragon would die." Heather looked up to see her mate leaning against the door jam.

"Why?"

"Children, if you keep asking your mother all these questions she'll never get through the story." He stepped into the room. "It's time for bed."

"But we're just getting to the good part."

"And you say that every time. Come on," Storm picked up his son. "You need your rest, and we need ours."

"More tomorrow night, Mommy?"

"Yes, my little hearts." She kissed each of them once they climbed into bed. "See you in the morning."

———

The weeks were flying by. She had assigned the soldier who had caused the trouble earlier to guard Henry. He had acted the way he did because he needed to act like he would be a good candidate to try to turn. The people working with him to protect Henry would worry about him. Wonder if they could trust him and she assumed Reasta would pick up on that. Now she wondered if it was all for nothing. Henry had gone out to his fields several times with no trouble. Heather figured Reasta didn't see him as an interest, or she would have pounced by now. She was happy he'd be safe but at the same time, she needed the information she was sure he could get if Reasta did kidnap him.

Oh, well. She had a lot of other things that needed to be accomplished.

Heather sat on the massive table the council sat around, meditating while she had a moment. What she wished she had was a drink. Leaning back, she put her hands behind her to brace herself and her hand hit something. What the heck did she hit?

It broke her concentration, and she had to look down. There sat a beverage container. "Now where did that come from?"

"Where did what come from?" asked Sam as she entered.

"What?" Heather opened the container and found it filled with an energy drink. "Oh, nothing. I just found this on the table. Mark must have left it for me before he went for lunch."

"Which he should be bringing you in a minute or two. I just saw him ordering your meal."

"Thanks." Heather uncrossed her legs and slipped to the floor.

"I didn't mean to interrupt your meditation time."

"It's fine, Sam." Heather touched her arm. "Your father watches me like a hawk and makes sure I get enough time every day." She needed to change the subject. "How is mated life?"

"It's not that much different than being bonded, although I feel more relaxed."

"That's because your hearts have bonded as well as your bodies." Heather smiled. The doors opened as she continued to talk. "It was the same for me. Once I mated with your dad, I found I was a lot more comfortable around him."

"I did overwhelm your mother a bit in the beginning." Storm stepped up to them and wrapped one arm around his mate and the other around Sam.

"I wasn't used to having someone constantly there." She gave him a one-arm hug. "Every time I turned around, he was there, in my space. Once we mated, I found I wanted him to be in my space."

"How much meditation did you do, my heart?"

"Not enough by your standards." She looked up at him. "But I did get a little time in."

Fridon's voice came across their inserts. "We have activity."

"We're on our way." She headed out the door with Storm right behind her.

"Heather, it's Henry."

"Is he okay?" She took off running.

"Yes."

"Do we have eyes on him?"

"No."

That made her move faster. She entered the command room and stopped next to where Fridon stood in front of one of the massive screens. "Show me."

The image of Henry with his guards appeared in front

of her. He was working on his crops, testing the soil, and adding what was needed as he went along. One minute he was there, the next he and his team were gone. Heather grabbed Storm's hand. Excitement coursed through her because they now could get the information they needed, but she was also afraid because she didn't want Henry to get hurt.

"We have to get them back."

"I know, but she took him onto her ship. We'll have to wait until she moves him back to the planet before we can rescue him."

Heather frowned. "Too bad we don't have someone to trade him for."

"What are you thinking, my heart?"

"We need leverage to get Henry and his team back and I know how to get it."

———

The other men Heather assigned to him stood nearby as Henry wondered where the hell he was. He had the full suit on like the rest and he was very uncomfortable. They had weapons pointed at them, but no one had made a move toward them. He watched as a woman entered the room. She was quite pretty in her own way but what caught his attention was her eyes. They were snake-like in design. This had to be Reasta.

"Gentlemen, I know you have standing orders to remain in your uniforms no matter what, but the pads you are standing on will heat up your suits if you don't remove your helmets."

"What if I remove my helmet?" Henry knew he wasn't military like these men with him, and he didn't want them harmed.

"And who are you?"

"Henry McNamara." He released the seals on his helmet.

"One of the humans." Reasta's gaze honed in on him. "Why were you outside working in the fields?"

"Because I'm the cook and I needed to check on my plants." Henry looked at the men behind him. "You going to leave them alone now?"

"Sorry Henry, I have my rules. The helmets must come off. I don't want Heather to try to gather information through those things." She smiled at him. "But if you tell me what I want to know I'll let two of them go back so they can report to their fearless leader."

He looked back at the men who were removing their helmets before returning his gaze to Reasta. "What do you want to know?"

————

"Do you want me to contact her?" asked one of the communication techs.

"No. That's what she wants and I'm not going to give it to her. She'll contact us when she is ready." Heather looked at her mate. "In the meantime, we need to get ready."

He slipped an arm around her and led her away from the command center. They hurried to their rooms, hoping they had enough time to set up everything before they heard from Reasta. They entered their bedroom and stripped off their uniforms. Heather went to grab one of her shifts, but Storm's warm hand stopped her. He crowded her back against the wall.

"Storm?"

"My heart, what is the one thing that annoys Reasta the

most when she sees us?" His breath brushed against her throat as he pressed his weight into her.

"When she thinks we been intimate."

"Exactly." He nibbled on the soft tissue just above her mark. "And if I arouse you just enough, you'll have that beautiful flush to your cheeks and that sparkle of desire in your eyes."

She wanted to argue with him; the gentle caress he gave her core had her wanting more. His mouth worked against her mark, pushing her need for him up. His fingers entered her, caressing her sensitive walls. Her response was a moan.

"Heather?" She heard Fridon's voice through her com. "Reasta wants to talk to you."

Now? It wasn't what she wanted. Her desire wanted to feel her mate buried deep inside her.

"She's ready, Fridon," Storm answered for her. He released her and gave her one of his bone-melting smiles. "We'll finish this later."

"Beast."

"Your favorite."

Heather took a deep breath as she heard Reasta in her ear.

"I'm sorry. Did I interrupt something?"

"You are always interrupting something." Heather turned on the screen in their room so she could see her nemesis. Storm had his arms around her, holding her close. She knew Reasta didn't miss the fact they were nude. "Are you contacting me to tell me that you're returning my people?"

"Now, Heather, you know me better than that." She narrowed her eyes. "Where are you?"

"Why?" Storm's erection pressed into her back. Heather turned around and smiled up at her mate.

"Never mind." Reasta averted her eyes for a moment. "If you want your people then you're going to have to share some of your grain."

"Hmm, you want to trade? My people are soldiers. They knew the risks when they joined security." Heather waited for her to come back. She'd be very surprised if Reasta didn't try to use Henry as leverage.

"And what about your farmer? He doesn't strike me as much of a soldier."

"Henry also knew what he signed up for. If you harm any of my people, my retaliation will be swift and destructive."

"My, my, such big words from you. How, Heather? How do you plan on performing this attack? You going to shoot my ship out of your space? If you could have done that you would have already."

Heather didn't comment. The only way she'd shoot at Reasta's ship would be after they rescued the rest of the ancients trapped in the pods. If she could pull them off the ship Reasta wouldn't be a problem anymore.

"I'm enjoying Henry's company so I will give you a day to figure out that you need to give me grain for your people. If I don't hear from you in time, I will be terminating my guests one by one until you give me what I want."

"Your threats don't frighten me, Reasta. Now if you're done, I'd like to spend some time with my mate." She turned in Storm's arms, dismissing her outright.

She heard Cim tell them the communication had ended.

"Is everything in place, Cim?"

"Yes, Heather. There are guards discreetly placed within the palace to make her think you are actually living in it."

"Good. Now we wait."

"And I know how we can spend the time." Storm lifted her up so they could look each other in the eye. She wrapped her legs around him, trapping his erection against her moist heat. "And if you keep this up, we won't make it back to the bed."

"Those never idle hands told me you didn't want to make it back to the bed." She gripped his buttocks, pulling him closer.

A growl escaped him as he pinned her to a nearby wall. He centered himself and drove into her, drawing a gasp from his mate as he filled her. His lips captured hers as he started to move within her. Each time he entered her she felt her body hug him. She quaked in his arms as he picked up the speed, increasing the exquisite sensations racking her body. The need for her release clawed at her.

She was close.

He broke the kiss and worked his way down to her mark. His tongue traced its intricate pattern.

It intensified everything she was feeling. "So close," she whispered.

Heather felt her release bubble up inside her, filling her veins with a euphoria only Storm could bring in her. She felt like she was floating. Storm's orgasm happened right after hers ended. They clung to each other during the aftermath.

"My heart." Storm pressed a soft kiss against her temple. "That was glorious."

———

Reasta glared at the blank screen. "She is back at the palace, and we didn't know that?"

"I'm sorry, ma'am, but they have the palace shielded so we can't see inside it."

She turned her glare onto the man who spoke and smiled when he cringed in front of her. "Get me the details. Now!"

The man scurried off to do her bidding. She turned to Henry, who cocked an eyebrow at her.

"I'm not going to cringe at your feet like your men. I tell the truth, even if it's not what you want to hear."

"Good, that means you won't lie to me when I ask you questions." She gave him a smile as she wrapped an arm around his shoulders. "I have the best cooks here. They can make anything you want."

"Even pizza?

She laughed. She had been on Earth and knew what he was asking for. "Even pizza."

Reasta took him to her private eating area. The man probably wouldn't want to see her race eat so she decided to wait until later to have her meal. One of her guards set a plate in front of Henry.

"What is this?"

She looked at the guard. He swallowed hard. "It is pizza from Earth."

"No, it's not." Henry stood. "Am I allowed to make my own meal?"

"Of course." Reasta looked at the guard. "Give him access to the food processors."

"No food processors. I cook my food from scratch."

"Sorry, Henry. We don't have a need for stoves. My race eats our food raw, and the rest use the replicators."

"That's fine." He sat back down. "I know you didn't isolate me from the rest because of my good looks. What do you want to ask me?"

"Has Heather moved back to the palace?"

"Now, she doesn't confide in me like that. Storm is her confidant."

"You saw the same image I did. That is her room at the palace."

"Well, since I haven't been to the Vespian palace I wouldn't know. Why does this bother you so much?"

"Heather deserves better than Storm."

"Not by what I've seen. He makes her happy and that girl deserves to be happy."

"You know her well then?"

"I'm sure you've done your homework."

Humans used the oddest phrases. What was homework? Her resources told her that Henry had been there for Heather since she started at the academy. She went to him whenever she felt threatened or overwhelmed.

"Do you know if she's staying in the caves?"

"No." Henry shook his head. "We don't talk about stuff like that. I tend the garden. Sometimes I'll go into their command center, but my contact with Heather is minimal."

"Living quarters must be at maximum." Somehow, she needed to get the answers she wanted. She could use the mind control drug but knew she didn't have any to waste unless Heather gave into her demands.

"They've done a good job accommodating everyone." Henry studied her for a moment. "Why is knowing where Heather and Storm is sleeping so important to you?"

"It's not." She smiled. Reasta didn't need him to become quiet because she pushed too hard. "I was just surprised by the background in our last conversation."

"One you had your man high steppin' to fix."

"True, but they are tasked to know the whereabouts of all Vespians. With so many in hiding now, it's not that hard a job."

"You can't track anyone underground?" Henry's brow

furrowed. "I thought technology could read through just about anything."

"No, the caves have a natural shielding that our scans can't penetrate. The palace is made out of the same material so we have the same problem with it."

"Why are you after Heather, anyway?"

"She doesn't see it because of her mate, but she has a much bigger destiny than being with these Vespians."

"Really?" Henry propped his elbows on the table. "Why not just talk to her?"

"I tried that, but she wouldn't listen."

"Now, that doesn't sound like my girl. Heather is a smart woman, if she didn't listen that's because she disagreed with what you had to say. Plain and simple."

"Why would you say that?" Had Heather confided their fight to him? If she did, then he had to be lying about not knowing if she was back in the palace.

"I've known that girl for a long time and she has always had really good instincts. It has kept her alive."

"Would you like a tour of my ship?" She decided to see what else Henry might let slip. Maybe he would prove his trustworthiness by what he said as they walked.

"Sure. I haven't been on too many, so I am a bit curious."

Reasta stood. So did Henry.

"How long have you known Heather?"

"Me? A long time. Me and Archie watched after her while she was at the academy."

"Archie?"

"The admiral. Heather and Storm gave him their room when we arrived."

So they weren't staying in their original room. That made her believe they were back in the palace. "This is our command center."

Several of her officers were there working on checking the palace out. She smiled. They would find out if there was any activity around the place.

"Are those two twins?" asked Henry when he spotted two of her clones. When he saw three more, he paused. "Oh, those are some of your clones, aren't they?"

"Yes. So Heather told you about them?"

Actually, I hear people talking when I bring food to them. People don't really pay attention to someone like me." Henry was quiet for a moment. "Can I ask you a question? How do you keep them from disintegrating? Earth hasn't been successful. We can create clones to keep our scientists safe while their clones do the hazardous job, but they don't last very long."

"What do you think is their problem?"

"The feeds say they haven't found the proper stabilizing agent." Henry shrugged. "I personally think it's a good thing."

"Why?"

"They can't create soldiers to fight in wars. It makes them sign a lot more treaties."

"You don't like war." She ushered him out of the command center.

"It's a waste of lives."

They continued down another hall. "Yet you are here."

"To feed our people."

"So, you don't plan on fighting?" Reasta stopped and turned toward Henry.

"I'm not trained. Now don't get me wrong, I know how to shoot a gun, and if your people start shooting at me, I will shoot back, but I cook for a living. That's what I love and it's my passion. I'd be much happier making the meal that brings our people together." He spotted a machine nearby. "Is that your cloning machine? It looks a lot like the ones we use."

"It is." She brought him to it. "The design is my own."

"Really? How did you create it? It took a team of about fifty of our people to even come close."

"I've had a lot of training and a lot of time to come up with the proper combination to create the perfect clone."

"So, you're not re-cloning constantly?" Henry looked at her.

She wasn't about to tell him she needed to constantly replace her clones because they did start to break down after a few months. She needed a mineral that she had found years ago but it was rare, so she didn't use it often. The last time she used it was when she created the other Heather and Storm. "Some of the clones are used for manual labor only so they are created for short-term use."

"You must have a lot of resources to do that." Henry shook his head. "Heather did tell me you made copies of her and Storm. Were they short term too?"

Smart man.

"Did she tell you what she did with them?"

"Sorry, no." He looked at the machine. "Is he making a clone right now?"

One of her guards was working close enough to the machine to give Henry that impression.

"Why?" His question made her suspicious.

"I'm just curious." He shrugged. "Never seen a humanoid created this way before."

He did seem harmless, and she knew he couldn't read the language on the machine, so she signaled him to step up with her.

They stayed out of the way and watched as the guard worked on the clone he was creating. Reasta watched Henry to make sure he wasn't trying to gain information he could pass onto Heather somewhere along the way. She could clone him then send the clone back when Heather gave into her demands, but Heather would know rather quickly.

Humans were fascinating. They could be tricked easily, and she knew Henry was no exception.

The clone had been developed, and the guard injected the fast-aging formula to the bed the infant sat in. This was its second dose. Next, they would pump in the balancing chemical to stop the aging process once they were at the age she wanted. This was one of the derivatives of the grain. She used it for so many things and now gaining it was becoming a problem. If Heather didn't give in to her demand, it would make matters worse.

Reasta felt Henry had seen enough.

"Time for you to rejoin your men, Henry."

He nodded and turned away from the cloning area. "How long are you going to keep us if Heather doesn't give in to your demands?"

"Oh, she'll give in, Henry. She is a little too soft-hearted not to."

———

Henry was ushered to the cell where the rest of his team was being held. He did notice several of the men were missing.

"Henry, are you okay?"

"Yeah, I'm fine. She just had some questions."

"You didn't tell her anything did you?"

"What do I know? I'm a cook not a soldier like you." Henry looked at the three soldiers surrounding him. "Where's the other two?"

"They've taken each of us away to question us too. I

just worry about Perkins. That attitude of his could get him in trouble."

One of the other men shushed the one talking. "Let's change the subject."

"They don't know how to cook human food," said Henry. "They gave me a pizza that looked like a rock. It was all grey."

"Henry, never turn down food. They might never feed you again."

"You wouldn't have touched it either if you had seen it," he countered.

Two of the guards with him shook their heads. They all turned at the sound of the door opening. One of the guards dropped a tray to the floor and pushed it through the barrier of their cell.

"That is the pizza she tried to serve me." The crust was a medium gray, what should have been red tomato sauce looked almost black and then it was covered with a sprinkling of white. No odor came off it.

"I see what you mean," said one of the team.

"We will need nourishment."

"And you trust her to give us something edible?" asked Henry.

"It sure would make me feel better if I could use my helmet to scan it." The woman who spoke stood and faced the guards. "I need my helmet."

They ignored him.

"Do you plan on starving us? None of us are eating this thing until we know what is in it. My helmet will allow me to analyze the ingredients in this meal."

"I can't allow that." Reasta walked into the room.

"Then we can't eat this."

"Then you'll starve."

"Let me use the helmet then."

Reasta looked at Henry who had spoken.

"I'm not a soldier. All I want to do is make sure that is edible." He pointed to the platter still sitting on the floor. "I know what to look for in the food and I'm sure you can set the thing to only scan what I want."

Reasta smiled. After she nodded to one of the guards, he placed the requested item on the floor and set the force field to accept it.

Henry picked it up. "I always feel like I'm going to suffocate in this thing. Don't know how you wear them all the time." Henry turned his attention to the gray mass. The system in the helmet analyzed everything. "It's clean, just monochrome."

He pulled the helmet off and turned to stare at her. "Your race is colorblind."

TWELVE

Heather sat in the war room waiting for the rest of the council to join her. Her thoughts went to the strange things that appeared when she needed it. Could she do it on purpose? The room was empty so she decided to try. Closing her eyes, she focused on creating something simple. Within seconds she had a small pebble in her palm. She grinned. This was a lot easier than the candles. She palmed the small stone and wished it away. She stood and bounced off a boulder over eight feet high and five feet wide.

"What the hell?" She walked around it. Did she create this when she made the pebble? She tried to wish it away, but it didn't budge. "How do I get rid of you?"

Heather closed her eyes and focused. "Begone." When she opened her eyes, it was still there. "No." She tried again but it hadn't moved. "No, no, no!"

Her staff would be there any minute. If she can't get rid of this, she would have to explain it. If it was only family, it wouldn't be a problem but there were people who didn't know about her power. Heather tilted her head as she looked at it. Could she make it invisible? Right, that would work until someone walked into it. The damn thing was massive and right behind her chair. There had to be a way. She created it and she had to get rid of it. "I will figure this out."

Heather waved her hand at it as she thought and stared as it faded from sight. Just as it did, Mark, Bear, and Storm walked in. Her mate arched his eyebrows at her, and she smiled back.

Fridon, Sam and Skye walked in, giving her a reprieve from explaining anything to Storm.

———

Heather studied the schematics Fridon had floating in the center of the table. The palace sat above caves that Storm admitted he explored as a child, but he didn't remember any entrance to the caverns they now inhabited. She wondered if the ancient computers there had kept any entrance hidden from him while he played.

The data streaming beside it showed it was part of the caverns she hadn't had a chance to explore to see if any other ancient computers were hiding in them. She would have to be the one to check it out to see if there was a passageway to the palace.

"We have the upper hand with this. We have several places where we can hide our soldiers without detection." Fridon highlighted the places he felt would work best for them. "We already have placed guards here, here, and here."

The image glowed where he touched so everyone could see their placement along with the new additions.

"Once we are sure we can enter and exit through the caverns I'll plan the rest of the teams' placement."

That meant she needed to explore that part of the caverns. She looked at Storm, who sat opposite her. The smile he gave her made her smile back. Their elite teams were ready. The panel had been pushing them since they had been fully assembled and would explore with them. It would allow them to work through the area faster.

Heather pulled up their schedule for the day. Most of it could be moved so they could get started right away. She saw a request from her brother to stop by the medlab. The one thing she couldn't ignore. "Have the teams warmed up yet?"

"No," responded Storm. "I'll take care of that."

"We'll move out when I get back." Heather stood. Her mate always stopped her when they separated for a kiss that could melt her bones. This time she was going to be the aggressor. She walked up to Storm and wrapped her arms around his waist.

"You're not going to let me mark my territory today?"

"I think you have marked it enough for everyone to know who I belong to. I felt it was my turn. I don't like to share any more than you do."

"Very true." He pulled her into his arms. "Shall I put you on simmer so you can focus or build that flame nice and high and watch as it works its way through you as we search for that opening?"

"I don't think it matters. Either one will have the same effect on me."

"That's what I like to hear." His mouth covered hers.

She felt his tongue brush softly against the inside of her mouth as it searched for hers. Once they connected, they moved together in perfect harmony. Storm's hold on her tightened as their tongues danced together. When they finally broke apart Storm rested his forehead against hers.

"This always backfires on me, but I can't seem to stop."

He lifted his head, and she saw the amorous glow in his eyes.

"Then we'll both be thinking the same thing today."

He smiled down at her as he brushed his fingers along her jaw. "I know what I'd rather be doing than exploring a bunch of caves."

"Me too, but we also know the longer we wait the better our intimacy is."

"True, I just hate waiting."

She laughed as she stepped in for one more quick kiss then headed to the meblab.

Her brother was waiting for her. He didn't say anything, just handed her a pad. The data spoke volumes.

"This is the biggest spike yet." Heather looked up from the pad. Something *was* going on inside her.

Her brother watched her and waited.

"I don't know." She looked around to be sure no one was paying attention to them. "Let's walk."

"You haven't seen anything?" Kuarto kept his voice low, but she could still detect the shock.

"Not really." She brushed a stray hair out of her face. "I mean a few strange things have happened but nothing I thought was something to report."

"Maybe you should now."

"I don't know what to tell you. One time, I wanted something to drink and found a bottle on the table that I was pretty sure wasn't there before." She looked at him. "I was able to create a small pebble."

"Really? When?"

"A few minutes ago." She decided not to tell him about the boulder.

Kuarto took the pad from her and pulled the data up. Heather placed her hand on the pad. "I'd like to try to figure out what has changed before you stick me under a microscope."

"You know I would never do that." He sat the pad down.

"But you have something you want me to wear or carry."

"No. That updated insert will record everything anyway. It recorded that spike."

Heather picked the pad up and looked at the date code. Now that didn't make sense. It was when she was sleeping, or at least in bed. What caused the spike? It was obvious it wasn't this new ability trying to show itself. She looked at her brother. What should she tell him? "I'm still going to need time. You know that. Half the time Storm sees it before I do."

"Okay, but please don't try to learn how to control this new ability without anyone knowing about it. I still remember the last time."

"I promise." Heather grinned. That last time gave her the hiccups so bad Kuarto had to put her in the medlab until they subsided. They had walked back to the lab and stopped just outside it.

Micali worked within the lab. She noticed the young woman didn't look happy. "What's going on with Micali?"

"The shots haven't worked."

"And she's afraid she'll be sent back to her planet."

"Pretty much. She'll deny it, but you can see it in her eyes."

"Are we finished? I'd like to go talk to her."

"Yeah."

Heather gave her brother a kiss on the cheek before she headed back into the lab and approached her friend.

"Hi Micali."

"Heather!" She gave her friend a one-armed hug as she

balanced whatever she was working on in her other hand. "Fridon told me that the council would be busy all day and unreachable."

"We will be, but Kuarto needed to speak to me before we headed off." Heather watched as she finished what she was doing. "How are you doing?"

"Kuarto told you, didn't he?"

Heather nodded.

"I am fine."

She gave Heather her brightest smile, but Heather knew better. Her brother was right, the smile didn't reach her eyes, "Micali, it's me. I know how badly you wanted to get pregnant."

A tear ran down her cheek.

Heather grabbed her hand and brought her into a room her brother had used before to speak to her privately. "Micali, you can't let this get to you."

"I am trying really hard not to, but Fridon deserves a son. We want a child that is a little bit of both of us."

"And it will happen." She grabbed Micali's other hand so she had a hold of both. "My brother will continue to work until he is successful."

"I know."

"Look at me." She squeezed her friend's hands to get her attention. "You will get pregnant, and it will be a healthy baby."

"I hope so."

"You don't sound convinced."

"I have helped with one birth and seen the size of the Vespian babies." Micali bit her lip. "What if I'm too small to carry?"

"I'm sure there have been a few women on your planet that had very large babies and survived the birth." Heather smiled. "And Kuarto will make sure you and the baby are healthy. Since I've been here, I've seen how these men care so much about us and any child we might bring into this world. If Kuarto thought you'd be too small I'm sure he would have told you that."

"You're right. "But…"

"No buts." Heather lifted their hands a bit to refocus. "I want to see that beautiful smile of yours. You have to believe that everything will work out."

"I do." Micali smiled and squeezed her hands.

"Good. Repeat after me." Heather locked her gaze with Micali, her voice became melodic, flowing over and around Micali. "You will get pregnant."

"I will get pregnant."

"Tonight, when Fridon gets home, you will fix his favorite meal."

"Okay. I will fix his favorite meal." She smiled. "I will also seduce him in my own way. The way he likes. Tonight, will be the first night that will lead to my pregnancy."

"Exactly." She stood and hugged her friend. "You are going to be a wonderful mother."

———

Heather caught up with the rest of her team in their private workout room. She had felt a little tired so had stopped by the galley to grab a snack and a drink.

Storm spotted her first. He noted the drink in her hand. "We're ready."

"Good."

"And what did the good doctor want to talk to you about?"

"Something a little odd in one of my readings," she said softly. "I'll explain more later."

"Is that why you stopped to get something to eat?"

When she looked at him, he touched his nose. "It doesn't miss much."

"I spoke to Micali and felt a little tired afterward."

"Is she okay?" His gaze slid to Fridon for a moment. "I sensed something in him."

"Yes, but the shots didn't work." She didn't want to be overheard. "Something else for later."

"I don't plan on talking when I finally get you all to myself." He wrapped his arms around her and pulled her close.

"You do have a one-track mind."

"When it comes to you, I do." He pressed his lips to the top of her mark which was just peaking up above her collar.

"We're ready, Ansira."

Storm straightened and touched her cheek before stepping away.

Time to take control. There was a total of thirty-three of them. Ten people in each elite team. They had expanded the elite teams because of the war, plus Heather, Storm and Fridon. Arc had wanted to join them, but Heather commanded him to stay in the war room. He could access any communication between her group and the command center from there.

It shouldn't take them long to hopefully find the connecting corridor they wanted to find. Troop movement to the palace would be a lot easier if they could keep them hidden from Reasta's scans.

"Let's go." She took point and led the teams to the air bikes they were using. She would break down the teams once they got to their destination. They headed out and worked their way quickly to the unexplored caverns. Once they reached the unexplored section they set down for a quick briefing.

"Your helmets had been fitted with the scanners needed to map out this area." Heather then spoke to Sam and Skye. "You'll take point and use the bikes to cover as much as you can. Everything you record will come to my helmet so if you come across several tunnels, I'll be able to see them and break down the teams so all of them can be covered. The rest of us will be on foot so we can do the detailed mapping needed of sections we have to travel to the palace and back."

Skye, Sam, and their teams snapped on their helmets and took off. Heather and Fridon stayed with Storm, Bear, and their team. They worked their way through, taking in each area to expand their maps. Nothing jumped out at her, but with all these people with her the other computer systems wouldn't show themselves. Every time she had found one in the caves, she had been alone.

They moved along, methodically recording. She found it boring but knew it was necessary. They had stopped for a break when Storm spotted two of the airbikes rejoining them. They landed close by and gave her the proper bow.

"Rise." She was afraid she was getting a little too used to this.

"Ansira, Skye has requested your presence." He gestured to his airbike.

She walked toward it, knowing Storm was right behind her. Once she climbed on, he joined her. In seconds they were air-born. Following the data she received from Skye's helmet, Heather worked her way to where Skye was waiting for them. The two guards on the other bike pulled in behind them.

Skye stood there, helmet dangling from his hands. He looked at the two guards who had returned with Heather and Storm then looked at her.

She turned to the guards. "Go on to your next section. Skye will catch up with you."

They bowed again then took off.

Skye didn't say anything, he just turned on his heel and reentered the small cavern to his right. He didn't say anything, just waited for Heather's reaction.

In the center of the area was a waist-high smooth cylindrical crystal. She stepped up to it and studied it. It reminded her of the podiums created by the ancients. Heather pulled off her helmet and set it down next to her feet. Next, she pulled off her gloves and placed them into the helmet.

"So, you walked in here and found it?"

"Nope. It wasn't up like this when we first came in. I was the last one to leave the cave and stepped right on it as it began to rise."

"It sensed your ancient blood?" She walked around it. "But it didn't activate for you."

"I don't think so." Skye looked at the podium as well. "I touched it the way we have with other consoles like this, but nothing happened."

She lowered her hand to touch the surface and found it halted by another warm hand.

"My heart, we have a mission at hand."

"And I'm not veering from it, but I need to see why this showed up now. It might be something we need for the mission."

"And if it's not?"

"Then we'll leave it and come back when we have the time." She rested her hand on the surface. The crystal started to glow, filling the cavern with a soft white light. Heather felt it start to vibrate, and she stepped back. After that, she couldn't move. A beam shot out and encased her. Without her helmet, she knew she could be in trouble.

Storm moved toward her, but thankfully Skye stopped him.

The scan stopped and released her. She moved to Storm's side, grateful when he wrapped his arms around her.

"Are you okay?"

She nodded. The cylinder's sides slid down into the floor, revealing a hilt. She frowned when she walked up to it and picked it up.

"I see you have found it."

That was her voice. Heather turned to see an image of herself. What the hell?

"I know, not what you expected, but you found the hilt, so it connected to me." The image looked around. "My heart, Skye. I'm glad you're here."

"That recording is acting like it is live."

"I am live."

"How?"

"That crystal is an amplifier for me to speak to you from the future."

"The future?"

"I know. You have ten thousand questions, and I can't tell you much, but I wanted to explain the hilt. It is a tool for you to use to control the computers as you find them. You have found two in the caves so far, correct?"

"Yes."

"And Arc has been quite annoying." The Heather on the screen added.

Heather nodded.

"And as you find the other systems you're going to find it harder to keep them all in line. That will allow you to do that."

Heather looked at it. "So, you're going to show me how to use this?"

"That's why I'm here, but this is for your ears only." She turned to look at Storm, and Skye. "Sorry gentlemen, but we need a little girl time. I'm going to turn off your communications and lock your helmets on. This Heather will explain everything later."

Storm's hands went toward his helmet, but it had already locked in place.

"Oh, he's going to be very mad. This better be worth it."

"What I'm about to tell you is what happened to me. I have to follow it to keep the timeline right. I never felt my future self said anything that Storm or Skye shouldn't have heard, but that device is very sensitive. Our mate has frozen it a few times when he tried to help me reprogram it."

"He means well." Heather looked at her mate who was trying to move. "What did you do, lock them in place?"

"Powered down their suits so they can't move."

"Oh, he is going to be very mad. Thanks."

"I remember, but the intimacy we shared after we fought was amazing." The future Heather smiled at the memory. "Anyway, the hilt handles slide down so you can slip it into the back of your suit. If you pull them up and out the laser will appear."

"Then it is a sword."

"You can use it that way. First, you'll notice the seven crystals running down the hilt. Two of the stones are glowing. Those stones represent Mac and Arc. The rest of the stones are dark. As you find the other computers the stones will start to glow like the first two. One thing. Don't show this to Cim until you have found the other four. If you do it before then he will be aware of the other computers."

"Understood," said Heather.

"If you were to press the lit stones, you'd call Mac or Arc to you. I recommend you try that once you get back to the main compound. The stones going across the handle is how you control the weapon. Press the green stone."

The laser solidified.

"Now you have a walking stick." Heather nodded. "Pull the handles out from the hilt."

A steel blade replaced the solidified laser.

"And how is this supposed to help me control the andriods?"

———

Storm growled his frustration.

"You want to stop growling in my ear?"

"Skye?"

"Yeah. This other Heather might have blocked us from hearing what they are saying but we can still communicate with each other."

"Fridon? Can you hear me?"

No answer.

"Looks like she cut us off from everyone but not from each other."

"Can you move?"

"Nope. She powered our suits down to just the right point. Our vitals won't be compromised but we can't move."

"Why would my mate do this to me?"

"I know this is semantics, but she's not your mate. Your mate is standing there holding a hilt. The woman responsible is from the future."

"It is still Heather."

"True." Skye paused when he watched as their Heather manipulated the hilt. She brought forth a beam then converted it to a staff as well as an old-fashioned sword. "That's a little awesome."

"It doesn't explain why she shut us out."

"You do have a tendency to try to take over."

"I'm only trying to protect my mate."

"From herself. A future self who knows what's at stake."

That quieted Storm. Skye was right. Maybe he did push a little at times, but he did it to keep his mate and their children safe. He needed to trust his mate.

Heather continued to manipulate the hilt, converting it into a knife, a baton and a staff. He could see her lips moving as she spoke to her future self. If only he could hear her.

———

"When you get back to the main complex show this hilt to Mac and Arc. They will give you a non-descript tube. If you press it against the hilt the tubes will be absorbed. That helps us control the two at a deeper level. It connects us to the androids. A stronger bond will develop, and it will help you pass Arc's test."

"Then you know my location in time?"

"I lived it, remember? I do have one question for you. Have you spoke Micali recently?"

"Today. She was so upset that she hasn't gotten pregnant yet."

"Good. That is what happened with me as well. You need to give it two days before you contact her."

"Why?"

"Just do it and think about what you've been told by Bert and other ancients when you talk to her."

"Isn't that going against the timeline?"

"Not when I was told the same thing."

Great.

"I'm going to release our mate now. You know how he's going to react." She powered up their suits then spoke once more. "I'm sorry that I had to lock you out, my heart, but I know you too well. Just remember this. Your Heather didn't do this to you. I did."

Storm whipped off his helmet. "You locked me out?"

"I did not. My future self did."

"Explain to me what the difference is. Isn't she still you?"

"How can I defend something I haven't done yet?"

"Right." Skye had taken his helmet off as well and had listened to them. "I'm going to catch up with the rest of the teams."

He knew what was going to happen between them once the arguing stopped.

"What was so secretive that we couldn't hear?"

"I don't know." Heather shook her head. "She showed me the different shifts of the weapon and explained how the hilt would control the androids, but I didn't think she said anything she couldn't have shared with you and Skye. She did tell me you have frozen this thing from working when you tried to help."

Skye came back in flying their bike.

"I didn't think you'd want to be disturbed so thought I should move this in here." With that he was gone.

"You allowed her to block me."

"And exactly how was I supposed to stop her? My future self has learned a few tricks I don't know." He was pissing her off again. There were moments when she wished she could hit a pause button when he got like this.

He just glared at her.

"What would you have me do?" Why wasn't he

moving? Heather brushed her hands on her legs. She was just overreacting. There was nothing wrong with him. "Reach into the future and give her a good thrashing?"

That made him laugh.

"I think watching you wrestle with yourself might be quite arousing." And like that his anger passed and desire took over.

"Who said I'd let you watch?" She placed her hand on her hips.

"Because you like it when I get aroused." He stepped up to her and drew her into his embrace. "You like how I become so hyper-focused on you that nothing else matters."

Heather rested her head against his chest. He was right. She loved being the center of his world. Lifting her head, she looked up at him, offering her mouth to him. He claimed it quickly. His tongue swept in, searching for hers. Once it found hers, they twirled and danced together, drawing a sigh out of her when the kiss ended.

"I wish we were in our rooms. This place isn't conducive for intimacy."

Heather looked around and knew he was right. The walls weren't smooth, and the floor was covered with sand. If they used the floor, they'd be picking sand out of the nooks and crannies of their bodies for days. She noticed the airbike and smiled. Taking Storm's hand, she brought him over to it.

Her hands skimmed over his uniform, releasing the seals and exposing his body to her gaze. When his hand went to her uniform, she stopped him. "I want to do this for you."

Heather moved to where she was just out of reach before she started to remove her uniform. It wasn't the easiest strip tease she ever done because of the way the uniform was designed. Her hands took their time opening the seals. Starting at her ankles, she slid her fingers against the seam. As her hand moved up her leg the seals parted and exposed her skin.

Storm watched every move.

Once she opened the seals as high as she wanted, she started working on her sleeves. Lifting her arms above her head, she worked on the seals there. She made sure she opened them on the top of her arms, working up to her shoulders. When she had those seals separated as far as she needed, she turned her back to Storm.

"My heart, you're killing me."

She turned her head toward him. "You just want to touch my body so you can take control."

He gave her a bone-melting smile. "You know me well, my heart."

She released the seal on one shoulder and the material slid down her back. Storm groaned when the other shoulder separated and dropped. Now the only thing holding her uniform on was her hands. Heather turned toward him and let go of her uniform. It pooled at her feet. Taking a step toward Storm, she stepped out of the circle of cloth at her feet.

Her braid was the next thing to go. Heather knew she was close enough to Storm now that he would take advantage of it and touch her the way he had wanted to earlier. Dropping her head back, she closed her eyes and pulled her braid forward to work it loose.

The heat of Storm's hand surrounded her right breast as she worked the braid free. He wrapped an arm around her waist and pulled her closer. She felt his warm mouth close around her left nipple. His tongue swirled around the tip, and she felt it all the way to her toes.

"You're not making this easy," she whispered. Each

time he sucked on her she couldn't undo the plat in her hair.

"I'm only returning the favor, my heart."

"If that is the way you want to play this then I will continue to tease you." She had released her braid and had her hands free. She gave him a smile that normally meant trouble.

Storm narrowed his eyes. "What are you planning?"

"Me?" She offered her hand to him. The moment he gave it to her she put the airbike between them. She patted the seat so he would sit down. "Now straddle the bike as you turn to face me."

The moment he did she climbed on the bike as well, facing him. She opened her mind and brought Storm in.

"My heart?"

"I thought I would try to create something special by using my mind."

"Like you did when we ducked into that alcove?" He gave her his bone-melting smile.

"No." she gave him one of her own. "When I tried to get the upper hand."

"You know I won that."

"You know I didn't lose that." She walked around him, letting her hands slide along his chest, over his muscles. Feather-like caresses she knew affected him. This time she made sure she had his undivided attention so he couldn't take control in the real world while she tried to arouse him in their minds. "We both won, but I didn't get to see how far I can push you before you lose control."

"I see." He tried to move but once again he couldn't. "If I remember I was able to arouse you physically while you tried to arouse me mentally."

"True." Her hands physically touched the places she knew increased his desire while she caressed him in her mind. "But just like I learned to let you have your way I'm hoping you'll let me have my way. You know we'll both enjoy our intimacy that much more."

He wanted to tell her no. She could see it in his eyes.

"Have you forgotten the wall?"

That made him smile. "That was glorious."

"I promise this will be just as glorious." She waited for him to agree. Heather knew her mate. He liked to experiment. The problem was, would he let her take the lead. Then she remembered what her future self said and smiled.

"You have that smile."

"What smile?" Her hands continued to move about his body. This time fleeting touches that she knew would arouse him. She held a feather in her hand, brushing along where her fingers had touched.

A deep growl filled the air.

"You like that." She switched the feather to a fur mitt. It followed the same path as the feather. Heather moved it over his skin, soft brushes everywhere. She wrapped her furry mitt around his erection for a brief moment, getting another growl.

Storm took as much as he could but when she wrapped that fur mitt around his erection once more, he grabbed her hand. "Enough."

"You sure?" Heather's mind flowed around him, taking his breath away. She broke the mental hold she had on him.

"It's my turn." His hands started to glide across her skin. Soft sensual caresses that had her desire spiraling.

"I am already aroused from trying to arouse you. I don't know how much more I can take."

"I know I can't take much more myself," said Storm. His voice deeper than normal.

"I can fix that." Heather lifted herself so she could slide down his shaft. They both sighed at the contact. She set a quick pace, but Storm placed his hands on her hips to slow her down. "Storm."

"I am ready to explode too, my heart, but we've never rushed our intimacy before, and I don't want to start a bad habit."

"Ha! Quick or slow our intimacy is a habit we are addicted to." Heather let Storm set the pace. She knew he needed a little time to control his body. She had pushed him to his limits, and he had let her. Joy at the thought filled her. As Storm liked to say it was glorious.

He tilted her back, and every muscle tightened. Just the slight movement had him touching a sensitive spot inside her and she knew this orgasm would be mind-blowing. She feared she would scream and bring everyone running.

Her orgasm raced through her, taking her breath away. She felt it fill her body with a euphoria she couldn't describe. Storm stiffened and he joined her as his climax took him to the stars with her.

He touched her face with gentle fingers. "That was glorious."

———

Heather and Storm decided to join the advanced team instead of returning to Fridon and the other two teams. The bike had a lot to do with their decision. They joined the group as they were resting. The moment they landed and pulled off their helmets all the people stood and bowed to her.

"That never gets old," she said under her breath. She didn't want all this attention.

Storm slipped an arm around her and pulled her closer. His silent reassurance made her feel better.

She smiled and nodded, and they went back to what they were doing. Skye and Sam stepped to greet her and Storm.

"We're under the palace now. If there is an opening, we should be finding it soon."

Heather nodded. Sitting with everyone else wasn't an option. Ever since she became the leader of this war people treated her a little differently. They watched her as if expecting something. When she mentioned it to Storm, he reminded her that they wanted to make sure she wanted for nothing and that they had been doing it since the moment she mated with him. It still felt different than before. Maybe she was just more sensitive to it.

"I used to play in some of the caves under the palace when I was a child," said Storm. "But nothing here looks familiar."

"We could look while they rest." She looked up at him with a smile.

He took her hand and headed toward one of the passageways in front of them. "Any particular way?"

Heather looked at the different passageways. "Hmm, let's try this one." She headed to the right, tugging him with her. "What was it like living above and playing down here."

"Like you, Toki and I grew tired of all the attention from the people. We just wanted to play like children so Mom had guards go into the caves and clear it out so we had a place to escape to."

"Then they could have used forcefields to keep you from going too far." Excitement filled her. "They wouldn't have used anything too advanced, right? Just something to keep you and your sister away from any opening they didn't want you to know about."

"Why are you so happy about this?"

"It means there is an opening. It could be hidden but our helmets should be able to find it without a problem."

Skye stepped up to their side and handed them their helmets. "The rest of the team is ready for your orders."

Heather hadn't planned on interrupting what they were doing. "What was your next step?"

"We were going to check out the right quadrant first."

"Then have everyone set their helmets to look for a low-grade forcefield as they move through."

Skye nodded. "You believe the entrance we're looking for is hidden?"

"Storm told me his mother allowed Toki and him to play in the underground caves below the palace. Her guards were ordered to make them safe first. I'm pretty sure there must have been a reason and hiding an opening to the underground caves make sense."

Skye pulled up the schematics of the palace. "Your rooms are here."

Storm looked at the three-dimensional image Skye brought up. "I wasn't given those rooms until I mated with Heather. When we were children Toki and I lived in my mother's suites." He touched the spot where his room was when he was a child. "The entrance to the cave was close to our rooms." He worked with the image, adding the caves he remembered as a child below the area where his mother's suites were. It wasn't far from where they stood.

Skye sent the info to the rest of the team, rearranging the order so Heather and Storm could take point. They headed out toward the area Skye had planned to investigate. Nothing out of the ordinary appeared as they worked their way through the place. They moved from one passage to another until they had cleared more than three-fourths of the area.

"Nothing?" Heather shook her head after she pulled off her helmet. "I don't believe it. There has to be something here."

"We haven't looked everywhere yet, my heart." Storm pulled his helmet off as well.

"I know, but we haven't found anything, and the chances are getting smaller and smaller."

"Just because we don't find an opening doesn't mean we can't pretend we have one."

"I know, but she does have ancient technology, and I always worry about what she can detect. To keep our people safe, I'd much rather have a way for them to enter the palace that didn't require transporting them."

"We could create our own opening."

"And that could take too long. What if she decides to attack in an hour?"

"Heather, you need to see this," interrupted Skye.

Storm followed behind her.

"We found a marker, but it's not where we expected it." He pointed up. "We still haven't found an opening yet."

Heather saw the marker then started to look around. The story she had been telling the children about the cursed dragon came to mind. The last scene she told them about was where the heroine had found a secret room. It looked like a wall but when she accidentally kicked some loose pebbles against that wall they disappeared.

"We need something to throw."

THIRTEEN

S torm didn't question. He went to Skye and came back with a few small cylinders. She took them from him and threw the first on right at the device they found. She felt if she broke it then the shield would drop.

A high-pitched wail filled the air as the cylinder shot right back at her. The sound had everyone ducking then looking at her.

"Sorry. Thought I could take it out. Looks like the shield is covering it as well."

"A heads-up next time would be nice," Skye whispered next to her ear. She grinned. He was right.

"My thought is to test the wall beneath that device. Either the sphere will pass through or make the shield glow."

"You're hoping it only blocks one way."

Heather nodded. She threw her sphere at another section, but it just bounced back to her as well. Soon she had several people helping her out. The area lit up when the shield was hit. "Okay, so it goes both ways. We need to disable that thing so we can get into the opening."

She looked at Skye. The man had an ability with computers and would figure it out much faster than the rest of them.

He sighed as he snapped his helmet back on. Sam fired up one of the bikes and lifted him up. "The thing has an odd color to it. Most security devices are blue in hue, but this one is green."

"Green?" Storm stepped forward. "You need to get away from that..."

The bike started to wobble beneath him.

Heather heard Skye tell Sam to keep the bike steady just before he pitched off the back of it.

———

Storm moved first, racing to place himself at the right spot to catch Skye before he hit the floor. He turned up his suit so he could take the punch of Skye's fall.

He could hear Heather shouting orders to Sam and the rest of the crew to get the bike on the ground without anyone getting hurt.

Skye landed on him like dead weight. His suit had shut down. They crashed to the ground together. Heather was at his side with Sam. They slid Skye off him.

"Storm, can you hear me?"

He raised his hand then gave her a thumbs up, so she knew he was okay. His mate focused on him while Sam and a few of their guards focused on Skye.

Heather released the seal on his uniform and pulled his helmet off. "You okay?"

"I'm fine, my heart." He took her offered hand and sat up. "His suit shut down completely. He's not getting any air."

Heather turned to look and saw someone trying to use the tool to pop his helmet off, but they weren't getting anywhere. She left Storm's side and took the tool from the soldier who was failing at removing Skye's helmet. Forcing it into the seal, she jerked it up and down before shoving it right and left until she broke the seal. Two of the other guards grabbed the helmet and pulled, giving her a small space to jam the tool in so they could wedge the helmet off.

Storm had stood and watched as they were able to release Skye, but he wasn't breathing. Heather slapped him hard, and nothing happened.

"Oh no you don't," said his mate. "I need you as my second." She slammed him in the chest, making his body convulse before he dragged in a huge breath.

"Damn, that hurt." His voice was raw, and he had a little trouble sitting up.

Their medic ran a scanner over him. "He's fine but needs a full workup once we get back to the command center."

Heather nodded. She looked up at the device. "We need to find a way up there." She pressed the button on her uniform. "Fridon? We need you and the rest of the teams here. I need something that can scale heights that doesn't have any technology in them."

"How high?"

"Twenty meters. Oh, and we need clothing without tech as well."

"On it."

Storm looked at her then the device. "Who do you have in mind?"

Before she could answer Skye piped up. "Me. I'm the one who can disarm it the quickest."

Heather looked at him.

"Are you sure?" asked Sam.

"Yeah. I'm fine. That damn thing might have gotten the best of me the first time, but all that did was make me determined to disable it." Skye struggled with his suit. "But the first thing we need to do is power up this stupid thing."

Sam went and retrieved his bag. Pulling out the spare battery pack he needed to power up his suit. She pulled the old pack out and snapped in the new one. Storm had made that mandatory for any mission. The moment it had enough power for him to move he pulled it off and climbed into another one he had in his pack.

Heather was surprised he had a second suit. Most of the time everyone worked with the one. "Lucky guess?"

"Sam recommended it."

"That was a good call." Heather looked at her daughter. How did she know Skye would need the second suit? That was something to watch. Perhaps her daughter's power was starting to show.

Storm came up to her and wrapped his arms around her. Now what? She leaned back against him and rested her head on his chest. Was he jealous?

Fridon and most of the other teams came into view.

"Everything you requested will be here soon. I sent five back to gather everything and they are on their way here now."

"Good." Heather straightened and pointed. "We need to get to that."

Three airbikes came into view, pulling an air sled each. They should have everything they need to turn that device off.

Skye slipped off his uniform once more and Heather found Storm at her side. She lowered her voice so only he could hear her. "Jealous?"

"Are you interested?" he murmured next to her ear.

"Eww. That is my son-in-law."

"And you have the right if that is what you wish."

She turned in his arms. This was something he had said before. Being raised on Earth taught her to be a monogamist, but Vespians didn't see sex the same way humans did. What did Storm want from her? She didn't want anyone but her mate. He knew that. Was there something she needed to do to claim him as her only sex partner? Something public that would satisfy her mate and stop these crazy questions?

"Why do you keep asking me this? You are my mate and all I want."

"My heart, you gave up everything to come here and become part of our society. Now you have the people you grew up with. I want you happy."

"I am. I have you." She touched his face with her fingers. "Is there something I need to do to prove this to you?"

"We'll talk about this later." He gave her his heart-stopping smile. "Skye is ready to go after that device."

She sighed as she turned in his arms once again. Not getting the answer she wanted frustrated her, but she needed to focus on the task at hand. Skye had changed once again. He climbed the makeshift stairs and disabled the shield in seconds. An opening appeared to his right about two meters up.

Several soldiers went to the stairs once he came down them and moved them over so Heather could enter first. She could have climbed up but knew they were doing this to honor her. She entered the room and grinned. It looked like a play area for children. This could be it.

Storm came in behind her and she turned to watch his

face. Recognition filled it when he looked around. "This is where Toki and I used to play."

As much as he wanted to wander around and reminisce Storm took her hand and led her to the doorway that led to the palace.

"Mother had it widened so the guards could stand by as we played." They walked out into the main hallway.

Heather knew where they were at this point. Now all they had to do was get their sentries here and prepare for Reasta's attack.

———

Several days later Heather sat at the table in the war room. She ran her hand over the hilt she had gotten from herself. So all she needed to do was show it to Mac and Arc and they would give her a tube. It sounded a little crazy, but she knew her future self wouldn't lie to her.

Arc was standing in a corner and since it was just the two of them, she walked to him. She held the hilt out to him, not sure if she needed to say or do anything else.

He looked at the hilt then looked at her. "You found the hilt."

"I did."

He pressed his hand against his side then held out a small piece of metal. It did look a bit like a tube.

Heather laid it on the hilt and watched in amazement as it melted into it. Some migrated to the stone creating a ring around the stone as well as in the stone itself. Now all she had to do was test it. After she got the piece needed from Mac.

The door opened and Fridon walked in. He looked a little shell-shocked and had this dopey grin on his face.

Heather had heard her brother page him to the medlab earlier. She jumped up. "Oh my God!"

She bolted out the door, tried to run down her mate, bounced off him, and continued running.

"Heather?"

"Sorry, my heart." She turned to look at him. "I'll explain later. Better yet. Talk to Fridon." Heather then took off running again, sliding into the medlab as she reached the doors.

"Wow, can I assume you're not here for me?" asked her brother.

"Um, no. I just saw Fridon."

"Figured. She's with a patient." He pointed to a small alcove with a bed. The medlab was built there because of all the natural alcoves. It gave his patients privacy.

Heather turned toward the alcove he pointed at just as Micali stepped out. "I saw Fridon."

"You know?"

Heather nodded. "Fridon's look of shock gave it away."

"The doctor just told us." She grabbed Heather's hand. "Thank you so much. Your faith in me getting pregnant allowed me to relax and just let things happen. I know it's still early and we don't know what to expect since I'm the first of my race to carry a Vespian baby, but I've never been so happy."

"I'm so happy for you." Heather hugged her. "I need to get back to the war room but wanted to congratulate you."

———

Storm walked into the war room, still looking behind him. "My mate says you'll explain why she bolted out of here?" Storm turned to look at Fridon and realized he wasn't focusing. "Fridon."

"What? Oh sorry. I was just thinking." He looked up at Storm. "I'm going to be a father."

———

That evening Heather sat on the floor with the twins. It was late because she had spent hours in the command center setting everything up and was tired, but she wanted to finish the story she had been telling them. They looked up at her in anticipation.

"So where are we?"

"Mom! You don't remember? You're telling the story!"

She wanted to laugh. "I just want to know what you remember."

"Our heroine has decided to work for the dragon. She has the days to herself but at night she must take care of the dragon," said Sunni.

"Yeah, cleaning his lair while he is out then cooking for him when he gets back," added Turrik. "He would bring back animals for her to cook. Sometimes she would do it that evening and sometimes she would have it ready the next evening."

"Yeah, she has been doing this long enough to get into a routine."

"And the last time you told us she found a secret doorway." Turrik leaned in. "Where did it go?"

"To Freedom. She found that it was nothing more than an illusion and walked through it."

"She didn't leave him, did she? He needs her."

Heather touched Zunni's face. "No. After working with him all those months she realized that too. She also knew since the dragon and the man were locked in the curse together if she left one, she'd be leaving the other."

"Oh, good. I was afraid she wouldn't do the noble thing."

So young and already knew so much. "She had found the dragon not to be as scary as she had been told as a child. He had a sense of humor she hadn't expected. It just took her a little time to get used to the way he talked."

"Because speaking was hard for him. We remember Mommy," said Turrik. "So she stayed?"

"Yes. She continued to cook and clean for him. One night, when she went in to give him his meal, she noticed a dress near one of his claws. Now she had cleaned the area earlier and knew it wasn't there before." Heather looked at her children who were watching her in rapt attention. "She kept looking at the dress as she brought out the dragon's meal."

"How did she do that? You said it took a lot of food to feed him and she cooked all day to have enough food for him."

"I thought I explained that before."

"Yeah, pulleys and levees and lots of carts to move everything. I mean her focus on the dress. She should be focused on making sure he eats the food and not her."

Heather wanted to laugh. Wait 'til they heard what she had to say next. "Now the dragon noticed she was looking at the dress. He lifted his claw and told her it was for her. She couldn't help but ask where he got it. When he asked why she couldn't stop herself from asking him if he ate the woman who wore it first."

"Ewww."

"I told you Dragon needed a lot of meat."

"I know, but still eww, Mommy."

"Well, when he heard her ask that, he demanded to know why."

"What did she say, Mommy?"

"She told him that she had been told since she was a child that she couldn't go out at night or the dragon would snatch her and gobble her up. That little girls were a special treat to the dragon." Heather watched as their eyes grew wide. "The dragon snorted, sending a bit of ash through the air. She coughed as some of the ash filled her nose and mouth.

"'Sorry,' said the dragon. 'I sometimes forget myself. The dress didn't come from anyone I ate. I had my man pick it up for you. A gift. Take it.' Our heroine looked at him. 'Thank you but where would I wear it?' She shook her head. 'I am quite happy in the dress I'm wearing now.' A growl emanated from the dragon's throat, and she knew she had upset him. She had learned by now that if she asked the right questions, she would find out why she was given this dress."

"He's mad at her, isn't he?" asked Terrik.

"Yes. He was trying to thank her but wasn't sure how to explain it."

"So what did she ask him?"

"Well, first she asked if he was happy with his meal."

"I bet he said it filled his belly," said Zunni.

"Yeah," said her brother. "That's what he always says."

"Then she asked if he was happy with her."

"Ohh, good question. Did he say yes?"

"He said the dress, and she knew it was a gift thanking her for all she had done. She smiled then and picked up the dress. Instead of waiting for him to eat she asked to be excused and although the dragon wasn't happy she didn't want to stay with him he let her go to her room." Heather looked up and saw Storm leaning on the doorframe. She knew she would have to wrap this up. "So she went back to her room and put the dress on. It was beautiful and fit her perfectly. She spun around and listened as the soft material swished with her movements. Once she was happy with the way the dress fitted, she ran out of her room and back to the dragon's lair."

"Time for bed."

"Aw, Dad, can't we hear what the dragon said when she came back in?"

"Tomorrow. You two need your sleep." He gave his mate a heart-stopping smile. "And your mom and I need to rest too."

Heather knew what he wanted. She stood after she kissed her children and joined him. Storm would get his intimacy, but she would also get some answers.

———

Storm rested in the bed as he waited for Heather. She had asked to be excused, and he knew what it meant. A smile filled his lips when she stepped back into the room with her silk wrap on. Vespians saw nudity and a clothed body the same way, but these wonderful little outfits she created just for him to help stimulate their intimacy were something he always enjoyed. It didn't need stimulating, but the fact that she did these things for him filled him with joy. It showed how much she cared for him. How much she loved him.

When the wrap dropped to the floor and he saw her outfit for the first time he knew she wanted something from him. What was the question. It was beautiful. It was a soft cream the same color as her skin.

He scooted toward the center of the bed when she climbed on it. As she crawled toward him, her hair cascading around her, her breasts straining to come out of the demi-cups that held them made his heart stop for just a moment. His heart.

She watched him as she got closer. A smile spread across her face when she saw his erection jump when she touched his leg. Heather settled herself on top of him, trapping his erection beneath her heat. Those crotchless panties came in handy.

Heather leaned forward and brushed a few fingers against his mark. "So why do you keep reminding me that I can take another partner if I want to? Is there someone you're interested in but won't approach her if I don't take another partner?"

"Of course not. You are my heart."

"And I have told you over and over that I want only you. I followed proper Vespian etiquette and showed that to everyone by feeding you and wearing our marks on my dress."

"So there is no other man that has caught your eye?"

"No."

He wrapped his arms around her and flipped them over so he was above her. "Then what have you been hiding from me?"

She blushed.

"We have never had secrets."

"Okay, but it's going to interrupt our intimacy."

He frowned at her. What did she mean by that?

"I'm still learning to control this and want us to be safe."

"A new ability?"

She nodded. There was a spark of fear in her eyes. He rolled off her and stood then offered her his hand.

"Clear room," she commanded. Once the room was bare, she looked at him. "I haven't hurt myself and I don't want to hurt you, so I need you next to me."

He wrapped his arms around her. "Is this close enough?"

"Yes." She leaned against him. "Okay, watch."

Heather held out her hand and it trembled a little as he focused on it. Then suddenly she held a small pebble.

"You created that?" He picked it up out of her hand. His mate still looked nervous. "What is wrong?"

"One time when I did that, I also created a bolder as tall as me. Scared the crap out of me."

"Is that why you've been sneaking off during breaks?"

"Yes." She let out a breath when nothing else appeared. "Was I that oblivious?"

"I know you, my heart, and felt you pull away from me mentally like you didn't want me to pick up your thoughts at certain times. It didn't take me long to figure out it was happening during breaks and lunch. Whenever anyone gave you a chance to be alone."

"Oh, crap. That's why you kept asking me if I wanted another partner. You were afraid I had already taken one and didn't want you to know about it. When the only reason I kept it from you was because I didn't want to hurt anyone if something went awry."

"And what would have happened if you had gotten hurt while you were alone?" He turned her in his arms. "You are my mate and my heart, and I want you safe."

"Um, my brother has been aware. He called me to his office to show me a spike in my mental readings then these things started to happen. One time I swear a stool appeared under my feet when you held me as we kissed. I also think I created a drink because I was thirsty."

"You shouldn't disappear without a word. What if you were needed?"

"I would have heard the page. Storm, I wasn't out of contact. I just didn't want to hurt anyone."

"And now?"

"Now that you know about this, I promise not to sneak

off anymore." She rested her head against his chest. "In fact, I'm glad you know now. I didn't like keeping it from you."

"Promise me you'll never keep anything from me again?" He shifted his hold so he could slip one arm under her knees and lifted her.

"Promise." She wrapped her arms around his neck. "Our standard bedroom."

"You think our conversation is over?"

She looked up at him with wide eyes. "I thought we'd like to be more comfortable."

"Fair enough." Their bed reappeared in front of them, and he laid her on the bed. Before she could move too far, he had her pinned with his body. "Now, why did you feel the need to keep this from me?"

"It frightened me." Her voice was soft.

"My heart, you have to stop this lack of faith in yourself. You and Skye have lived with humans too long."

"And we've seen what happens when power goes to someone's head."

"You forget that you're not human. You're Vespian and ancient. Have you ever seen a Vespian think they were better than any other Vespian?" Feeling her body beneath his had him wanting to drop their conversation and do what they did best. His hands moved up and down her sides.

"No."

"And Bert probably has a few gifts we don't know about, but he doesn't think he is better than any of us."

"True." She shifted under him, making him smile.

A simple brush of his fingers against one of her sensitive places, her ribs, had her desire rising. He could smell it.

"Then there is that soft heart of yours." He moved

down her body so he could press his lips against her mark. "You always find the good in everyone. I don't think you have a selfish bone in your body."

"I know but…" Her breath hitched.

"You need to trust what everyone else sees. So does Skye." He lifted his head and captured her lips with his. His tongue swept in, touching hers and inviting it to dance the dance they knew so well. Joy filled him as he felt her tongue brush up against his. It took him a few minutes before he broke the kiss. "I have faith in you, and you need to have that same faith in yourself."

She looked up at him and smiled. "It will take me time to trust myself the way you want me to, but your trust in me will make me try."

"Good." He bent his head and nibbled on her mark again. "Yet, I know you will still question yourself."

"It's a hard habit to break." Heather tilted her head to give him better access.

"One I will enjoy helping you break." He focused on her body then. Storm continued to touch Heather's sensitive spots. He pushed their intimacy whenever he could. Tonight, he wanted to remind her he was her protector. Everything she did needed to go through him first. He had been a little lax in making sure she knew who was the dominant one. It was time to remind her. Taking one hand then the other he used the restraints already attached to the bed.

"Are you mad at me?" Heather was quick to figure out what was happening.

"Not mad." He brushed his fingers against her cheek.

"But you're not happy."

He centered himself and drove into her. She sucked in her breath as he filled her. "Why did you hide this new ability from me?"

"I explained that."

"As your mate, what do I do for you?"

"Do?" she gave him a confused look. "Everything."

"Good answer." He pulled out then drove back in, putting a smile on her face. "Name a few."

"You're my mate. The father of our children." She studied his face. "Not what you're looking for. Um, You're my sounding board, my protector."

"Yet you decided to keep me out of the loop."

"I didn't want you hurt. I was only trying to –"

Storm slid out then filled her again, breaking her concentration. "I am your protector. I can't protect you if you keep things from me."

"Can I ask you a few questions?"

He could tell she was serious. "Of course."

"I want to ask you the same questions." She wrapped her legs around him. "Who am I to you?"

"You are my heart. My mate and the mother of our children."

"And as your mate am I to leave all the protecting to you? If one of the children were to be in danger, am I supposed to wait for you to protect them?"

"Of course not." He figured out what she was trying to say.

"Good. I'm glad we cleared that up. Now. What is my job right now?"

He frowned. "You are the leader of this war."

"Which means I'm responsible for the health and well-being of my soldiers, right? Once he nodded, she continued. "Remind me what my Vespian title is?"

"Ansira."

"And what does that mean?"

"Protector of all."

"Aren't you part of that all?" When he went to answer

her, she tightened her legs against his waist. "I understand you want me safe. I feel the same way about you and our children but if I feel an ability could harm anyone, I will try to master it before I show it to anyone. I couldn't live with myself if something happened to anyone, especially you, because of a new power."

———

Heather had trouble sleeping. Her mind was running through so many scenarios she found getting her mind to shut down was not working. Maybe she should try meditating. She sat in a comfortable chair and closed her eyes. She started with relaxing her toes, then her legs, and moved up her body relaxing as she went. Focusing on her breathing, she let her mind wander.

She found herself walking through the palace halls. Door after door was closed, which surprised her. In the real halls there were no doors. Why was she seeing this?

"What is going on?" She said it mentally but knew whoever set this up heard her. "Am I being tested? Arc?"

He appeared in front of her. "I have tried to test you several times, but you kept going to your mate to get his imput. I need to see what you would do without him. Mac was the one who recommended that I be honest with you. That you would be willing to go through any test if you knew the parameters."

"Mac is right. I understand you need to test me, but making my mate do something he would never do to separate us is the wrong way to go."

"I learned that," Arc said. "Behind the doors are different scenarios. Pick one. That will be your test."

"It doesn't matter which one?"

"No."

Heather nodded, then studied each door. She took a deep breath, faced a door, and waited for it to open. It opened to chaos. People running everywhere. The moment she stepped into the room the doors behind her closed and disappeared. There was no turning back.

"Soldier."

One of the people running by skidded to a stop when he realized who had spoken to him. "Ma'am."

"What is going on?"

"Sorry, Ma'am. I don't know. All I know is that I've been told to join my elite team."

"Carry on." She knew she wouldn't get any answers that way. She followed the soldier as she looked around. This was the command center? Why were the screens blank?

"Arc, this would seem more real if you had the screens working."

She walked to one of the terminals and programmed the screens to reactivate. Heather needed to know what was going on or she wouldn't pass this test. Reasta's people were everywhere outside the caves. They were searching for the entrances. "That can't happen."

A few keys pressed and she blocked Reasta from finding the entrances. Now all she to do was wait.

"That won't work forever."

Heather turned to find the soldier she had spoken to beside her. "Why not?"

"Because you'll fail the test."

"It's all about the weapons, isn't it? Which one I would use at what time."

"How do you want to handle this situation?" Everything switched back to the scenario she walked into.

"Keep them under surveillance." Now she had to figure out how to pass this test. Her first thought was to go to the council chambers. That was where they had put the other weapons they had found. Maybe Arc followed suit.

The doors opened to an empty room. The walls were loaded with weapons Heather had never seen before. As she touched each one its use and capacity filled her mind. She knew what they did and how much damage they could do in the right situation.

She still hadn't seen anyone she knew. No Storm, Sam, Skye, Fridon. No one. Heather walked out of the room. Now she had to face the gauntlet that would prove she was worthy of the power the computers would give her. She knew that each computer would test her to some degree. Each in the expertise of that computer. Right now, she had to show she knew how to use the ordinances available and how to use them properly. Not knowing what was going on made it difficult.

Heather was surprised when she was called back to the command center. What was Arc up to? She ran back the way she came. Not knowing what she needed to do made her wonder what the test was. Would she know when it started?

A guard came up to her. "We're awaiting your orders."

"Not until I have a few questions answered." Heather kept her emotions locked down. "Who can answer those questions for me?"

"I don't know, Ansira but I will find out." He took off. Leaving her in front of the screens once again.

She studied them. At least they weren't blank anymore. There was something odd about the images. One by one she took each image and enlarged them so one filled all the screens. The people in the images moved oddly. They didn't fit the scene. Heather smiled. Reasta and her people weren't really outside the cave openings. The question now was if the feed was live or something prerecorded.

Arc was keeping her away from her council so who was going to be the one to answer her questions? Would it be him?

"I am here to answer your questions, Heather."

"Mac. I had wondered who Arc would send. What are you allowed to tell me?"

"I've been told to answer your questions. If you ask one I can't answer, I'll make you aware."

"Okay." Heather rubbed her hands together. "Let's talk about what I think I know. This is a test to see how I would handle ordinances with my battle with Reasta."

"That is correct."

"I don't like to use weapons. How is this going to work? Without my council to help filter what is going on outside it's going to take longer for me to figure out what's happening."

"Arc knows this." Mac touched Heather's forehead and watched as she fell to the floor. "Which is why the test starts now."

———

Heather found herself in the white room. How did she get here? She was being tested by Arc, but her mind was a little fuzzy.

Mom?

Sam? She felt stress emanating from her daughter. *Is everything alright?*

I did something very stupid. I wasn't paying attention and got captured.

What? How?

I'm sorry, Mom. I'm on Reasta's ship. She plans on doing to me what she tried to do to you.

Anger filled Heather. *We've got to get you off that ship. What happened to Skye?*

I don't know, but you need to find him and make him aware. I'll get back to you. Sam? We are going to rescue you.

Love you, Mom.

Love you too.

———

Storm walked into the council room to see Mac carry Heather over to her chair. A growl escaped him as he came at Mac.

"Stop. Heather hasn't been harmed. Arc needs to test her without any interference from you. He knows he can't do it without your help. He has tried several times, and Heather constantly reaches for you to help her with the decisions he needs her to make on her own."

"Why does she look so lifeless?"

"Arc sent her to the white room. He's hoping she will believe it's real. She has heard from your daughter and has been told that she has been captured by Reasta. Arc knows Heather will reach out to you. You must get her to make the decisions on her own."

"And if I refuse?" Storm crossed his arms over his chest.

"Arc will continue to test Heather until he accomplishes that goal. If you decide to not help this time he won't try to use you again. He'll find another way to achieve his goal."

"And I'd dislike that one even more." He paused. "She's contacting me."

"Please make her do this on her own."

My heart?

Storm, have you talked to Sam?

No. I just learned about her capture. What is your plan?

I'm not sure yet. I know we can't try what we did when we rescued the ancients, and we can't use the way you rescued me either. What about we try capturing some of her troops? We were going to do that for Henry and the team she already has. If we can get someone high enough in her army, she might be willing to release Sam.

Then I'm going to leave that to you. I'm helping reinforce the caves so Reasta can't gain access.

Do you need me?

We have it under control, my heart. You work on getting our daughter back safe and sound.

I'll do my best.

"I have done as you asked. You know Heather will still ask for my opinion. Why is that such a problem?"

"Arc would have to answer that." Mac looked at Storm. "Heather has to prove herself to Arc the way she did to me."

"Didn't Heather figure out that you were testing her pretty quickly?"

"Yes, but that was part of the test. We know her mind is unique, and she can grasp things quickly. It's one of the reasons we were created for her."

"Is that part of the test for her now? That she realizes she's in the test, even though you made her think she's already finished it?"

"Again, you need to ask Arc."

"Since you can't answer me, I'm going to assume that I'm right. Aren't you afraid she'll pick that up somehow when she's communicating with me mentally?"

"It's a chance Arc is willing to take."

"Then he has watched her and learned more about how she handles things. That's good because I know my mate and she is very good at her job."

Heather was told to go to the council chambers and her team would join her as soon as they could so she sat there by herself, which was odd. Even if the rest of her staff were elsewhere, normally someone would walk in with information for one of them or to ask a question, but she had been there for at least a half an hour without any interruption. This wasn't real.

"Computer? I need to see what is going on. Load the cave entrance everyone is working on."

"There are three."

"Then show all three."

She watched as people moved about. There was no sense of urgency in them. She frowned. This wasn't right. This can't be real. Heather decided to go for a walk. Finding a way to rescue Sam was evading her anyway. Was the rescue fake as well? When she went close to one of the cave entrances she was confused. The people she saw on the screen were nowhere to be seen.

"Okay, there is something not quite right here." She spoke out loud to herself. "Arc? Come here."

Arc appeared in front of her. "Yes, Heather?"

"There is something not right here. With all the weapons you put at my disposal, why aren't these people wanting any of them? No one is here, yet Storm told me they were reinforcing the cave entrances to keep Reasta's people out. Is this your doing?" Heather looked at Arc. "I'm still being tested, aren't I? I thought you wanted to know how I would use the weapons."

"I do."

"Then why did you use such a lame program? Storm told me that they were working on blocking the caves. Why would they ignore one?"

"Because I wanted to see how quickly you would catch on. That took longer than I expected."

"I didn't leave the council chambers for about fifteen minutes. I was questioning things within five minutes."

"Then why didn't you leave the room earlier?"

"Because I was hoping someone would come in. People are always in and out of that room. The fact I was there by myself without seeing anyone had me suspicious."

"Did you reach out to Storm?"

"In the beginning when I thought it was real, but then I realized you made him go along with your plan." Heather studied the android. "Where is he by the way."

"He's sitting right in front of you."

"But we're not done are we."

"Knowing your abilities I have learned that I can't use the normal way I would test someone." He created the war room for them to be in. "Tell me, how would you rescue Sam if it was real."

"The same way we're going to rescue Henry and our soldiers."

"But they are soldiers, Sam is your daughter."

"Henry is family." Heather sat in her chair. "That man helped raise me. I was an orphan. I had no family, and he took me under his wing. He was the shoulder I cried on when I was having a bad day. He kept trying to put a smile on my face. I love Henry. He was a father to me."

"And Bear?"

"The other half of my childhood. He was my teacher. He made me think things through. I could talk to him about anything. Instead of having a mother and father I had two fathers. Each filled a different void that I had because I had no parents."

"You mentioned you couldn't use the other ways," asked Arc. "Why?"

"Mac was involved with the rescue attempt of the elders and ancients. I'm assuming you have that information."

"I do."

"We were able to fool Reasta once, but it would be foolish to think we could do that again. I was also trapped on Reasta's ship and Storm was able to sneak on the ship through the hydroponic bay. We used our clones to replace us and escape."

"The same clones you have allowed to blend in with Vespian society."

"Yes."

"Why do you feel that can't be done again? You have the ability to clone."

"That's true, but Skye came close to being caught when he was bringing us back to Vespia. Reasta also realized she had the clones pretty quickly. I have to assume she figured out that we got in and out that way."

"Don't you think you're giving her too much credit?"

"Are you kidding? Reasta isn't stupid. The only place she couldn't see what was happening was while we were in the hydroponic bays. I know the moment she realized she had our clones and not me anymore she figured out how that happened and has taken steps to fix that. We couldn't take that chance. I won't put my people in jeopardy like that."

"You are quite an enigma."

"I've heard that before." This was the first time she had heard it from an android, and it piqued her curiosity. "Why do you think that?"

"You acted like everything is fine when it isn't. You allow your mate to control you but you're the one who leads the council. You're passionate with Storm, yet when humans are around you fear what they think."

Heather made a face. "I think I need to give you a little history first. I was in Earth's security when I met Storm. I was assigned to guard him. Our relationship was forced in the beginning. The Vespians were searching for someone who fit a particular criteria."

"You."

"Yes." Heather nodded. "My government decided that they wanted me to get a treaty signed between Vespia and Earth. The only way I could go to Vespia was if I was mated to one. Earth had me marry Storm, but Storm's uncle did the bonding ceremony before that. We mated before we left Earth.

"Someone was after me. We didn't know why." Heather took a breath. "Storm and I had grown closer. The mating ritual changed something in us. We were more comfortable with each other, and I could keep up with his libido. The passion you mentioned was so beautiful and something I never experienced before."

"Who was after you?"

"Ialog," said Heather. "He tried to make me believe that the relationship I had with Storm wasn't real."

"Storm rescued you?"

"Yes, and Ialog wouldn't leave us alone. As long as I was on Vespia he didn't bother us. I'm not sure why but I was grateful. I was called home to earth because Ialog started a rumor that I was being mistreated. Once again, he kidnapped me. There always seems to be something trying to tear us apart. All that did was make our love stronger." She continued to tell him about their life together and everything that tried to tear them apart. She was honest with her ability and how Storm was always there to help her master some new talent. Arc needed to know how much they were entwined. She held nothing back.

"Why do you behave the way you do in public?"

"Wow, okay. Let's start with the Vespians. You commented on the way I behave around Storm. The males are very dominate, so are the women but the males are also very protective. The women know this and love the feeling they get from being protected. It's one of the reasons non-Vespians aren't allowed on the planet. They don't have to be afraid of a stranger. They can trust without fear. Our men would never harm us even when they get angry. So the women allow their men to be dominate. We still stand up to our mates. We just don't do it in public."

"But you weren't raised on Vespia."

"True but I am mated to the future leader. I must behave the way a Vespian woman of my station should. Believe me there was a lot of training so I wouldn't upset the people. In the beginning, they weren't sure I was a good choice for Storm."

"Why?"

She went through the way she and Storm behaved before and after they met. How she was treated when she first arrived. She told him about the device in her back. Why she trusted the people around her. Heather did her best to answer all the questions Arc had for her.

"You say you trust these people yet not all of them know your secrets. You even kept things from Storm."

"True, but I did that to protect my family."

"Family? Kuarto, Sam and the twins are the only ones that are biologically related to you."

"From a human standpoint family could be a close nit group you trust to be there for you. That is what I have. Bear and Henry raised me. They are my fathers. Kuarto is my brother. Toki is my sister-in-law. Fridon is my brother as well. The bond we share goes very deep. He is very good with computers. Skye is mated to my daughter. He is also wary of my abilities. I worry about the same thing so I trust him to do the right thing if I were to lose control of this power of mine."

"You fear your power?"

"At times."

"Yet you are the leader of this war, and all of your family is in the war council. Aren't you afraid they will be hurt?"

"Skye and myself were two of the best in Earth security and we were trained by Bear. Storm is the head of Vespian security, and he trained Fridon and myself as well as Sam and Skye so now we know Earth and Vespian security techniques. They have the same goal as I do. Remove Reasta from Vespia and take her power away from her."

"Do you want revenge for all you've been through?"

"Revenge?" Heather shook her head. "I want our life back. I want to be able to walk through the gardens at the palace without fear of someone trying to grab me. I want the Vespian people to be able to go back to their lives."

"And if you have a chance to kill her, will you take it?"

"You seem to be fixated on that. Why?" When Arc didn't answer she tilted her head a little. "It's about those weapons, isn't it? I'm not sure you're going to understand. I am trained to protect. I can kill if I have to, but I'm supposed to try to fix any issue without violence. This is no different."

"You know what Reasta wants. Why would you say that?"

"Because I'm not going to give her the child she believes I'm supposed to have that will allow her to live forever. I've been told that I'm a perfectly created ancient. Yet I'm not what she wants. That or someone lied to protect me." Heather brushed a piece of hair away from her face. "Reasta won't get that child, but I don't plan on killing her unless I have to. I'll try to use everything at my disposal, including using the prayer I used on Ialog to subdue her."

"Interesting."

"Is there anything else you wish to talk about? If not, I need to get back to the council."

"You may go."

"Have I passed your test?"

"Yes."

Heather opened her eyes to find Storm sitting across from her. "My heart?"

"Are you okay?"

"I'm fine. Arc just had a few questions for me." Heather stood.

"Mac said you were being tested." Storm did the same.

"He learned pretty quickly that I was aware of the test so knew his readings would be skewed. I'm pretty sure he realized that wouldn't work so he asked me questions. I don't know if I told him what he wanted to hear, but I answered his questions the best way I could."

Storm wrapped her in an embrace. "As long as he doesn't take you from me again, I'll be happy. I don't like it when I can't reach you."

"Sounds like I need to give you a little me time."

———

Heather hated waiting. The elite teams worked in shifts at the palace because no one knew when Reasta would strike. She and Storm had moved back in because they needed to be there the whole time. At least she had passed Arc's test. The cache of weapons he had released to her was overwhelming. Right now, she was working with the weapons they had already been using. Hopefully, she'll have a little time after this to work through some of the new ones. She turned her focus to the sweet little faces she saw on her private screen. It was the way they had communicated with each other for the last few weeks. "So how is your training?"

"Bert says he needs to challenge us more."

"I was the same way. Some of my teachers saw how quickly I learned and gave me college-level questions when everyone else was at a mid-education level. Others had me do special projects on the subject to become well-versed in it." She wanted to give them a kiss, a hug. Instead, she had to pretend everything was all right and this was normal.

"Mommy, you okay?' asked her daughter.

"Of course, my hearts, I just miss you so much. The first thing I want when I see you again is kisses and hugs."

They nodded as they looked at each other. "We can't wait."

"Me either." She knew they didn't have a lot of time to speak, but she took every second she could to contact them.

She felt the heat of Storm's hand on her shoulder just as he leaned down and smiled at their children.

"We miss your hugs very much." He pressed a kiss against her cheek.

"Daddy."

Storm touched the screen, and their children returned the gesture. "You need to get back to class and we'll contact you later today if we can."

They nodded.

"My hearts."

"You're our heart, too, Mommy." They blew kisses to their parents then disconnected the com.

"I miss them so much."

"I know, I miss them too, but we're doing this to keep all of the children safe."

Heather nodded as she stood. "Why is Reasta dragging her feet? Does she honestly think she's going to catch us off guard?"

"I doubt that, but she could be waiting to see if we become complacent."

"Which won't happen."

"Or she could be waiting for us to make a mistake."

"Another thing that won't happen." She leaned against her mate and snuggled closer when he put his arms around her. "I might be irritated but I'm not rash. We will wait as long as it takes, and we will be diligent."

As if on cue Fridon contacted her. "Reasta wishes to speak to you."

"Well, I don't wish to speak to her."

"I will make her wait then."

"How long do you plan on making her wait?" asked Storm.

"Long enough to make her mad." She looked up at her mate. "I'd love to ask her when she plans on attacking."

She waited until she was pretty sure Reasta was fuming before opening the com. The moment she saw the woman on the screen she sighed. "What do you want?"

"I want you to answer when I contact you."

"Really? Do you know what I want Reasta? I want you to go home and leave us alone. I want to be able to have three uninterrupted days with my mate." She mentally said *and her children* but wouldn't dare say that aloud since this woman didn't know about the twins. "I want to be able to walk through the palace gardens without fear of being kidnapped by one of your goons. I want my people to be able to get back to their lives. I want you gone."

"Then give me what I want."

"No. What I will give you is a chance to walk away. If you leave now, I won't kill you, as long as you stay away from any planet known by Earth or Vespia. Now as we explore and make more allies our paths may cross again, and this deal will be void but you would have a little more time to live."

"Have you forgotten that I have some of your people?"

"They are soldiers and know the risks," was all she said. "Are we done here?"

When Reasta paused she hit the disconnect button.

Heather turned and looked at Storm. She laughed nervously. "You think that will rattle her a little?"

"By the look on her face, I think you rattled her a lot."

FOURTEEN

It didn't take long before she received word that there was movement from Reasta's ship.

"Let's get everyone together so they are ready." Heather waited until everyone gathered around her. "Our goal is to get to the high-ranking soldiers. If she follows her normal routine, she'll send a bunch of her disposable clones with a handful of her more trusted men controlling them. One thing we have learned in dealing with her disposable clones is if you kill them as their bodies decompose, they smell awful, explode and make a real mess. I'd like to spare the palace if we can. Set your weapons on low. I want them knocked out so we can focus on the people we need to capture."

"What are you going to do with the clones?" asked Bear.

"We will give them back before they expire. Let her deal with the smell and exploding bodies."

Everyone had their assignments. It now was just a matter of waiting again. At least this time she could see how far away they were and would be able to estimate their arrival. This was the moment she needed to focus.

Storm stood beside her as they drew closer. He handed her helmet to her. "Are you ready?"

"Yes." She took her helmet and snapped it on. They took their positions next to their soldiers.

The first wave was just as Heather predicted. The clones dropped one by one. Once they shot the last one several of their soldiers came out of their vantage points and slapped tags on them so they could be moved to a safe place.

Wave after wave of clones came at them. They methodically disabled all of them.

Heather thought they'd never see the end of the clones. They kept coming, but she also noticed that some of Reasta's people were intermixed with them now. Their uniforms were different and easy for her to spot.

"Now we need your skills. The clones still need to hit with a low setting but the soldiers from Reasta's race need more power to knock them out." Heather used a virtual screen she brought up through her helmet to show the strength needed to make them unconscious. Once she had the information ready, she shared it with the rest of her soldiers.

As she shot their adversaries, she kept watching for the uniform to change once again. If Reasta followed her normal routine, one of her inner circle should be showing up soon. And since Reasta thought they would be capturing Heather and Storm there might be more than one of them with this group.

The moment she saw him she felt excitement fill her. There were two in control, and one was Reasta's general.

After explaining what she wanted to do and receiving resistance she was able to convince everyone that her idea was the best. She touched her mate's arm before standing. "It's time."

The general stopped moving forward when he spotted her. He raised his weapon and pointed it at her.

Heather released the seals of her helmet and smiled at him. "Welcome. General."

"Welcome? I'm here to take you back to Reasta."

"Is that what Reasta told you would happen?' Her smile brightened. "I'm sorry but she misinformed you. You see, you're surrounded and you two as well as the rest of your soldiers are now my guests."

Her mate poked him in the back with his weapon to let him know she wasn't lying.

"Now, be nice and surrender your weapon so we won't have to kill you."

He stared at her with such hatred she wanted to take a step back. After a few seconds, he reversed the weapon and handed it to her. One of their medics came up and put a tranquilizer into his neck. Another did the same to the other officer. They dropped to the floor.

"Let's get them back to the med lab."

———

Heather entered the med lab and looked for her brother.

"I'm detoxing them now. The clones are in stasis so their bodies shouldn't disintegrate until we give them back to Reasta."

"Good. Any adverse reaction?"

"Not yet, but it will be a few hours before I let you speak to either one of them."

She nodded as Storm entered the lab. He walked up to her when Kuarto stepped back to his computer.

"I wish to speak to you."

Heather pointed to one of the rooms where they could have some privacy. She knew what he wanted to talk about. His anger rolled off him in waves.

Leading the way, she tried to gather her thoughts so she could defend herself. Storm had a right to be furious with her. In his eyes, she had put herself in danger.

He waited for the door to close before facing her.

"Before you start, I wish to speak." She stepped up to him and pressed her hand against his heart. "I know you're upset with me because you think I put myself in unnecessary danger. I want you to know that I thought it through before I revealed myself. There was no way they'd harm me. I am far too valuable to Reasta. I also know that her general wouldn't have believed me if all he heard was my voice. Showing my face meant they wouldn't shoot for fear of striking me. Where they could have if they didn't believe it was me."

Heather waited for him to growl at her or yell at her. Something. But all he did was stare at her.

"You have become the leader I knew you could be." He sighed.

"Wait. What?"

"You're right. He would have demanded to see you if you had kept your helmet on and we could have had soldiers harmed because the tension would have escalated, and they would have laid their lives on the line to protect you."

"I hear a but in there somewhere."

"You must talk to me about this beforehand. You told us minutes before you did it. I didn't have time to prepare.

I'm a soldier but all I wanted to do was grab you and run until I was sure you were safe."

"I didn't know I was going to do that until I knew who Reasta had sent. How am I supposed to warn you when it is the spur of the moment?"

"I don't know. How about sharing it mentally? Maybe we need a code word so I know when you're going to make me swallow my heart."

She wrapped her arms around him. "I don't do it on purpose. Most of the time when I put myself in harm's way or take chances that make you cringe it's instinctual. I believe I'm safe. At least most of the time."

"And it's those moments when you could be hurt that fills me with fear." He slid his arms around her and held her close. "I don't care if you heal quickly, my heart. I don't want you harmed."

"I know that." She leaned back to look at him. "I never plan on being harmed."

"So, the next time I think you're taking a risk you shouldn't be I can wrap your braid around my hand and keep you at my side?"

"Only if you want a very angry mate at your side." She listened to his heart with joy. "So, I guess there's no hot sex?"

"I think that is why you push sometimes. You enjoy our intimacy after we fight."

"I don't get to see you lose control that often and sometimes your anger gets you to lose control when we're having sex. Plus, there's the makeup sex where you are so tender it takes my breath away."

"And you had hoped that would have happened here? What happened to my shy mate?"

"That door seals and the windows can become opaque."

"But everyone would know what we did."

"They're probably wondering what's going on in here right now."

"True." He loosened her collar so he could brush his fingers across her mark. "Yet I'm still not happy with you and feel I should show you my displeasure."

"How do you plan on doing that?" She had an idea of what he wanted to do and wished she could get away from him.

He urged her back against the cave wall that the office was built around and lifted her so they could see eye to eye. "By bringing you to the brink and not letting you have your release."

"What?" He had spiked her desire and walked away to heighten their intimacy later, but he had never just done it to punish her.

His mouth latched onto her mark and his hands opened the seals of her uniform so his hands could reach her core. She had no defense against his attack. As usual, she was putty in his hands. Soft caresses had her sighing. He brushed against her curls before slipping into her folds. He knew just where to touch her to heighten her desire.

"The scent of your arousal fills me with the same need, my heart," Storm whispered against her neck. "I knew this would backfire, but I felt the need to frustrate you like you frustrate me."

Heather wanted to scream when he pulled his hands out of her uniform then resealed it.

"We will both suffer." He captured her lips for a quick but heated kiss. "But it will make tonight glorious."

———

Heather watched the general on the screen as he paced his room. Kuarto said he was clear of the mind control drug. Would he be her ally? Or still stand with Reasta? She'd soon find out.

After speaking to her council, it was decided that she speak to him one on one, but she would take Storm, Sam, and Skye as guards. They would be wearing their helmets and standing in the background, ready to move if he tried to harm her.

She was already in the room and waited as Sam and Skye brought him in. Instead of speaking, she gestured to the chair on the other side of the table she sat behind.

"Is that your mate?"

Heather smiled. "My protection."

"Like I can do any damage with these things on." He lifted his hands to reveal the cuffs.

"You are fighting for my enemy." She paused for a moment. "How are you feeling?"

He gave her a confused look.

"No headaches or pains in your body?"

"Why do you ask?"

"Because your fearless leader kept your body pumped full of drugs. Our doctor cleared your system of the chemicals, but he did say you might have some side effects."

"Drugs? What are you talking about?"

Heather could see the disbelief in his eyes. She pulled up a screen to show him his blood work. "You had a lower dose than others, but you have been given the same drug all of your soldiers received."

"She told me..." He shook his head. "I never received any injections."

"That might be true, but you could have gotten it many different ways. It could have been in your food or drinks."

"I scanned everything before I ingested it."

"So, you didn't trust her." Heather sat forward. "It could have been on anything. Equipment you handled all the time. In the air of your office or room. What about your uniform? The chemical could have been inserted in your uniform somewhere and gave you a dose at certain intervals."

He didn't respond, but she knew she had him thinking. Not having the drug in his system anymore allowed him to see what Reasta was doing. Now she needed to give him the proof. They had taken his uniform from him earlier.

"We took detailed scans of this." She set a pad on the table between them. "See for yourself."

As he went through the data Storm stepped forward and set his uniform on the table. He looked at Heather and then grabbed his uniform. "I was promised that I wasn't drugged. Why would she lie to me? I was her second-hand man. I did everything she asked of me."

"Did you, or did the drug help you follow her commands without question?" Heather let the question hang between them. She needed his help, but she wasn't going to force him. That was what Reasta did to him.

"What do you want from me?"

"I want you to see the truth. That she isn't the one you should be following."

"And you are?"

She shrugged as she sat back. "That is for you to decide."

"And what have you done with my soldiers?"

"The clones are in stasis. I didn't want to deal with the mess they make when their time is up. The rest are in separate rooms. When they started to detox, they became quite violent. Your second in command is sitting quietly in his room as well." Heather tapped the screen a few times then split the screens so he could see all the members of his team at once.

"And what do you plan on doing with them?"

Heather smiled. "Trade them for my people."

"You know she could send you clones."

"And I could do the same thing." She cleared the screen. "And we have a way to scan for clones so one of my demands is that I get the real thing."

"She's not going to be very happy."

"I'm hoping she'll be furious."

"You know she has a way to scan too."

"I'm not worried about it." She watched him. "You have two choices. Either help us and stay here or go back to Reasta after I've angered her once again."

———

"There are a half a dozen of them that are already clones," Kuarto informed her when she walked back into the med lab.

"Then let's not waste our technology on them. The ones I really want to clone are her general and his assistant."

"He's a clone too," said the general after he entered the lab with his two guards, Sam and Skye. "Reasta seems to take her anger out on him when she gets mad at me."

"How many generations?"

"I've lost count." He looked up when three of the soldiers stepped up to their barrier.

The nod was slight, but Heather caught it. She wondered who they were to him.

"Several others are also clones."

He looked at Kuarto. "Which ones?"

Kuarto pointed to the soldiers who were clones. The general seemed to release a sigh of relief when the three who had approached their force field weren't included. "The rest are the originals."

Heather nodded. "Is everyone now clear of the drug?"

"Yes. If you wish to speak to any of them it is safe."

"I was thinking of allowing them to be with another soldier or two. Make them feel a little more comfortable. I do want to keep the clones away from those who are clear."

"I can do that."

Heather used her screen to make the ones she wanted together. The first thing she did was put the three that the general acknowledged together. She'd watch them to see if she could get any clues about their relationship to each other and to the general. Then she paired the rest up with a few groups having three in their group as well. The only two who remained alone was the general and his second.

Her mate had been behind her, waiting. She looked at him. "Your turn."

Storm nodded and headed to the room where the second was being held. Heather wanted him to intimidate the clone to see if he would crumble.

Heather stayed with her brother. "What can you tell me about the first three?"

"Well. They're very young. Eighteen years. They haven't picked their sex yet, although it looks like one will be female."

"Really? I've never seen a female other than Reasta. Do we know who their parents are?"

"They seem to have come from the same group of eggs, but those could have been frozen."

"Why do you say that?"

"Because they aren't from Reasta. I have matched their DNA with someone here though."

"The general."

"Yes." He looked at her. "How did you know?"

"It was the way they all stood and walked up to the edge of their rooms when he came in. He also acknowledged them, and he didn't do that with any of the other soldiers." She looked at the three in the room. "That does give me a little more leverage if he resists."

"You want him to stay?"

"He's a wealth of knowledge, Kuarto. He could give us details that we're missing. Having him on our side would turn the tide in our favor. He could give us intel on Reasta we have lacked in the past."

"You think it's wise to trust him?"

"I'm not saying to give the man the key to the city, but if I offer to keep his children safe, I hope he'll give us what we need."

———

Storm came up to her and wrapped his arms around her. "Reasta is asking to speak to you."

"Then she's figured out that we have her people in custody."

"Do you wish to speak to her now?"

"Yes, but I want to speak to her from the command center. No need to get her suspicious until it's too late." Heather walked with Storm.

"Do you believe the general will help us?"

"Yes. I found out three of the soldiers are his children. I'm hoping he'll see we'd be a much better choice than going back to Reasta."

Storm ushered her to their command center. He stayed at her side as she answered Reasta.

"Why, Reasta, I'm surprised to hear from you. Have you called to gloat or make some demand of me?"

"Oh, Heather. You can pretend all you want but I know you have my guards, and I want them back."

"Really? How about that. You have a few of my people and I want them back."

"You want a trade?"

"I do have more of your people than you have of mine."

"Fine."

"And I want the originals. We can test for clones, and I won't release your people until mine are tested."

"Now Heather, why would you think I'd send you clones?"

"Because that was what you did when you thought you had killed my mate." Heather waited for her reply.

"When do you want to do this trade?"

Heather smiled.

———

Heather, with Storm at her side, spoke to the general once more. "Reasta has agreed to the trade."

He gave her a look.

"I need your decision."

"I have to go back."

"You're that loyal to her?"

"You don't understand. I have people who rely on me to keep them safe."

"Like the three children you have with you." Heather watched as he straightened.

"What are you talking about?"

"Come now, general. We have your DNA and I saw

how you acknowledged three soldiers. It didn't take too long to put two and two together."

"She'd know."

"And that is why you're willing to go back?"

"I have two more children on her ship. I can't leave them."

"And what if I promised to get them free as soon as it is possible to do so."

"I can't take the chance that she'll figure out you sent a clone in my place."

"That's what I thought." Her mate, who had been quietly standing behind her, stepped to the door of the room they were in and opened it. One of his three children entered. "Your daughter asked to stay."

"Daughter? They haven't picked a gender yet and being female isn't a smart move."

"Sometimes it can't be helped, and she knows the danger. That is why she decided to stay." Heather paused. "She wanted to speak to you."

The door opened and one of his children walked in. She stood next to the table he sat at. "Father."

He looked up at his daughter. Heather stood and offered her the chair she was vacating. Storm escorted her out of the room so they could watch on a monitor. Kuarto walked up to her side.

"Do you think he'll be able to tell the difference?"

"He shouldn't, but this is a good test for us. I've done a lot more research and testing since we adjusted the clones of you and Storm and with the ancient technology, I think we've perfected it. There are ways to check, but only we have that technology. If he can tell the difference, then I need to start all over."

"We are talking about his children. I'd like to think I'd know my children from a clone."

"You have a mental link with your children. You would know, no matter what. I'm testing him with his real daughter. Let's see if he gets suspicious.'

Heather turned her attention to the conversation between the general and his daughter.

"Why would you become female?"

"I have tried to stop it, but no matter what I do the female hormones continue to control me." She looked at her hands. "She will kill me, Father. This is my only choice."

"And how do you know these people won't do the same thing? They know very little of our race and will want to learn from you."

"And they explained that to me. The doctor told me I would be scanned and there would be some DNA testing but nothing invasive."

"And you believe them?"

"What choice do I have? Here I have a chance to live longer. If they are true to their word, I have a chance at a real life. I want that chance."

"And your brothers?"

"I want them away from her before she destroys them."

———

"How can you fool Reasta?"

Heather handed him one of Kuarto's scanners. "To prove that it works I've lined up your soldiers so you can inspect them to see which soldiers are clones. I never gave you that information and this will prove that I'm not trying to trick you."

"And how do I know you didn't set this up to show me what you want?"

"Scan yourself. Check the data."

He palmed the scanner and dropped it from one hand to another for a few minutes before he stood and ran the scan.

Not wanting to show any of their technology yet, Heather pointed to an insert next to the screen so he could view it.

He didn't speak as he looked at the data. He stood and slipped it into a pocket. "Take me to my people."

Heather nodded and led the way. The only one they had cloned so far was his daughter and the clone now stood with the rest of the soldiers. She already had the woman's memories up to the point of being cloned. Would he be able to detect it?

She had shielded the conversation he had had with his daughter inside his head so he wouldn't ask the clone something she wouldn't remember from their conversation. This had to be as clear as possible. Heather watched as he walked in front of his people, pausing a moment without speaking. He would glance at the scanner as discreetly as possible after he passed each person.

"There are three missing." He turned to Heather.

"You may check the people we have in stasis, but we thought they were all disposable clones by their uniforms." Heather gestured for him to walk with her.

"Then you have all my guards. The three I'm looking for must have run away."

"Does that happen a lot?"

"Enough. Reasta can track them, but sometimes she is in a good mood and leaves them alone."

"How does she track them?" She asked.

Do they have some sort of insert we're not aware of? She heard her brother through their insert. *I found the one at the nap of their neck and I removed all of them when they first arrived just in case Reasta has a way to penetrate our shields.*

"You don't know?"

"I was hoping you would feel comfortable enough to tell me."

"It's in the nap of my neck." He was quiet for a moment. "Can I assume you've already cloned my daughter?"

"We have."

"You did a good job. I didn't know she was a clone when I tried to talk her out of staying here."

"That wasn't the clone."

"Oh, when do I get to meet this clone."

"You have."

"What? When?"

Heather pointed to the scanner he still held.

"That was the clone? This said she was the real thing."

"I know. Now do you think we can fool Reasta?"

"If you will show me how you did this I will stay."

Heather smiled. She'd have to talk to the council first, but they had the ally they needed.

———

"The general has agreed, but he wants to see how we were able to fool the scanner." She looked at her brother. "That's why I asked you to join us Kuarto. I want him to stay, but I also don't want to give all our secrets away just in case he can't be trusted."

"The best way to prove what we can do is to clone him. Let him study himself and see how good this cloning system is."

"Then all I need to do is convince him."

It took a couple of hours, but she was able to convince the general to allow them to make a copy of him. Kuarto walked him through their process. He took the DNA sample and inserted it into a fabricated egg.

"I know this is a bit disconcerting. Heather and Storm had issues with their clones. Heather said it was like looking in a mirror, but she didn't have control over her mirror image."

"Your technique doesn't look that much different than what Reasta uses."

"Basic technology will be the same. To clone properly you need to start with an egg. Since I don't have one from your race I start with a synthetic and insert your chromosomes into it. Once the egg reads as your species, I then insert your full DNA to recreate you."

"How long does this take?"

"About eighteen hours Earth time. Then I have to age the embryo to adult." Kuarto took him to the cryotube the egg had been inserted to. "I constantly watch for errors to pop up and correct them so the DNA doesn't become corrupted."

"You can correct them? That is something Reasta can't do. Not with limited power."

"Limited power? I thought the ship was powered by the ancients you have in those pods."

"It is, but Reasta has made so many clones over the years she has drained the ship." He stopped talking when he realized he might have said too much. "The ship has a mind of its own at times."

"Heather brought some of those pods back with her when she realized people were in them." Kuarto looked at him. "We have studied them to know who they were and what those pods did."

"And I spent time on that ship," Heather said from behind him. "I noticed a few odd things while I was there. The ship is protecting the ancients Reasta has trapped in those pods, isn't it?"

The General nodded. "That is what I believe."

"I'm happy to hear that. She has taken so many lives it's good to know something is stopping her." So she had drained the ship in her greed. That was good to know. Maybe they could add to the strain by pushing her even more.

"She wasn't always that bad, Heather."

"Really? That's not what Ialog told me. She stole that ship from him when she learned about how he planned on creating me."

"She told me she found that ship."

"Why did you become her general? What did you see that made you trust her?"

"I saw a lost person trying to find her way." He shrugged. "Then she learned that Vespia had reawakened Ialog."

"How did she find that out?"

"The ship told her. It keeps files on all ancients that it can find, but Reasta has had trouble accessing them. Ialog's was on the screen when I started working for her, but it sat dormant. When it showed activity again, she knew he was awake, and we made our way here."

"This is the type of thing we need to know. You know I'm going to pick your brain. I want her to leave Vespia alone and I want to live my life without fear."

"I know and I'm ready."

———

Henry was the first one she saw. Her heart leaped into her chest. Heather hoped he was okay.

Kuarto was the one dealing with their returning soldiers. He was scanning each person to make sure they were getting their original people back. They were trading ten at a time. Heather saw Reasta make a big deal out of scanning her own people as well.

"This one is a clone."

"That's not going to work, Reasta. He came to us that way." Heather swiped her pad, sending the data on each soldier to her. "The one's in red are the clones."

Reasta didn't say anything else. Once they had all their people Reasta saluted her and had her ship land.

"Oh, almost forgot." Heather touched her pad and watched as all the clones they had in stasis appeared in front of the ship. "Don't forget them."

Reasta shot her a hateful look. She herded those soldiers into the ship as well.

"So how much time do they have?" Heather asked her brother in a quiet tone.

"A few seconds at most. Our stasis field will dissipate the moment she takes off."

"And leave her with an ugly mess."

———

Henry walked beside her as they talked. "She is quite obsessed with you. All she wanted to know was what you were up to. If you and Storm were still in a strong relationship."

"That doesn't surprise me. I've been her focal point from the beginning."

"Why you?"

"She wants to control me."

"Is that why you're in charge of this war?"

"Part of it." She looked at him. "I'm in control because the Vespian council chose me. It's not something I wanted."

"But you're not Vespian."

"To them I am." When Henry gave her an odd look she continued. "Vespians don't allow anyone on their planet unless they are related to them, right?"

He nodded.

"That's because of the way they view things. The moment I mated with Storm I became one of them. They don't care where I was raised or how little I know about their ways."

"Have you told Bear this? He has been trying to figure this out since we've been here."

"Then why didn't he just ask? He is still acting like he's on Earth and I need everyone to think the way the Vespians do. I need people to ask questions. I need them to think on their own, not follow others blindly."

―――――

"I'm torn between keeping them secluded and introducing them to the rest of our soldiers." Heather had all her high-ranking officers around the massive table in their war room. She wanted everyone's input on this. There were so many things that could go wrong, and she wanted to see what everyone else felt would be the biggest barriers.

"What if they end up double-crossing us?" asked Bear.

"That is something I thought about. I wouldn't give them any top-secret information, but I want to show them how wonderful the Vespian people are. Understand why we're fighting to keep our way of life."

"Are you sure you want to bring in such an aggressive

race? The way they procreate could make them the dominant species in a few short years," added Skye.

"Vespians are also quite aggressive," said Storm. "And
Heather isn't talking about allowing them to live here
forever. I would assume they would want to go back to
their home planet when the war is over. I doubt there are a
lot of humans who want to stay here once we're no longer
fighting."

"They would have to pass the same requirements of
anyone who wants to live on Vespia," she answered,
drawing the conversation back to what to do with their
new guests. "My thoughts are to introduce them to
everyone because I think it would be a good moral booster
but limit their interactions with our people until we feel it's
safe to have them fully integrated."

Storm gave her a wink. Sam nodded. As she looked
around the table, most agreed with her.

"Good." Heather stood. "Then we'll introduce them
tonight."

"During our honoring of our returning soldiers?"

"That will be a formal event. Afterwards, we will allow
everyone to mingle. That is when I plan on introducing
them."

"You people sure like your parties," murmured Skye.

A low growl escaped Storm just as Sam elbowed him in
the ribs.

"Skye, how does Earth's security handle missions?"

"They have been known to celebrate a bit too. Never
understood that either."

"Everyone is trapped here. I can't keep morale up if we
do nothing but drill and fight. We all need a way to burn
off our frustration. Help us forget that we're trapped here
for a few hours."

"I'm sorry I said anything."

"It's okay. I'm sure there are a few others who have thought the same thing."

She dismissed everyone and headed back to their rooms with Storm.

"I don't like the way he questions you all the time."

"It's part of his nature, my heart, just like how you dislike it is part of yours." She put her arm around him and hugged him. "He can't help but question and you can't help but protect."

"Does it bother you?"

"No, I find it endearing." She smiled up at him. "Just like the way you always find ways to arouse me while we're working."

"Those are my favorite moments too." He pulled her close. "The stolen moments in odd places excite me. Thinking about them excites me."

"My heart, if it pertains to me, it excites you."

"You know me well." He captured her lips with his.

———

Everyone had been honored, and they were now mingling. Food filled the buffet tables while some of the cooks moved about offering small bites to those who didn't want a full meal at the moment. Heather sensed her mate coming up behind her just before she felt the heat of his hands. His left one slid across her abdomen to her right hip while his right one went across her ribs to rest just below her left breast.

"I think Mother did a wonderful job with your formal uniform. It almost feels like fur," Storm whispered in her ear.

Heather smiled and leaned back against him. "I swear

your mother creates some of these outfits with you in mind."

The long gown was dove gray, her council color as well as the color of all her other uniforms. She didn't even know she had a dress uniform until the box arrived at their rooms a few hours ago. Unlike Earth uniforms that were designed to make everyone look the same, Vespian dress uniforms accented each sex. Women always wore gowns and men wore suits.

Storm wore a long jacket over a tunic and slacks. He wore the standard black, with piping that showed his position with the war council. It was the light gray of her dress. The second piping was his command color. A bright blue that his elite squad wore as well as anyone in his command.

Fridon had the same thing. His command color was green.

Skye had a violet piping along with the gray. It didn't take her very long to figure out her command color was violet but because she was the leader she didn't wear any colors. It made her want to sigh.

"Are you ready for the introductions?" He turned her in his arms so she was looking at him.

She nodded. "I hope I'm making the right decision."

"Everyone is behind this decision."

That was true. She had spoken to everyone on the council personally and asked if they thought she should allow them to mingle with their people. They told her to follow her heart.

She moved to the dais and waited for everyone to quiet down.

"I have four people I want you to meet. They worked for Reasta and have decided to join us. Please show them Vespian courtesy and show them respect as they learn the

Vespian way. With their help, we will defeat Reasta and take our planet back."

The general and his children stepped out on the dais with her.

She smiled at them as they faced the Vespian people. Now they would defeat Reasta and send her back where she belonged.

The End

THANK YOU FOR READING

Did you enjoy this book?

We invite you to leave a review at your favorite book site, such as Goodreads, Amazon, Barnes & Noble, etc.

DID YOU KNOW THAT LEAVING A REVIEW...

- Helps other readers find books they may enjoy.
- Gives you a chance to let your voice be heard.
- Gives authors recognition for their hard work.
- Doesn't have to be long. A sentence or two about why you liked the book will do.

ABOUT THE AUTHOR

Writing for Barbara Donlon Bradley started innocently enough, like most she kept diaries, journals, and wrote an occasional letter but she also had a vivid imagination and wrote scenes and short stories adding characters to her favorite shows and comic books.

As time went on, she found the passion for writing to be a strong drive for her. Humor is also very strong in her life. No matter how hard she tries to write something deep and dark, it will never happen. That humor bleeds into her writing. Since she can't beat it, she has learned to use it to her advantage.

Now she lives in Tidewater Virginia with a cat who thinks he owns everything, her husband and daughter.

www.barbaradonlonbradley.com

ALSO BY BARBARA DONLON BRADLEY